# BEYOND THE LITTLE BIGHORN

# BEYOND THE LITTLE BIGHORN

ROBERT VAUGHAN

WOLFPACK
PUBLISHING
— EST 2013 —

**Beyond the Little Bighorn**
Paperback Edition
Copyright © 2025 by Robert Vaughan

Wolfpack Publishing
1707 E. Diana Street
Tampa, FL 33610

wolfpackpublishing.com

Paperback ISBN 979-8-89567-793-3
Ebook ISBN 979-8-89567-792-6
LCCN 2025947335

# BEYOND THE LITTLE BIGHORN

# PROLOGUE

THE WIND BLEW ACROSS THE DRY COUNTRY THAT bordered the Powder River, stirring up the dust of the Oregon Trail. A wagon train, with ten families, had stopped in a shallow hollow near the river. Smoke was drifting from the cook fires with the smell of boiled coffee and charred rabbit meat still on the evening air. Somewhere, a harmonica player could be heard playing a well-known hymn as the camp prepared for the night.

Twelve-year-old Jacob Andrews and his mother, Martha, sat on a small log beside the campfire. They both stared at the flames as Jacob absently poked at the embers. They both could hear the voices of his father, Marcus, and the lead scout, Eldridge Everett, as they stood some distance away. They were speaking in hushed tones.

"You know we're being watched," Everett said, keeping his voice low. "We spotted sign two days back up in the draw. Saw travois marks and lots of fresh pony droppin's." He glanced over his shoulder. "All we can pray for is that it's Lakota and not Crow."

"If it's Crow," Jacob's father said as he rubbed his chin, "do you think they'll attack?"

Everett scanned the ridgeline. "So far, they've been quiet, but we're definitely in their territory." He paused, then added, "If they come after us, I reckon it'll be tonight."

Jacob wasn't supposed to listen to such talk, but he always did. He had heard the same tone of voice when they talked about cholera, or potential outlaws, or even the threat of a bad winter in the mountains. He knew men only whispered when some sort of danger was about to happen.

His mother, having overheard the same conversation, laid a gentle hand on his shoulder. "Jacob, fetch your sister from the Murphys' wagon. It's time you two got some sleep."

Jacob rose and crossed over to the next wagon, where little Susan was playing with her rag doll.

"Come on, Susan, Mom says we need to go to bed," Jacob said.

"How come? I'm not sleepy," Susan said.

"It doesn't matter, come on." He lifted his sister down from the wagon, and she ran off toward their mother.

That's when he heard it.

A high-pitched whistle from the ridge that sounded like a hawk's cry.

A war cry rose through the night, and that was followed by the thunder of hooves.

The men shouted as they grabbed their rifles and began to fire. Everything around the peaceful little campsite erupted into chaos.

Jacob stood still, his heart hammering in his chest. Along the ridge, what had appeared to be shadows, exploded into a throng of mounted warriors, their bodies painted for war. Arrows flew through the air, many finding targets. A man screamed. The still-burning campfires lit up faces painted with red and black.

"Jacob!" his mother screamed.

He turned, sprinting for her, but a nearby Crow warrior barreled past him on horseback, swinging a club. Jacob stumbled as the blow struck someone behind him. He saw Mr. Murphy collapse in a heap. Jacob, gasping for breath, scrambled under the nearest wagon.

From the shadows, he saw his father take cover behind an overturned crate, as two warriors rushed toward him. He dropped one rider before the other ran a lance through his chest. Marcus Andrews fell without a sound.

Jacob bit his fist to keep from screaming. Then he saw his mother standing in the firelight as she clutched Susan to her chest. A Crow warrior grabbed her arm and pulled her forward.

"No!" Jacob whispered.

The warrior raised his knife. Martha Andrews didn't beg. She didn't scream. She held Susan tight as the blade came down, striking her in the throat.

The second thrust found Susan, her blood mixing with that oozing from her mother.

Jacob shut his eyes and pressed his face into the dirt as hot tears ran down his face.

Then after what seemed like an eternity, the sounds

subsided. Daring to open his eyes, Jacob saw Indians moving among the fallen bodies. One by one, they began scalping the men, not even checking to see if any were still alive. For some reason, they did not touch the women or children, leaving them where they had fallen.

Jacob's breath was coming in gulps. He knew if they found him, he would be next. With his heart pounding, he did the only thing he could. He played dead.

He lay still, with his face in the dirt, forcing himself to ignore the smell of blood and gunpowder. He did not move when he sensed hands were turning over the bodies close to him, stripping them of their clothing. Jacob did not react when a warrior kicked dirt over his back.

Time passed. He did not know if it was minutes or hours, but at last, total silence came except for the sound of gathering vultures.

When dawn began to break, Jacob lifted his face from the dirt and slowly opened his eyes. When he was sure no one was nearby, he crawled out from under the wagon.

What he saw caused him to wretch. Bodies, broken wagons, and scattered belongings were everywhere. Some fires still smoldered from the night before, while the buzzing of flies was everywhere.

He found his mother, and he knelt beside her, too shocked for tears. He took her hand in his. It was cold, oh so cold. Susan, who lay across his mother's body, was gone, too. He held her delicate little hand in his, as a sob broke from his throat.

It was at that moment that a stark realization came to Jacob. He had no one. He was alone.

But then a horse's low snort broke the silence.

Jacob turned quickly, his pulse racing.

On the ridge above him, he saw three mounted warriors. Were they Crow? Their hair hung in thick braids, but their faces were unpainted. One man, who appeared to be their leader, studied the wreckage below.

Jacob remembered the conversation he had heard between his father and Mr. Everett. They had said they hoped those Indians watching them were Lakota and not Crow.

And now, Jacob prayed these men were not Crow.

A man with one feather in his braid dismounted and slowly walked toward him. Jacob wanted to run, but his legs would not move.

The man knelt beside him, his dark eyes searching Jacob's face.

"Washté, wicasha čikala," he said gently. Good, little boy.

Jacob began to shake uncontrollably.

Another warrior spoke. "Crow did this. Boy not Crow. He is alone."

The leader nodded as he looked around the massacre. "A bad thing. The child will come to Lakota village."

Jacob did not understand their words, but he did understand Lakota, and he understood they were not going to kill him.

The warrior offered Jacob his hand. At first, he hesitated, but then he took it. Looking around at all the carnage, he had no choice.

The warrior lifted him onto his horse and then

climbed on as well. Behind them, the sun was rising while the valley still smoked.

Jacob could not look back.

At that moment, he knew he would never be Jacob Andrews again.

# CHAPTER ONE

THE EVENING OF AUGUST 30TH, 1875, FOUND THE NEW York Art League's Show Gallery bathed in the glow of chandeliers and gas jet lamps. The League was sponsoring a showing of the work of Silas Thomson, one of America's best-loved artists. Among the patrons in the gallery foyer stood his daughter, Emily Thomson, who was acting as one of the hostesses.

Thomson's fame and reputation did not end on this side of the Atlantic—he had also shown in Paris, London, and Vienna, and was nearly as highly acclaimed in Europe as he was in America.

He counted among his friends such men as Renoir, Monet, and Albert Sisley. He studied in Paris under Eugène Isabey, but was not unduly influenced by his teacher's academic romanticism. Silas's unique style was best explained by a noted art critic for the New York *Tribune* in a glowing account of Silas's work, *Train Shed*:

. . .

*IT GIVES one a remarkable feeling of presence in the interior of a train shed. This is accomplished in part by a brilliant use of diffuse light, but also by the optically perfect perspective of his subject. Atmosphere is captured in a bold and imaginative way. Thomson is a major artist with an exquisite feel for form... It is most noteworthy to discover that Silas Thomson is constantly growing as an artist. A new spirit and vitality has appeared in his work. Certain elements in the canvases displayed in this show did not appear in his earlier paintings. Thomson has developed an eye for the variations of light and color that breathe life into his work.*

WHEN EMILY READ the last comment, she and her father held a small, private celebration. Such a statement, they both knew, was a compliment to Emily's own skill with the brush.

Silas suffered from rheumatoid arthritis. Unable to handle the brush with his former precision, he had trained his daughter to carry out much of the work. She was nearly equal to him in skill, and she now made most of the preliminary drawings as well as some of the finished work.

It was not simply vanity that caused Silas Thomson to keep secret his arthritis, it was to protect a dream. For years, Silas had nurtured the ambition of going to the Indian territories to paint the natives in their natural habitat. Finally, he was given the opportunity when the New York Art League commissioned him to create a series of paintings that would accurately portray life among the Plains Indians.

Emily was as delighted as her father. She had been

so long a part of his dream that she felt a compulsion just as strong as his.

They both knew that the commission would be in jeopardy if the Art League knew of Silas's affliction, so they kept it, and Emily's involvement in his work, a closely guarded secret.

Despite their caution, the venture was almost stopped before it could begin. The Indians were beginning to make trouble in the Black Hills, and the Department of the Interior refused to grant permission for Silas and Emily to undertake their assignment.

But Silas was determined to complete this commission. He and Emily proceeded to Washington to call on the President.

President Grant was a great fan of Silas Thomson's work, and had hung what was possibly Silas's most famous painting, *Toward Higher Office*, in the White House. This work depicted President Lincoln lying on the bed after having been shot, surrounded by the anxious friends who made up the deathwatch. Above Lincoln, painted in glowing colors, was his soul being transported to heaven by a host of angels.

Moved by the Thomsons' appeal, Grant overrode the Department of the Interior. He granted a presidential order enabling Silas and Emily access to the Indian lands.

"You understand," Grant had cautioned, "that this merely clears you with the United States Government and her military forces. I cannot promise how the Indians will accept you."

"I understand, Mr. President," Silas replied. "But I am told that the Indians have a way of measuring the intention of a man's heart. If that is the case, then I need not fear them, for they shall see the peaceful purpose to which my mission is dedicated."

"We can only hope that there is some validity to your belief," Grant had said. "Though I fear that there may be dishonorable Indians as well as dishonorable White men. I give you this pass with reluctance. But I give it to you in full appreciation of your contribution to preserving our culture for generations to come."

"Thank you, Mr. President."

"Now, when do you intend to leave?"

"I have an art show in New York on the thirtieth of August, and I have booked train tickets for the following day."

"An art showing, eh? Oh, how I wish that I could quit Washington for a brief spell and enjoy the show with the other patrons of the arts."

"Mr. President, I shall reserve one of the canvases of my Indian campaign just for you," Silas promised.

AND IT WAS JUST that promise of which Paul Gideon was now voicing his disapproval. Gideon, Thomson's agent, was standing quietly with Silas and Emily in the back of the gallery, sipping wine and watching the people file through the show.

"You have just promised the president two hundred and fifty dollars of my money," Paul said, flatly.

Silas raised an eyebrow. "And what makes you say that?"

"Because that painting would sell for something like twenty-five hundred dollars and you know it. Ten percent is two hundred and fifty dollars. But no, you had to give it away, so no commission for me."

"After what President Grant did for us, I felt he deserved it," Silas said, as if that simple statement explained everything.

And in a way, it did, for Paul Gideon had worked with the artist long enough to know that arguing with him over some sentimentality was a wasted effort. But he returned to another subject that had been troubling him—the trip into Indian Territory.

"Have any of my convincing arguments made an impression yet?" he asked.

Emily laughed as she shook her head. "No, Paul. We're still going."

"You are both crazy," Paul said.

"Tell me, why do you object so much? By your own admission, this project will bring in a lot of money from the Art League. And ten percent of that is yours."

"Yes, but suppose some Indian takes your scalp? Ten percent of nothing is nothing," Gideon countered.

Silas ran a hand across his nearly bald head. "I doubt I have much to offer any Indian who is bent on scalping me."

"What about Emily? I'd hate to think of that copper-colored hair hanging from a warrior's belt, or from the tip of his lodgepole," Gideon countered.

Silas looked down at the floor, his face troubled. Emily knew that Paul had struck a telling blow with his argument, for this was the same argument she and her father had been carrying on for some while. Therefore, it was up to her to convince her father once more, she should make the trip out West with him.

"Paul, we've been through this a hundred times," Emily said. "Neither you nor anyone else can say anything that will make us change our minds. We're going, and that's that. Am I not correct, Father?"

"Emily, I don't know," Silas said. "Perhaps..."

"Perhaps what?" Emily asked. "Father, we've come too far, and our dream is right in front of us. We cannot falter, not now."

Silas smiled at his daughter's insistence, then looked back at Gideon. "There," he said. "Has any man ever had a daughter more deserving of admiration than I? She has spirit and determination to match my own. I tell you, Paul, nothing shall prevent our going. And no evil will befall us upon the way."

"I hope you're right," Paul said, though he was clearly skeptical. He saw a well-dressed patron admiring one of Thomson's more expensive canvases, and setting his drink down, he excused himself. "Ah, perhaps we will have a successful evening after all. If we sell that piece, it will little matter whether anything else sells at all, for that painting alone can cover the season's expenses." He hurried off.

"Ah, good old Paul," Silas mused. "Show him the promise of money, and all his other problems vanish."

"Don't scoff," Emily said. "I'd just as soon he find something to occupy his thoughts other than focusing on our trip West. And we'll need every cent we can scrape together if we can afford the trip."

"Yes," Silas agreed. He sighed and ran his hand across his head, a characteristic gesture. "I hope, Emily, my dear, that we are truly making the right decision."

"We are," Emily said. "I'm certain of it."

Before Silas could answer, a man approached them. "Mr. Thomson, sir, I am Stuart Philson of *Harper's Weekly*. Might I have a moment of your time?"

"Of course," Silas said, smiling politely.

"Do you believe, as many others do, that color photography, should it ever be perfected, would render a death blow to the artist?"

"Not at all," Silas answered easily.

Emily stepped aside, allowing her father to handle the interview. Philson would not want her opinion, and indeed, she knew she would be unable to provide answers with her father's articulate exactness. The reporter began to scribble furiously in his notebook in an attempt to keep pace with Silas's words.

Emily observed the two men under the light of the gas jet and composed a painting in her mind. Her father was tall with a nearly bald head and heavy, expressive white eyebrows. He was very dignified looking, even handsome, she thought, and she was proud of his appearance. The reporter, by contrast, was short and rather plump, with no distinguishing features.

If she were to paint the scene in oils, she would use subtle tones. She would want to show the quiet intensity of the conversation, with the measured pauses before her father's answers were given. No color photograph could ever do that, but she was confident she could capture the mood.

Emily turned to the paintings that graced the walls, and her gaze went immediately to those where her own handiwork was most evident. Each painting was a record of history, and no mere words on a page could ever duplicate that. She smiled, knowing there would always be a place for the artist.

# CHAPTER TWO

EMILY AND HER FATHER SPENT A MAGNIFICENT FIVE DAYS in the remarkable comfort of the train's Wagner parlor car as they began their westward journey. It was outfitted with deep plush seats upholstered in velvet, carved wood paneling, and soft kerosene-lit lamps. Their nights were passed in a comfortable sleeping compartment, and all their meals were taken in the well-appointed dining car.

Silas sat in one of the overstuffed chairs of the parlor car, absorbed in a copy of the *Lightning News*, a newspaper composed daily for the benefit of the passengers. He frowned as he read an article.

"Can this be true?"

"What is it, Father?" Emily asked.

"According to this story, a man named Alexander Graham Bell is working on a device that would send the human voice over a wire. He calls it a telephone, and claims it will one day replace the telegraph."

"My," Emily said, as she leaned forward to look at

the article. "Isn't it remarkable what marvelous things are being invented?"

Silas folded the paper and glanced out the windows at the vast plains that were flashing by. "Yes, it is indeed remarkable. This train, for instance. Now, in comfort rivaling that of a person's own living room, one can span the continent. New York to San Francisco in seven days! Why, it wasn't so long ago that trip took nearly six months, if all went well." He was quiet for a moment, and only the rhythmic clacking of the wheels over the track joints intruded. "That's why this mission is so important, Emily. If we don't capture life among the Plains tribes as it is now, I mean, as it truly is, then their way of life may be lost forever. And that would be a sin."

She put her hand on her father's and smiled at him. "You are right when you say this record must be recorded by an artist, and not by a photographer."

"Photography!" Silas scoffed. "Any fool can squeeze a bulb, and any mechanic can develop a plate. And then what do you have? A flat, lifeless black-and-white shadow that they call a picture. There has never been a photograph taken that could compete with a painting. A photograph slices just an instant out of time, but a painting is much, much more. A true painting has a breath of its own."

Emily hid a smile. "You don't have to convince me, Father. I'm on your side, remember?"

Silas put his other hand on top of Emily's and smiled at her, as he shed the harsh expression that had come over his face while he discussed photography.

"Of course you are." He held up his hands, now knotted and bent from arthritis. "You are more than on my side," he added quietly. "You have become my hands, my talent, my expression. I don't know what I'd do without you."

"Everything I might be, I owe to you, Father," Emily said. "You taught me everything I know."

"I cannot teach talent, my daughter. That has to come from God, and from Him, you received a generous share."

"Excuse me, Mr. Thomson, Miss Thomson," an approaching steward said, interrupting the moment, "but your table is ready."

"Thank you," Silas said, standing. "Well, as this shall be our last meal aboard the train, we wouldn't want to be late, now would we?"

"No," Emily agreed. She was hungry, and the meals had been excellent, but she always approached the trip to the dining car with trepidation. Emily braced herself, as if she was about to plunge into an icy stream. When she opened the rear door of the parlor car, a deafening roar filled her ears as the wind whipped against her dress and hair. The car's normal rocking motion was magnified out here, forcing her to hang onto the railing tightly.

There was a gap between the platforms of the two cars. It was narrow enough to be stepped across but wide enough that if one were to misstep, an unfortunate passenger could fall onto the tracks below. Though Emily had negotiated that gap many times before, each time, it was a frightening experience for her. The gap between the cars was small, but it was enough to show the ties of the railroad bed rushing past, stark evidence of the train's fifty-mile-per-hour speed.

Emily timed her move carefully and then crossed. She held her breath, only exhaling when both she and her father were safely on the other side. Then she opened the door and they stepped into the dining car.

Inside, the dining car matched the elegance of the rest of the train—there were draped curtains, polished wood paneling, and as an unexpected nicety, fresh flowers on each table. A waiter greeted them and directed them to their table.

They settled in and perused the menu that featured blue-winged teal, antelope steaks, roast beef, boiled ham and tongue, fresh fruit, and hot rolls among the offerings. Emily ordered boiled ham, while Silas chose the roast beef.

As they were finishing their meal, Emily noticed a man in a military uniform seated across the aisle. He had been watching them, and now, he leaned forward to speak.

"Excuse me," he said. "I am Colonel Olin Gray, with General Terry's staff. Would you by any chance happen to be Mr. Silas Thomson?"

Silas turned, looking puzzled. "Yes. Do I know you, Colonel?"

"No, sir, I'm sure you do not," he replied. "But I once attended a lecture you gave in New York. May I tell you how much I admire your work?"

"Well, thank you, Colonel," Silas said, genuinely pleased by his remark. "That means a great deal to me. And may I present my daughter, Emily."

"An honor, Miss Thomson," the colonel said as he inclined his head politely, but now it was his turn to look confused. "If I may ask, what brings you out here in the middle of nowhere? Or, are you bound for a lecture tour in San Francisco perhaps?"

"No, my dear fellow," Silas said. "We are going to Fort Lincoln."

"Fort Lincoln?" the colonel asked. "What on earth are you going there for?"

Silas set his fork down. "We will be going on from Fort Lincoln into the Black Hills. We are commissioned to do a series of paintings depicting the Plains Indians in their natural environment."

"What?" the colonel asked, nearly choking on his drink. "Mr. Thomson, you can't be serious, sir! Don't you realize there's a war going on right now?"

Silas reacted to the colonel in a calm voice. "I knew there was some Indian trouble, but I didn't realize..."

"*Indian trouble*, you call it?" Gray interrupted as he raised his voice. "Mr. Thomson, what is happening is considerably more than Indian trouble. The situation in the Black Hills is escalating by the day, and General Custer and his men have their hands full trying to keep things under control. I wouldn't advise you to go through with your plans."

Silas folded his hands on the table. "I appreciate your concern for us, Colonel, but we've come too far to be dissuaded now. We will be going on." Silas spoke with the air of one who had heard all this before

"I can't believe you are that obdurate," the colonel said, shaking his head. "I'm afraid I shall have to issue an order forbidding you to proceed with your preposterous plan."

Silas arched an eyebrow. "And on whose authority would this order be executed?"

"As deputy to the military commander of the region," Colonel Gray said. "I doubt the Department of the Interior knows of your foolhardy venture. Once they are informed, they will uphold my order."

"I'm sorry, Colonel, I appreciate your concern for our safety." Silas reached into his coat pocket and pulled out a folded document. "I'm afraid I have an order that supersedes yours. This letter grants me unrestricted access to the Indian territories." He handed the paper to Gray. "As you can see, it is signed by the President of the United States."

Gray hesitated, staring at the paper, then back at Silas. "You have permission from General Grant to go into the Badlands?"

"From *President* Grant," Silas corrected. "We will be going into the Badlands."

Gray rubbed his beard, studying the two of them before sighing in resignation. "Very well," he said, "but at the very least, I insist you allow me to arrange for a military escort to Fort Lincoln from the Bismarck depot. I'll wire ahead from Fargo tonight."

"If that will put your mind at ease, Colonel Gray, I have no objections to the escort," Silas said, "but I must make one thing clear, we have no intention of being confined to the fort."

Gray nodded. "I only wish there was some way to make you understand the danger you're walking into." He stood and wiped his hands with his napkin, then gave them a halfhearted salute. Then he turned and left the dining car.

Silas sighed. "Ah, Emily, I fear we shall encounter many more like Colonel Gray before we can begin our work."

"Then we will handle them as we handled him," Emily said. "Nothing can stop us now, Father. Nothing."

Silas studied her for a moment before nodding. "I hope you're right," he said. "And I hope they're wrong."

"Everything will be fine, Father," Emily said, pushing aside any uncertainty in her own mind. "I just know it will."

––––––––

EMILY SLEPT SOUNDLY THAT NIGHT. She had grown accustomed to the steady motion of the train, and the clatter of the wheels against the rails soon lulled her into a deep and dreamless rest.

"Bismarck! All passengers for Bismarck!"

Emily was awakened by the conductor's call. The train was slowing and within a few minutes, it came to a complete stop. Pushing aside the curtain, she looked out into the early morning light.

"Bismarck. This is the end of the line, folks. Everyone gets off here," the conductor called again.

The station was a low brick building with a simple white sign bearing a faded black-lettered word, *Bismarck*. At this early hour, only a few people had turned out to meet the train. She saw a pair of old men sitting idly on a bench near the depot, while a small cluster of people began greeting arriving passengers. Off to one side, a young man and woman stood silently, the sadness in their expressions suggesting they would soon be separated.

With an artist's eye, Emily surveyed the scene. She saw something that first made her gasp, then thrilled her.

Two Native American men stood apart from everyone else, watching the train with dark, unreadable eyes, as if trying to comprehend this marvel of the White man's world. Their expressions showed no curiosity, only quiet acceptance of the iron beast that had roared into their world.

"Emily," her father called up from the lower bunk. "Hurry and get dressed. I'd hate for the train to turn around and take us back while we're still abed."

"I'm hurrying, Father."

She let the curtain fall back into place and began the difficult task of dressing within the confines of the narrow berth without sacrificing her modesty.

A few minutes later, Emily and her father stepped out onto the station platform, adjusting to the cool morning air. They were approached almost immediately by an Army sergeant.

"Beggin' your pardon, sir," the man said, his voice having a distinct Irish brogue. "I'm Sergeant Flynn. I was ordered to meet a Mr. Silas Thomson and his daughter, and escort you both to Fort Abraham Lincoln. I take it that would be the two of you?"

Silas sighed, shaking his head. "Yes, Sergeant, that's us. I see Colonel Gray wasted no time in carrying out his promise."

"No, sir," Flynn said with a broad grin. "'Twas easy enough to find you now, bein' as how the colonel said 'twould be a tall handsome figure of a gentleman, and a lass as lovely as any colleen I'd ever likely see."

Silas chuckled. "Sergeant, I suspect you've a bit of the blarney in you."

"Aye, perhaps so," the sergeant said. "But by the saints, I've never spoken truer words. Where would your baggage be now?"

"Well, if the Northern Pacific has done its job properly, it should be unloading now," Silas said.

"If you'd like to take yer breakfast now, me 'n the men'll see to your things," the sergeant offered.

"Thank you, Sergeant, that's most kind of you," Emily said. She rewarded the sergeant with a smile that caused him to brighten visibly.

Breakfast was disappointing. After having been spoiled by nearly a week of omelets, pancakes, and other delicacies, the tough steak and fried potatoes offered at the Bismarck station were a stark contrast to what they were used to. But realizing that meals ahead may be even less appetizing, they ate without complaint.

The sun had climbed higher in the sky by the time Silas and Emily left the restaurant and was already promising the heat of a late summer's day.

"Here, ma'am," Sergeant Flynn called as Emily stepped out on the platform. "We've got General Custer's personal coach for you. You'll like it, it rides like a cloud."

The vehicle was a *spring coach*, built along the same lines as the Concord stagecoach, but smaller and much lighter. The sergeant held the door open while Emily and her father climbed in.

"Hold that coach!"

Emily had already taken her seat, but she turned to see a man running toward the coach.

"Oh, bless me, it's Cap'n Tom," Flynn muttered under his breath.

"Who?"

"Cap'n Tom Custer, the brother of Gen'rul Custer himself," Flynn said. "By the looks of it, he likely spent the night in Bismarck, 'n he's a bit *likkered up*. Wouldn't do for the gen'rul to see him in sech a condition."

"Surely if the general is his brother, the captain need not worry about anything," Emily suggested.

"No'm, that ain't the case a'tall," Flynn said. "You see, the gen'rul...he's quite a stickler for military courtesy and the like. Cap'n Tom now, he don't rightly give two hoots 'n a holler for sech things. So when you got two brothers like that, 'n one of 'em bein' a commandin' officer 'n all, why it just naturally means trouble."

Tom Custer reached the coach, dusting himself off. "Sergeant Flynn," he said, addressing the soldier, "my brother wouldn't be in town now, would he?"

"No, sir, Cap'n Tom," Flynn said. "He just sent the coach in to pick up a couple of guests."

"Guests? Well, now, I hadn't heard that we were to be honored with guests," Custer said, squinting toward the coach. He walked to the door and looked in. When he saw Emily, his smile disappeared.

"Sergeant," he whispered, though it was loud enough for Emily to hear. "Why didn't you tell me you were escorting a lady?"

"I didn't get the chance, sir," Sergeant Flynn answered.

"I've been drinking." Tom exhaled as he rubbed a hand across his face.

"Cap'n, why don't you stay in town a while longer?" Flynn suggested. "The gen'rul's likely to be tied up with these folks for a time, 'n he won't be lookin' for you right away."

Tom let out a short, deprecating chuckle. "Meaning I can sober up before I come in, is that it?"

"No, sir," Sergeant Flynn said. "Why, I wouldn't..."

"That's all right, Sergeant," Tom cut in. "It makes sense. No point in giving Autie another reason to get angry if I can avoid it, eh?"

"Yes, sir, Cap'n, that's the way I see it," Sergeant Flynn said.

Tom came back to the coach and tipped his hat. "My apologies, ma'am," he said. "I was going to ride back to the fort with you, but to be honest, I am ill-fit for female companionship. I am, sorry to say, besotted. If you will forgive me?"

"Of course, Captain," Emily replied evenly.

Tom straightened, saluted Emily and Silas, then, executing a crisp, military about-face, turned and headed back toward town.

Silas watched him go, then turned to Flynn. "Is he often in that condition, Sergeant?"

Flynn hesitated. "Yes, sir, more often than the gen'rul would like," he admitted. "But don't let the whiskey fool you, none. He's as brave a soldier as ever fought in a battle. Aye, 'n as good a man too. There's not a manjack in the Seventh as wouldn't soak his trousers in kerosene and march through hell for the cap'n...if you'll excuse the language, ma'am."

"If, as you say, the captain is a good man, why does he drink so much?" Emily ventured to ask.

"He's got a few demons to contend with, ma'am," Sergeant Flynn said. "Picked 'em up at Washita."

Before Emily could ask more, a mounted soldier rode up.

"Sergeant, the detail is formed."

"Aye," Flynn said. "Put two men up front, two in the back, and two outriders. I'll take the reins."

"Right, Sergeant," the soldier said. He relayed the

orders, and six mounted cavalrymen fell into position around the coach.

"Hope you folks have a right comfortable ride," Flynn said as he climbed up onto the driver's seat.

Emily watched the last buildings of Bismarck fall behind them as the coach rolled toward the open plain. She was curious what the sergeant had meant about Washita and Captain Custer, but that question would have to be answered later.

# CHAPTER THREE

TIMOTHY PATRICK FLYNN, SERGEANT, UNITED STATES Army, Seventh Cavalry, studied the terrain around him as he guided the coach carrying Emily and her father. General Custer had told him Silas Thomson was a very famous painter.

Flynn had never heard of him, but that didn't mean anything. Flynn was not a man given to much reading, but he did have an appreciation for art. He liked one painting in particular. He would often stand in front of it and look at it in silence. He was ashamed to admit that he had no idea who the artist was. In fact, the painting was so real to him that he sometimes forgot that it was just a picture and not a window onto real life.

At Fort Abraham Lincoln, the painting hung in the Sutlers' Store. It was of a cavalry unit on parade, and the artist had captured it perfectly. When Flynn looked at it, he could almost lose himself in the picture. He could feel the sun on his back and smell the horseflesh beneath him.

It was a fine, fine painting, and Flynn often wished

that he were one of the soldiers in the picture, suspended in time and space, immortalized forever in an important moment of your life. Of course, Flynn did not think in those words, but the meaning was there.

It would be nice, Flynn thought, if Silas Thomson would create something like that for the Seventh Cavalry. A portrait of General Custer and his soldiers, encamped perhaps, or on the march, or maybe even in battle. But not a battle like *Washita,* Flynn thought. He had no desire to have *Washita* immortalized.

"Sergeant!"

Flynn snapped back to reality at the shout from one of the point riders.

"Aye, lad?"

"The bridge is burning!"

"What?"

From his seat, he saw the bridge ahead, flames licking at the wooden planks while thick black smoke was rising into the sky.

"My God, lads, there must be Indians about! Call the riders in, we're going back to..."

Flynn was interrupted by a swishing, thumping sound as an arrow buried deep into his chest. He let out a bellow of surprise and pain.

Inside the coach, Emily grabbed at the side of her seat as the vehicle lurched to the side. "Sergeant Flynn, what's happening?"

"Ma'am, get down on the floor!" Flynn called out, his voice strained. "We're under attack!"

Even as he spoke, two of the outriders fell from their saddles, mortally wounded as arrows pierced their bodies. From out of the smoke, a wave of warriors, at least fifty strong, emerged. They were yelling and screaming as they charged toward the escort party, wielding bows, rifles, and war clubs.

Sergeant Flynn gritted his teeth, fighting to keep control of the vehicle. With a crack of the reins, he managed to turn the coach around and whip the panicked horses into a full gallop. From Emily's position in the coach, she could see through the dust that the Indians were gaining on them.

"They're going to catch us!" she cried, her voice shrill with panic. Never in her life had she been more frightened than she was at this moment.

Silas muttered under his breath, "Is it to end here?"

Another soldier went down, then, to Emily's horror, the last two soldiers broke off the running fight with the Indians. They disappeared into the prairie, abandoning the coach with its wounded driver and two terrified passengers.

Sergeant Flynn, weakened from loss of blood, lost control of the frightened horses as the coach swayed violently. In moments, the Indians had surrounded the coach. One of them leaped from his horse to the coach, and clinging to the window frame, stared in at Emily and her father. His painted face leered at them, then he let out a war whoop and scrambled onto the top of the coach.

The coach rumbled to a stop. It was quickly surrounded by dozens of Indians, all shouting and yelling, and some laughing to celebrate their victory. One of them stepped forward, opened the door to the coach and motioned for Emily and her father to get out.

"We'd better do as he says," Silas said in a measured tone.

The calmness her father showed steadied Emily...

and helped calm her, too, as he had no doubt intended. As they stepped outside, Emily saw Sergeant Flynn slumped in the driver's seat, gripping the arrow in his chest. Instinctively, she started to move toward him.

"No."

The command was sharp, spoken in accented English.

"But I must see to him. Can't you see he's dying?"

Flynn coughed, forcing a weak chuckle. "Don't worry, ma'am, I ain't dyin'. The arrow didn't hit 'nythin' vital."

Emily let out a breath she hadn't realized she was holding.

"Thank God for that," she said.

Silas turned to Flynn. "What's going to happen to us? Are we going to be killed?"

"I don't think so," Flynn said, his breath shallow. "If we was, why like as not we'd already be dead. They'd'a kilt us the moment they stopped the coach."

One of the Indians spoke gruffly in Lakota and pointed to the interior of the coach. The Indian who had climbed on the roof, grabbed Flynn by the collar and pushed him off the seat, sending him crashing into the dirt. Flynn cried out in pain.

"Stop! Can't you see what you're doing?"

She moved toward Flynn, but he raised a hand. "I'll be all right, ma'am," he grunted. "Just help me get inside. That's what they're a wantin'."

"Father, help me," Emily said.

Silas bent to take one of Flynn's arms, and together they got him on his feet. Then, they hoisted the big man back inside. As soon as they were seated, the warrior on the roof took the reins. He snapped them against the horses' backs, causing the coach to lurch forward abruptly.

"Where do you suppose they'll take us?" Emily asked as the coach rattled and jerked across the rough prairie.

Flynn rested his head against the wooden wall. "They're Hunkpapa Sioux," he said. "Probably here on a hunting party, so my guess is they've got a camp somewhere nearby. They'll be taking us there, I reckon."

Emily unbuttoned Flynn's shirt. She winced at the sight of the jagged tear that was still oozing blood, though by now the blood had begun to coagulate. The shaft of the arrow protruded from the middle of the ugly hole in his chest.

Emily made a face and instinctively turned her head away.

"Sorry, ma'am, I should'a maybe told you. Ain't such a pretty sight," Sergeant Flynn said.

"Should I...try to pull it out?" she asked hesitantly.

Flynn managed a weak smile. "Bless you, ma'am, for thinkin' about it. But it's best to just leave it in there til I can get somewhere still to lay proper. Besides that, I'm not all that sure you could yank it loose, lass, even if you tried. 'Tis flared, you see, 'n the little devil goes in a mite easier than it comes out."

"Oooh," Emily said, flinching at the thought of pulling out the arrow.

"If the heathens ain't got it in mind to kill us right off," Flynn continued, "I reckon they'll have one o' their medicine men yank it out for me."

"Surely, Sergeant, you wouldn't let a savage medicine man operate on you?" Emily asked, shocked at the thought.

"Ma'am, I figure they've had a heap more practice jerkin' out arrowheads than most White doctors. Yes'm, I reckon I'd let 'im do it."

Emily glanced at her father and was startled to see him calmly holding a sketch pad. He was staring out the window, sketching a picture of one of the warriors riding alongside the coach.

"Father, what are you doing?"

Silas didn't look up. "Just what I came out here to do, daughter."

Emily didn't know whether to laugh or cry. Here she was, terrified, not knowing what was going to happen to them, and yet here was her father, sketching a picture as casually as if he were sitting in his own studio.

"Let 'im be, lass," Flynn said. "When the Indians see it, might be they'll realize you mean no harm to 'em. At any rate, it can't hurt."

Emily wasn't convinced, but she held her tongue.

———

THE NEXT HOUR was one of the strangest Emily had ever passed in her life. The coach bounced across the open plains, the monotony of the jolting ride broken only by the occasional sharp lurch and the grunt from Sergeant Flynn when they hit a large bump. Flynn was drifting in and out of consciousness, his head now resting on Emily's shoulder. Across from her, her father sat making sketch after sketch, having now drawn five of their escorts.

Emily was envious of both of them—Sergeant Flynn because he was unconscious and unaware of their circumstances for most of the trip, and her father for being so dedicated to his art that he left no room for fear in his heart.

They forded a small stream, and silver sprays of water shot out from both sides of the coach. Then, without warning, the coach slowed abruptly.

"Sergeant Flynn," Emily whispered. "We're stopping."

The door to the coach was yanked open, and a tall, fierce Indian stood there looking in. His face was covered with red paint, but his expression was blank.

"It's Crazy Wolf," Sergeant Flynn muttered when he saw the warrior.

"Who?"

"The fella at the door," Flynn said in a tight voice. "He's one of the war leaders. I don't think the gen'rul knew he was in the area, though. If he did, I doubt the Seventh would still be in garrison right now."

The Indian said something in Lakota, then motioned for them to get out of the coach.

Emily hesitated. "Sergeant Flynn is wounded. He needs help."

"Don't waste your breath, ma'am," Sergeant Flynn said as he grunted in pain. He braced himself, gripping the edge of the coach before stepping out onto the ground. "They see I'm wounded. If they aim to help, they'll do it without being asked. If they ain't gonna help, all the askin' in the world ain't gonna do no good."

Crazy Wolf looked at the three of them with a cold, calculating stare. Then he shouted something and pointed to Sergeant Flynn. Two Indians stepped forward, grabbed Flynn beneath the arms, and then led him away.

"Thank you," Emily said instinctively.

Crazy Wolf ignored her.

Emily and her father remained beside the coach, surrounded by the people of the village. To Emily's surprise, the people didn't seem hostile at all. Many were women and children, and they seemed more curious than anything else.

Several times, children would edge closer to Emily, fascinated by her long red hair. They whispered back and forth to one another. Then, when she smiled at them, they would turn and run back to cling to their mothers.

Silas, unfazed by their situation, got his sketch pad from the coach, and began drawing a picture of one of the children.

Crazy Wolf came back, stepping in front of them.

"Why do you come to soldier-fort?" he demanded. "Are you soldier-squaw?"

"You speak English," Emily said. "Am I glad to know you can speak to us."

Without warning, Crazy Wolf slapped Emily. The sudden blow shocked and humiliated her more than it hurt her.

"Here, what do you think you're doing?" Silas shouted. He dropped his sketch pad and started toward Crazy Wolf, but two warriors grabbed him by the arms.

"Father, no!" Emily cried out. She was holding her hand up to her jaw. It stung from the unexpected slap, but her face burned more in anger and embarrassment than anything else. "I'm all right. Don't make this worse."

Crazy Wolf's expression did not change. "When Crazy Wolf ask woman question, woman must answer. Why do you go to soldier-fort? Are you soldier-squaw?"

"No," Emily said. "I am...that is, my father and I are artists."

Crazy Wolf frowned. "What is artists?"

"We paint pictures," Emily said. She pointed to her father's sketch pad now lying in the dirt, its pages riffling in the soft breeze. "There. Look at that pad."

Crazy Wolf picked up the pad and began flipping through the pages. A strange expression came over his face, and he called to the others. The first Indian Silas had drawn came over to look at the sketch. He laughed and showed it to several others, and soon half the camp was yelling and straining to see the drawings. In the melee that followed, several of the drawings were torn.

The two Indians holding Silas released him so that they, too, could see the pictures. Silas and Emily exchanged uneasy glances, wondering what their fate would be.

"Why do you make pictures?" Crazy Wolf turned back to them, his face showing no sign of amusement.

"I am doing it to preserve your people's culture for all time," Silas said.

"I think you make pictures to show soldiers," Crazy Wolf said, his eyes narrowing. "Maybe you take to fort. Soldiers see the pictures, and they come to arrest us."

"No," Silas said. "That's not what I had in mind at all."

"Crazy Wolf," Emily said, interjecting. "We want to stay here on the Indian lands. We want to paint many pictures of your people."

"No," Crazy Wolf said.

"But why not? We mean you no harm."

"No."

Crazy Wolf spoke in the same short, guttural

language. Before Emily could react, she and her father were taken by several of the Indians and separated.

"Wait!" Emily cried. "Crazy Wolf, where are they taking us?"

Emily struggled against the grip of the two men who held her, but she wasn't strong enough to break free. They took her into a nearby tipi and shoved her to the ground. Before she could stand, rawhide thongs were wound around her wrists and ankles, and then secured to wooden stakes that had been driven into the ground.

"What are you doing?" she demanded. "Please, let my father and me go. We mean you no harm. Can't you see that?"

Despite Emily's entreaties, the captors left her helpless and vulnerable to any indignity that might befall her. They stepped outside without another word.

For a long while, she lay still, trying to hear anything from her father or Sergeant Flynn. But she heard nothing.

Then, she heard laughter.

She turned her head as a group of children ran into the tipi. They were playing a game, and they darted around her as if she weren't there. They jumped over her, squealing and laughing, paying no more attention to her than if she were a fallen log.

Later, an old woman came in. She sat down between Emily's legs and stared, unblinking.

"Do you speak English?" Emily asked.

The woman made no response. Not even a flicker in the eyes, or the slightest change of expression on her face, showed that she had heard Emily speak.

Emily tried again. "What are they going to do to us?"

Again, the woman was silent.

"My father, and Sergeant Flynn. Are they all right?"

Still no response. Finally, after the woman seemed to have satisfied whatever curiosity had driven her there in the first place, she got up and left.

No one offered Emily anything to eat through the rest of the day, but she was so frightened that she had no appetite.

———

NIGHT CAME, and the wavering orange of the campfires' glow bathed the inside of the tipi in eerie light. The Indians seemed to be celebrating, for they were dancing around the fires and singing, a strange, haunting, discordant chanting. The incessant pounding of the drums seemed to coincide with the rhythm of Emily's own pulsing heartbeat.

It all seemed so unreal to Emily. Only days ago, she had been standing in the foyer of the New York Art League Gallery...and now, she wasn't at all confident that she would survive this night.

A conversation began just outside her tipi. Emily twisted her head, straining to see who it was, but she could see nothing more than two shadows.

She couldn't understand the words being spoken, but she could understand their discordant intent. Finally, the two arguers drifted away, and Emily was left alone again. She lay there, listening to the drums, trying to reckon the passing of time. She had come to the somewhat irrational conclusion that if she could just make it until morning, she might have a chance to survive.

A moment later, the flap of the tipi was pulled aside,

and Crazy Wolf stepped inside. He stared down at her, the war paint still across his face. His dark eyes studied her, his expression unreadable.

Emily could feel her pulse hammering in her throat. She swallowed hard, willing herself to stay calm.

"Crazy Wolf," she said, forcing her voice to remain steady. "What have you done with my father? And Sergeant Flynn?"

He did not answer.

She licked her dry lips. "What...what do you intend to do?"

Again, Crazy Wolf did not answer. Instead, he knelt down beside her, pulling a knife from his belt. The blade pressed against her throat—not hard enough to cut, but enough for her to feel the knife against her skin.

She shut her eyes, twisting her head to the side, as she breathed a quick prayer. Then she waited for the pain, but it didn't come.

Instead, she felt the knife shift to her chest, to the neck of her dress. There was a sudden, sharp tug—then a tearing sound.

Her eyes flew open to see Crazy Wolf's hand grabbing the torn fabric, preparing to rip her dress further.

"No!" Emily screamed, more from anger than fear.

The single word came out strong, and it was enough to make Crazy Wolf stop. She glared up at him, her eyes filled with defiance.

For a moment, he hesitated. Then something in his expression changed.

Another voice could be heard from outside the tipi. It sounded commanding and urgent.

Crazy Wolf froze.

The voice called again. This time, it was followed by the shuffle of approaching feet.

Crazy Wolf yanked his knife away, stashing it back in its sheath. He stared at Emily for a long moment. Then, without a word, he rose and disappeared through the tipi's flap.

Emily exhaled shakily, barely realizing she had been holding her breath.

She lay still, staring at the flickering light against the tipi walls, her mind racing as realization settled over her. For the first time since being captured, she understood just how powerless she was. But for now, at least, she was still alive, and she had escaped the humiliation of what she was sure was about to happen.

She did not know what had just saved her, whether it was luck, intervention, or something else entirely, but she did know it would not protect her forever.

Her body trembled as the restraints bore into her wrists and ankles, her breathing ragged. She turned her head toward the entrance, trying to hear what was happening outside. The voices in the unknown language continued, each rising higher and higher. Another argument, she thought. Then footsteps faded, and the drums began again, louder and faster, as if they were setting the pace for the beat of her heart.

Emily shut her eyes and forced herself to lie still, waiting. For what, she didn't know.

# CHAPTER FOUR

SUDDENLY, A SHARP CRY RANG OUT FROM OUTSIDE, followed by the dull thud of a body hitting the ground.

Emily's eyes snapped open just in time to see Crazy Wolf fall to the ground as he stumbled sideways through the tipi flap. He was holding his jaw where he had been hit.

Another man followed him and stood behind him, his posture rigid. He stepped forward, the firelight illuminating his long, dark hair and his sharp features.

Crazy Wolf spat out something in Lakota, his voice full of anger, but the other man replied in the same guttural language. The two warriors stared at one another for a tense moment as the tension between them escalated. Then, with one last defiant look at Emily, Crazy Wolf jumped up and stormed out.

Emily exhaled shakily, hardly believing she was still alive.

But her reprieve was short-lived, because now the stranger turned to her.

He crouched beside her, and she stiffened, thinking

that this man would be no different from Crazy Wolf. Even in the shadows, his eyes startled her. They were not the dark brown of the others, but she was sure they were blue. His skin, though sun-bronzed, seemed lighter than theirs, too.

"Who are you?" she asked hoarsely.

He remained silent for a moment, then drew his knife. Her breath caught, but with a quick motion, he cut the rawhide thongs at her wrists, then her ankles. Pain prickled through her limbs as circulation returned, and she rubbed at her wrists, staring at him in confusion.

Why had he saved her? And what would he want in return?

Without a word, he rose, moved to the side of the tipi, and picked up a discarded blanket. He tossed it to her, and she caught it, wrapping it around herself as she covered her torn dress. The coarse wool scratched her skin, reminding her of her precarious position. She was still a prisoner and still at the mercy of these people.

And yet, she instinctively knew, this man wasn't like the others. There was something about him, something about the way he carried himself. He was definitely different.

He crouched near the fire, poking at the coals as he brought a small blaze back to life. When he finally spoke, his quiet, unaccented English surprised her.

"I was twelve when my family joined a wagon train bound for Oregon," he said evenly. "My parents, my sister, and everyone else on the wagon train, were killed when we were attacked by the Crow. I played dead and was left behind. The Lakota found me. They gave me a home. A new life. A new name. I am called Two Hearts, because I am both Lakota and White."

"When you...were White?" Emily asked, her voice barely above a whisper.

He gave a small nod.

"Jacob Andrews. That was my name before. Now I am Jacob Two Hearts."

Emily hesitated as her mind began to whirl. Then she stood, pulling the blanket tighter around her shoulders.

"Then you know our world as well as you know theirs," she said as she took a step toward him. "You understand what's right and what isn't. Please, Mr. Two Hearts, you have to help us. My father, Sergeant Flynn—we didn't do anything wrong. We were on our way to Fort Lincoln, that's all. We need to be freed."

Jacob's jaw tightened.

"I can't help you," he said bluntly. "The tribal council decides the fate of captives."

"But surely you have some influence here?" she argued, her voice rising slightly. "Can't you convince them?"

"I can try," he said after a moment. "Maybe they will listen. Maybe not. Crazy Wolf will have angry words, I do know that."

"You have to do it," she pleaded.

"The council decides," he repeated again. "Not me."

Emily balled her hands into fists as she let out a long sigh. "You are our only hope. I can see that, but if you won't speak for us..."

"I didn't say that," Jacob said with a faint smile. "Whether they listen is another matter."

"Oh, but Crazy Wolf! He will try to stop you," she

said, her voice anxious now. "Will you be in danger after what you did tonight?"

Jacob's smile widened slightly. "Crazy Wolf doesn't frighten me. We've fought many times since we were boys. He's never beaten me yet."

Emily took a breath before she spoke. "Be careful, whatever he tries, you should be ready."

Jacob nodded his head slightly, then gestured to the wooden trunk by the entrance.

"Your belongings were brought here," he said. "You may want to put on another dress. The council will decide soon, and they will want to see you."

"Thank you," she said, her voice low. "From the bottom of my heart, I thank you."

Jacob didn't reply. He stepped to the tipi entrance, paused, and added, "I'll try my best...we'll see what happens."

Then he ducked through the flap and was gone.

Emily let out a slow breath as the cool night air swept into the tipi behind him.

She had no illusions about her situation. Whatever debt Jacob might feel for what he'd done tonight, it wasn't a promise of safety. He was Lakota now. And in this world, she knew the fate of captives was rarely kind.

For now, she moved toward her trunk. All she could do was be ready.

———

THE COUNCIL FIRE BURNED BRIGHTLY, casting long shadows across the circle of men. Jacob Two Hearts moved through the gathered warriors, his face calm as he took his place among the inner circle.

Najinyanupi was already speaking.

"When the prairie is on fire," the elder said gravely, "you see animals surrounded by the fire, you see them run and try to hide themselves so that they will not burn. That is the way we are here."

Jacob sat quietly, his back straight, his hands resting on his knees. He listened to the ongoing discussion and knew it was not about the captives. This was a discussion the council had had many times before. It was a reckoning with their future.

"I wish to speak now," one of the council elders said. White Ghost stood up, and the others looked toward him, for he was older than most and considered very wise. His voice was quiet but carried weight.

"The White men have driven away our game," he said. "Until now, we have nothing left that is valuable except the hills they are asking us to give up. The earth is full of minerals of many kinds, and the ground is covered with forests of heavy pine. When we give these up to the Great Father, we know that we give up that last thing that is valuable either to us or to the White people."

The circle murmured its agreement.

Then Crazy Wolf leaped up and strode across the circle to stand before Jacob. He did not ask for permission to speak.

"He is a White man!" Crazy Wolf shouted, pointing accusingly at Jacob. "He was born White, and he cannot change what he is."

A mutter rippled through the circle, though no one spoke openly.

Sitting Bear, one of the elders, rose to speak, and said, "Jacob Two Hearts was born White, but now he is

Lakota. We welcomed him with the sacred ceremony. He is one of us."

Crazy Wolf, who had been holding something in a clenched fist, suddenly threw two stones into the dirt before the fire. One stone was red, one was white.

"Look at the two stones," Crazy Wolf said. "If you are not blind, you can see that one is red and the other is white. Medicine men cannot change the color of the stones, wishing cannot change the color of the stones, prayer to the Great Spirit cannot change the color of the stones, and no ceremony can change the color of the stones. I know, for I have tried all of these ways. And yet, as you see, they have remained the same. One is red..." He paused dramatically and walked back over to stand in front of Jacob. He leaned over so that his face was only inches away from Jacob's. "...and one is white!"

His voice dropped to a low growl. "And no ceremony will ever turn a white stone red. Just as no ceremony can change *you*."

The circle fell quiet as the men's eyes shifted uneasily between Crazy Wolf, Jacob, and the stones.

Crazy Wolf stood there in the light of the campfire, allowing the impact of his dramatic speech to sink in.

Finally, Sitting Bull held up his hand, and the murmurs died immediately. It was the first time that night the great chief had spoken.

"You have shown us that the color of the stones cannot be changed," Sitting Bull said. "It was a good speech with many wise words. But I ask you, Crazy Wolf, what does the color of the stones have to do with Jacob Two Hearts?"

Crazy Wolf straightened. "Just as stones cannot be changed, neither can men. Jacob still thinks like a

White man. Tonight, because I dared touch a White woman, he struck me. The Whites believe that a Red man is an animal, unfit even to look at their women. They tell their women to kill themselves rather than let a Red man even look at them. And so this is also true of Jacob Two Hearts."

The men around the fire had some angry remarks at that accusation, and Jacob could feel their eyes on him. He knew Crazy Wolf's words had struck a nerve, but he stayed seated, his hands tightening into fists in his lap.

Sitting Bull nodded once. "You have spoken. Now Jacob Two Hearts may speak."

Jacob stood slowly. His face remained calm, though his pulse was racing. He let his eyes sweep around the circle before he began to speak.

"It is true that I attacked my brother, Crazy Wolf," he said evenly. "Not because the woman is White, but because what he was trying to do would have been unwise. He was about to force himself upon her."

"And you could not see a Red man with a White woman?" Crazy Wolf challenged.

Jacob ignored him. He turned to the others.

"We are very close to the White fort now, but we do not have many of our warriors in camp. If harm comes to her, or to her father, or the long knife sergeant, Custer will come down on us before we are ready. And then it will not be just the warriors who die—it will be the old ones, the women, the children. Do you want another Washita?"

A few of the older men lowered their eyes at the mention of Washita.

Jacob continued, "It was wrong to attack the wagon that took the woman and her father toward the fort.

They are of no danger to us. But Crazy Wolf was foolish, and without the consent of the council, he led an attack. It is said that he killed four soldiers. But it is also said that two soldiers escaped. They returned to the fort, and they will tell Custer what we have done. If we keep the captives, Custer has many more soldiers than we have warriors, and he will come, and many will die."

"You speak like a White man. We are not afraid to die," Crazy Wolf shouted.

Jacob's cold stare bore in on Crazy Wolf. "No," he said. "I speak with the wisdom of one who is a member of this council, a Lakota. I have no fear of dying. But I will not allow our women and children to be slaughtered because of your foolish pride. I say we release them. Send word to Custer that we regret what happened and that his medicine wagon may come for the sergeant. If we do this, we can make a truce that will allow us to fight another day."

The circle sat in silence, the crackle of the fire the only sound.

After some time, Fool Dog spoke. "He speaks wisely. I say we should listen to him."

Crazy Wolf glared at Jacob.

"And I say he is a White man and will trick us with his White words!" Crazy Wolf insisted.

Then Sitting Bull spoke again. His deep, steady voice cut through the tension. "No, he is not a White man. He is Lakota. Your story of the stones has no meaning. You say he cannot change because he was born White, but a stone has no heart. Jacob Two Hearts does."

Jacob bowed his head in gratitude.

"Go," Sitting Bull said. "Bring the woman to me. She will hear my words."

Jacob left the council fire and walked back through the quiet camp. His chest felt tight, though his face betrayed nothing. He had cut Emily loose, but he hadn't told her to stay in the tipi. If she was gone, his argument to release her would crumble. He wouldn't be able to convince the others that she could be trusted.

When he stepped back into the tipi, he breathed a sigh of relief. Emily sat waiting, her hands folded in her lap. Her questioning eyes met his.

"Will I be released?" she asked, her voice steady despite the pounding of her heart.

"Yes," he said simply.

"Oh, thank God," Emily said. Then her thoughts turned immediately to the others. "What about my father? And Sergeant Flynn? Will they be released, too?"

"Yes. At least your father will be leaving with you."

"But not Sergeant Flynn?"

"Flynn must stay until Custer sends an ambulance wagon for him."

"How badly hurt is Sergeant Flynn? Will he live?"

"Yes, he will live," Jacob said, as he motioned for her to stand. "Now, come. Chief Sitting Bull wants to speak to you."

She rose, grabbing her shawl. "What will happen?"

"You will go before the council," Jacob said. "But Sitting Bull, alone, will decide your fate."

Emily nodded as she lifted her chin.

Jacob held open the flap, and she stepped through first.

The village, which had been imposing enough in

the daytime, was terrifying by dark. The flickering glow of the campfires cast eerie shadows, and Lakota faces that had expressed curiosity in the daytime now seemed like unreadable masks. The rhythmic pounding of the drums, that seemed to echo her heartbeat, filled the air.

Jacob led her toward the largest fire, where the council still sat in a circle, their faces lit by the flames.

"This is Sitting Bull," Jacob said, pointing toward one of the men.

Emily had read of Sitting Bull. From the preparations she and her father had done before coming to paint, she knew that he was the chief of the Hunkpapas and that he had never lived on a reservation in defiance of government orders. He was an impressive-looking man, and despite the uncertainty of her position, she looked at him with the practiced eye of the artist. The lines of strength and wisdom in his face comforted her.

Sitting Bull looked at her steadily. "What is your name?"

"I am Emily Thomson," she said.

"I am Tatanka Iyotake," he replied. "In your language, that means Sitting Bull."

"I have heard of you," Emily said, finding her voice. "It is an honor to meet you."

"Why have you come?"

"My father and I are artists," she explained. "We came to paint the Lakota and show the people in the East what you are really like."

Across the circle, Crazy Wolf sneered. "She speaks lies! She will give the pictures to the soldiers so they can hunt us down like animals!"

Emily turned her eyes to him. "That isn't true," Emily

said. "We want to take the paintings back to New York and let the people see you as you are, not just what the newspapers tell them. If people understand your ways, maybe they will demand that Washington keeps its word."

Sitting Bull nodded at her words, but his tone did not change. "Crazy Wolf says you should be killed."

Emily met Crazy Wolf's glare. "Crazy Wolf is a coward," she said firmly. "He tried to force himself on me while I was tied to the ground. Then he would have killed me when I couldn't fight back."

A ripple of laughter passed through the council at her blunt and direct words. Crazy Wolf glared at her with hate in his eyes, and she knew that she had made an enemy for life. She wondered if that would make their mission a lost cause, if indeed, it was not already. On the other hand, she would not be cowed by him.

Sitting Bull raised his hand for silence. "Jacob Two Hearts has spoken for you. He says you should be set free to return to your people."

"I am grateful to Mr. Two Hearts," Emily said, "and I do want to be free. I will return to the fort so I can make certain a wagon is sent for Sergeant Flynn. But I do not want to stay with my people. I want permission for my father and me to move freely among your people in order to finish our work here."

Upon hearing her answer, a murmur moved through the council.

"If you stay with us, you know, by your words this night, you have made Crazy Wolf your enemy," Sitting Bull said. "Does this not frighten you?"

"Yes," Emily admitted. "But I still wish to stay anyway."

Sitting Bull regarded her in silence, and then said, "We will speak of this."

Emily stepped back to the edge of the firelight and sat on the ground. She watched as the council discussed her fate and that of her father and Sergeant Flynn. Jacob Two Hearts and Crazy Wolf both spoke in Lakota several more times. She couldn't understand the words, but she could tell, as the voices rose and fell, that the words were heated at times, measured at others. Finally, as she heard Crazy Wolf's tone become even sharper, she knew that the council was turning against him. Then, with one final outburst, Crazy Wolf stormed out of the meeting, glaring angrily at Emily as he walked by.

The hatred of his stare sent a chill down her spine.

Jacob came to her, and with a faint smile, offered his hand to help her to her feet. "It has been decided. You and your father will return to the fort as I have said," Jacob said.

Emily swallowed the lump in her throat. "Thank you. And will we be able to return? To finish our work?"

Jacob looked toward Sitting Bull. "That is for him to say."

Once again, Emily found herself standing before the great chief. Sitting Bull stood, raising his hand, palm out. He bowed his head for a moment before he spoke.

"I have listened to your words, and I have spoken with the council," he said. "Now hear what we say. When you return to the fort, if the soldiers say you may come back, we will not harm you. We say it is good if people in the large, white villages know of our ways. Perhaps then they will tell the Great Father in Washington to let our children live in peace.

"But, you must take these words to Custer. Tell him these are the words of Sitting Bull, chief of the Hunkpapa Sioux."

Sitting Bull walked toward the fire. He gazed at it for a moment, as if composing his thoughts, then he turned back to Emily.

The circle grew quiet as he began to speak.

"Tell the Whites the Black Hills belong to me! Look at me and look at the earth. Which is older, do you think? The earth, and I was born on it. It does not belong to us alone—it was our fathers before us, and it should be our children's after us. When I received this land, it was all in one piece, and so I hold it. If the White men take my country, where can I go? I have nowhere to go... I love this land. Let us be. That is what they promised in their treaty.

"But what is the White man doing here? He comes to spy out the land, to build more forts, more roads, and to dig for gold? The Black Hills belong to me. The White man must go back."

Sitting Bull finished his speech, then walked out of the circle of light and disappeared into the night. Emily looked after him, staring into the dark for a long moment. His words, though simple, were eloquent, and they rang with the power of truth. She knew without completely understanding why what he had said was not just a message. It was a warning.

She swallowed hard, understanding the enormity and significance of what she had been asked to do.

"Mr. Two Hearts," she said quietly. "Please tell Sitting Bull I will be proud to carry his words to Custer. He will hear them."

Jacob's eyes held hers for a long moment. Then he nodded.

"Then we leave at dawn."

# CHAPTER FIVE

THE DREAM CAME AGAIN.

It had haunted Tom Custer for seven years, returning with relentless persistence. He had never spoken of it, not to his sister-in-law, who had always taken a maternal interest in him, and certainly not to his brother.

He would have spoken about it if he thought anyone could understand. If talking might help him get free from the grip of the nightmare, he would have told them everything. But no one could understand.

So he drank.

"Too much alcohol is inconsistent with the tenets of command," his brother said, chastising him for his intemperance. "It is unbecoming of an officer, and it is unbecoming of Custer."

But Autie didn't understand. Autie never had the devils of Washita chasing him.

To George Armstrong Custer, Washita had been a brilliant victory. Another tactical success. He could detach himself from the blood and the screams, reducing the battle to columns of men maneuvering across the field. He saw it as part of the campaign. A necessary operation.

How Tom wished he could approach Washita with the same sense of detachment. God knew he had tried.

But he couldn't.

And so, in his sleep, the past overtook him once again.

The oddest thing about the dream was that, regardless of how many times it returned, it was always so vivid that while he was dreaming, he could not distinguish it from reality. It forced him to relive the moment, again and again...hundreds of times over the last seven years.

In the dream was the fog, a thick blanket pinned to the earth by the tall pine trees. The fog shielded the Indian village where Black Kettle's people were sleeping in the predawn hours. There were no warriors in the village to give the alert of the cavalry's approach—only women, children, and old men.

The ground was covered with heavy snow, as if the fog had solidified and dropped from the sky. The snow and fog together deadened all sound, so that the horses and men moved in eerie silence.

Tom sat rigid in the saddle, in the front rank, and the others of the Seventh Cavalry were drawn up in line with him. He didn't know how he got there or how long he had been there. His breath steamed in the cold air, curling like ghosts around him.

Behind him, the band dismounted and began playing "Garry Owen", the regimental tune. It floated through the mist, bright and absurdly cheerful.

The horses stirred at the music, shifting uneasily.

Somewhere behind them, the band was just a shadow in the fog.

Then the order came, and the Seventh Cavalry surged forward.

The horses' hooves made no sound, as if the animals were running on thin air. The shouts of men, the rattle of equipment, even the first tentative gunshots—all of it was done in silence.

Though the soldiers and horses were mute, the band was not, and Tom could hear the incessant sound of "Garry Owen"—the band was invisible in the fogbank behind them, a ghostly orchestra, not of heaven, but of hell.

And then the savage butchery began. Tom could see it all as a slowly danced ballet, a grotesque, amazingly detailed choreography.

Women and children were cut down by flashing sabers. Old men were shot at point-blank range. Infants were trampled under horses' hooves.

It was a soundless dance of color—white snow, red blood, blue coats, and the golden hair of his brother flashing through the mist like a banner of triumph.

A sharp pounding shattered the dream.

Tom sat bolt upright in bed, breathless, his heart hammering against his ribs. For one terrifying moment, he was still in the valley, surrounded by fog, screams, and the dead.

"Cap'n Custer! Cap'n Custer, sir!" came the voice through the door, followed by more pounding.

He exhaled slowly, running a hand through his damp, dark curls. The dream was fading, but the sick churn in his gut remained.

Again, the knock came—more insistent this time.

"Captain Custer, sir? Beggin' your pardon, but the general wants to see you."

"I'm awake," he muttered, more to himself than the man outside.

He swung his legs over the side of the bed and put his feet on the rough-hewn plank of the floor. For a moment, he just sat there, staring down, reminding himself that he was in his quarters, not that blood-soaked valley.

The pounding came again.

"I said I'm awake," Tom called, pushing himself to his feet. He crossed the room, poured water from the pitcher into the basin, and splashed his face, bracing against the cold sting. As he reached for a towel, he called out, "Come in, Sergeant Kennedy."

The sergeant entered with a crisp salute. Tom returned it with a sloppy version.

"My brother would be proud," he said dryly. "Now, what's on the *general's* mind?"

"General wants you to take the search party out today, sir."

Technically, Autie wasn't a general anymore, his actual rank was lieutenant colonel, but the brevet title of general had stayed with him since the war. And with his reputation, few would argue the point. He was likely the best-known officer in the United States Army.

"Search party?" Tom asked, rubbing the towel across his face. "What search party? What am I supposed to be searching for?"

Sergeant Kennedy hesitated. "Oh, beggin' your pardon, sir, I thought you already knew."

"No, Sergeant. I, uh, was unavoidably detained in

Bismarck yesterday, and I didn't return to the fort until quite late. I spoke to no one. What's missing?"

Kennedy cleared his throat. "That artist fella. And Sergeant Flynn. And the artist's daughter. They was comin' back to the fort in the general's coach when they was attacked by Crazy Wolf."

Tom froze. He lowered the towel slowly.

He remembered her, the girl in Autie's coach. The one he'd only glimpsed yet couldn't quite forget.

"What? You mean the people I saw in town yesterday never made it back?"

"No, sir."

"That's incredible! And you say Crazy Wolf attacked them? How do you know?"

"Because Chance and Evans got away and made it back," Sergeant Kennedy said.

Tom's jaw tightened. "You mean they *abandoned* the others?"

Kennedy shifted uncomfortably. "Well...not exactly, Cap'n. We found the other guards. They was dead. But we haven't been able to find the village."

Tom took a long breath through his nose, working to keep the anger out of his voice. It wasn't the first time soldiers had cut and run, but this time, they'd left a civilian and his daughter to be taken by a man like Crazy Wolf.

He pulled a buckskin tunic over his head.

"Get my horse saddled," he said. "Have the men mounted up. I'll be there as soon as I see my brother."

"Yes, sir." Kennedy turned to leave, then paused. "Excuse me, sir, but will you be wantin' any breakfast?"

Tom made a face. His stomach roiled at the thought.

"No. I don't even want to think about eating."

Kennedy gave a knowing nod and slipped out the door.

After Sergeant Kennedy left, Tom lingered by the mirror. His brother was a stickler about his officers' appearance, and he would be no less strict with his own brother than he would be with the others. The figure who looked back from the mirror was of medium height, trim, with flashing blue eyes in which one could readily see a resemblance to his brother. But whereas the general had long, golden hair, Tom's was cut short, and was curly and dark. And he was clean-shaven.

Tom decided that he could pass muster for his brother's critical inspection. He strapped on the belt that held his service pistol, ammunition pouch, and saber.

"General Custer's shining example of military discipline," he muttered, as he gave a sarcastic salute to his image in the mirror.

Then he saw the half-empty bottle of whiskey sitting on a shelf.

For a long moment, he hesitated. Then he reached for it, tipped it back, and took a quick swallow. The burn hit his throat, then spread through his chest, and dulled the edge of the morning. It wasn't a cure—but it helped.

---

TOM'S QUARTERS were next door to his brother's house, and it was but a moment before he was knocking on the door.

Elizabeth Bacon Custer—Libbie, as everyone called her—answered the door.

"Tom, do come in," she said with a warm, practiced smile.

She showed no signs of early age from the rigors of military life in a remote fort. In fact, she seemed to thrive on it. She was a very pretty woman with skin that one New York reporter described as being *of the white transparency of alabaster*. The writer went on to say that *her cheeks were apple red. Her hair, luxuriant and wavy, was chestnut brown. Her features were well cut, and her eyes were the light, gray-blue of Lake Erie, from whence she came.*

"Where's Autie?" Tom asked as he stepped inside.

"He's taking his breakfast," Libbie said, leading him toward the dining room. "Won't you have something to eat?"

"No, thank you."

"Don't tease him so, Libbie," came Autie's voice from the table. "He has no time for breakfast."

Tom followed her into the dining room and saw his brother seated at the head of the table, elegantly dressed in a black velvet tunic with gold trim. His blond hair was combed to perfection, and he buttered a biscuit with slow precision, looking at Tom with a disapproving expression.

"Where were you yesterday?"

Tom met his gaze evenly. "I...uh...was detained."

"You were drunk," Custer said flatly.

"Autie," Libbie chided gently, "don't be too hard on him."

Custer pointed his knife toward Tom as if to press the point, then sighed and set it down with a clink.

"Tom, oh, Tom, do you think I enjoy reprimanding you?"

"I suppose not."

"No, of course I don't," Custer said, his tone shifting. "In fact, when Libbie and I go to New York this Christmas, I intend to leave you in command of the regiment. You, Tom. Not Reno. Not Benteen. You."

Tom blinked, caught off guard.

"That will surely mean promotion for you. And when I fulfill my manifest destiny...who better to lead the Seventh than another Custer?" He leaned forward, voice low and intense. "The Custers have an obligation, Tom. A pivotal role to play in the history of our nation. You must never forget who you are."

"That hardly seems likely," Tom replied dryly. Then, more pointedly, asked, "Autie, what happened yesterday?"

Custer waved off the tone. "Now, about yesterday."

"What happened?" Tom asked again, pressing now. He knew how his brother loved to lecture. He loved to hear himself deliver sweeping proclamations like he was already dictating to his biographer.

"Yes, well, a terrible business," Custer said. "I sent Sergeant Flynn and an escort detail to meet the train. Silas Thomson and his daughter were aboard. You've heard of him, I'm sure. Probably the most famous painter in America. I attended one of his gallery showings in New York last winter. He's brilliant. Absolutely brilliant."

Tom barely restrained a sigh. "But what happened yesterday?" He was used to his brother's digressions.

"As they were bringing them back to the fort, they were attack by Crazy Wolf. Four of our men were killed. Two escaped and brought back word, and we don't know about the fate of the others."

"Did you send patrols when you found out?"

"Yes," Custer said. "We sent out two patrols, one searched north and one went west. Today, we'll go east and south."

"There's no need to go east," Tom said flatly. "I know where they are."

Custer raised an eyebrow. "Oh? And how do you know that?"

"When I was in town yesterday, I overheard some buffalo hunters talking about a large stand. The herd was south of here, that's where we'll find Crazy Wolf."

"If Crazy Wolf is with them," Custer said, "then that means some of the other chiefs are there as well. White Ghost, Sitting Bear, Fool Dog...maybe even Sitting Bull."

"And Jacob Two Hearts?" Tom asked.

The briefest flicker of something passed across Custer's face before an expression of determination and hate set in.

"Yes," he said flatly. "Maybe even Jacob Two Hearts."

Tom frowned. "Autie, why do you have such a personal vendetta against him? He isn't the only Indian ever to beat you in a skirmish."

"Because he is a traitor to the White race," Custer snapped. "And when I capture him, I shall take great pleasure in hanging him for treason."

"It's only natural that he would fight with the Sioux. After all, he was raised by them. He knows no other life."

"I will not tolerate treason," Custer said, his tone unyielding. "And don't you attempt to defend it."

Before Tom could respond, there was a knock on the front door.

"That'll be Sergeant Kennedy," Tom said, stepping toward the entrance. "My troop is formed. I have to go."

"Tom."

Custer's voice stopped him.

Tom turned back. "Yes?"

"It would not look well for me if something has happened to these people," Custer said, his voice lowering. "The newspapers back East would tear me to pieces. You know how badly they want to discredit General Custer."

Tom suppressed a smile at hearing his brother refer to himself in the third person.

"Find them for me."

Tom studied him a moment longer. "Is your only concern how this will look to the Eastern papers?"

"No, of course not," Custer replied quickly.

"Good," Tom said. "I'd hate to think that was the only reason for this search."

Libbie stepped forward then, placing a gentle hand on Tom's arm.

"Don't be too hard on him, Tom," she said softly. "Your brother looks out for all of you. Custer is one of the best-known names in America. We are family...and we will always stand united as family."

Tom smiled. "You're right, Libbie. You don't have to worry about me. And Autie doesn't have to worry about the Thomsons. If they're out there, I'll find them."

"I have no doubt of that," Libbie said, as she kissed him lightly on the cheek.

Tom stepped out onto the porch. His horse was already waiting at the foot of the steps, brought up by one of the stable hands. He placed his boot in the stirrup and swung into the saddle with the ease of long habit. Standing in the stirrups, he surveyed the troop before him.

Sixty mounted cavalrymen sat tall and ready in their saddles, stretched out in a single line. Their carbines caught the morning light, and though their uniforms showed the wear of weeks of field use, the men exuded discipline, strength, and purpose.

"Sergeant, prepare to move out," Tom called.

"Troop! Form column of twos!" the sergeant yelled, his voice carrying cleanly across the parade ground.

The movement was swift and precise, as the line of horsemen shifted smoothly into formation. The cadence of command and the creak of leather mingled in the morning air.

"Guidon, post!"

A trooper moved forward, the red-and-white regimental flag snapping in the morning breeze as he galloped to the front of the column.

Around the edges of the parade ground, the few wives and children of the soldiers and the men left behind—the blacksmiths, cooks, and garrison troops, were standing by to witness the patrol's departure.

Tom, for all his laconic military attitude, couldn't help but be moved by the scene. He had ridden out on missions like this more times than he could count, but it never grew routine. Every ride held the same unspoken question: who would come back?

"Move 'em out, Sergeant," he ordered.

"Forward—ho!"

The command rang out. The column surged into motion as the troop passed beneath the fort's gate.

The regimental band, standing around the flagpole, struck up "Garry Owen".

# CHAPTER SIX

THE COLUMN WAS ONE HOUR OUT OF THE FORT, MOVING slowly but steadily. The plains stretched out before them in folds of hills, one after another, and as each ridge was crested, another was exposed, and beyond that, another still. The dusty grass gave off a pungent smell when crushed by the horses' hooves.

The golden light of morning had long since given way to the white brightness of day, and though it was already September, the heat of a long, hot summer lingered on. Tom had sweated away all the alcohol in his system, and the merciless sun gave him a headache. He held his hand up to bring the column to a halt.

"D'ya see anythin', sir?" Sergeant Kennedy asked.

"Have the men dismount, Sergeant," Tom said. "Give the animals a five-minute blow."

"Yes, sir," Kennedy replied, and he passed the order on to the men.

The soldiers dismounted and walked their horses to cool them down. Some of the soldiers stretched out on the ground for a moment, and several others used the opportunity to relieve themselves.

Tom handed the reins of his horse to Sergeant Kennedy, then took his binoculars and climbed the hill to scan the horizon. But he saw only dusty rocks, shimmering grass, and more ranges of hills under the beating sun. He started to drop the glasses when he saw one outcropping of rock that looked different from the others. He stared at it more closely.

"Sergeant Kennedy!" he called. "On the double!"

Sergeant Kennedy ran up the hill, puffing loudly by the time he reached Tom. "What do you see, sir?"

"The coach, Sergeant," Tom said. He handed his binoculars to Kennedy, who looked in the direction Tom pointed.

"Aye, it's the coach all right," Kennedy said. "But where are the horses?"

"The Indians took them, of course," Tom said. "The question is, where are the people?"

"My bet is they are inside the coach, sir."

"Or lying dead alongside it," Tom answered grimly. "Let's get the men mounted."

Sergeant Kennedy ran back down the hill. "Mount up, men!" he called. "We've spotted the coach."

"D'ya see Sergeant Flynn?" one of the men called.

"Just the coach," Kennedy said. "We don't know what else we'll find."

Tom reached his own horse and swung into the saddle. He wondered what they would find when they reached the coach. He had seen dead and naked bodies hacked to pieces and left to turn purple and bloated under the relentless plains sun. He knew what they looked like and what they could do to you inside.

He also remembered how beautiful the girl he had met yesterday was, and his stomach twisted as he thought of what she would look like without her long, radiant hair.

"Forward at a trot, Sergeant."

The column broke into a trot at Sergeant Kennedy's command, sabers, canteens, and rifles jangling and dust boiling up behind them. The coach loomed larger until they were within a few hundred yards of it.

"At a gallop!" Tom called, and he stood in his stirrups and drew his saber, pointing it forward. It wasn't just showmanship, it was a signal to the soldiers to be on the alert for a possible Indian ambush. Every soldier drew his rifle from the saddle scabbard and held it at the ready.

At first, Emily thought the Indians were returning. It didn't seem like they had been gone more than half an hour, and when she heard the hoofbeats, she was frightened that perhaps Crazy Wolf had changed the council's mind. But when she looked out, she saw that the approaching riders were cavalrymen.

"Father, it's the cavalry," Emily said. Happily, she opened the door of the coach and stepped outside to greet them.

"Troop, halt!" Tom called, and the soldiers reined in their mounts.

"Are there Indians about, miss?" Tom called.

"No," Emily said. "They've gone."

"Sergeant Kennedy, send out two squads. Clear the area for three hundred yards in every direction."

"Yes, sir," Kennedy replied.

Tom swung down from his horse and walked over to

Emily. It was only then that Emily recognized him as the officer she had met the day before.

"Are you all right, Miss Thomson? And you, sir? Have you been harmed?"

"We are fine," Emily said. "And you, Captain Custer. How are you today?"

"I'm fine," Tom said, then looked at her with a curious expression. "I must say, Miss Thomson, you seem in remarkably fine spirits for one who has just gone through such an ordeal."

"We were not harmed," Emily said.

"What about Sergeant Flynn?"

"He was wounded in the battle," Emily said. "The Indians removed the arrow. He is weak, but not in serious condition. Sitting Bull said you may send an ambulance for him."

"Sitting Bull? Did you say Sitting Bull?" Tom asked.

"Yes."

"Are you positive?"

"Would you recognize a likeness of him?" Silas asked.

"Yes, of course," Tom said.

Silas reached back into the coach and pulled out a pad. He thumbed through the pages until he found the sketch of Sitting Bull and showed it to Tom.

"Yes," Tom said. "Yes, that's him, all right. Well, my brother will be happy to hear this. He's been looking for Sitting Bull for this entire year...and you found him on your first day out here."

"I think it would be more accurate to say that he found us," Silas said.

"Cap'n Custer, the men report the area is clear," Sergeant Kennedy said, riding up to the coach.

"Good," Tom said. "Have a couple of the men hitch their horses to the coach. We'll form a screening detail and lead them back to the fort."

"Yes, sir," Kennedy said.

————

IT WAS early afternoon by the time the coach and escort reached Fort Abraham Lincoln. But Tom had sent a fast rider out ahead, and by the time the coach rolled in through the front gates, the entire garrison had turned out in full parade dress uniform. The band struck up a crisp march as the detail came through the gates.

"Look sharp now, men," Tom said to his tired troopers. "Sit tall in the saddle."

"Oh, Father, look," Emily said. "There, over there by the flagpole. That's General Custer, isn't it?"

Silas nodded. "That's Custer, all right."

The escort detail passed in front of the flagpole. "Eyes—right!" Tom called, and as the cavalrymen, two by two, snapped their heads toward General Custer, Tom held his saber out in a salute. General Custer returned the salute.

"Troop, halt!"

The coach creaked to a halt in front of Custer. "Dismount!"

Emily could hear the jangle of equipment as the men swung off their horses.

"Sir, Captain Custer and A troop returning from the mission," Tom said. "Pleased to report, sir, both civilians are safe and well."

"Thank you, Captain," Custer said. "Well done. You may dismiss your men."

"Dismissed!" Tom called, and at that instant, pure bedlam broke out. There were cheers and shouts of hurrah, and the men who but moments before had been blue statues in the sun now came running toward the coach.

General Custer was the first one to the coach. He opened the doors and helped Emily and her father out.

"Are we glad to see you!" Custer said, smiling broadly. "I must say, you certainly gave us a scare."

"Well, thank you," Emily said, somewhat flustered by all the attention. "I must confess to a moment or two of fright myself. Oh, and General Custer, Sergeant Flynn is alive, though wounded. Sitting Bull said you may send an ambulance for him."

"Yes, I will lead the party myself," Custer said. "We will get underway right after lunch. Have you eaten?"

Suddenly, Emily realized that she was hungry. Her appetite, suppressed by fear and uncertainty, had returned with a vengeance.

"I am starved," she said. "We haven't eaten since yesterday morning."

Custer laughed. "Well, Libbie will be happy to hear that you are hungry. She has been cooking ever since she heard you were safe and returning to us."

Emily touched her hair, which was hanging in unkempt strands. "General, would it be possible to take a bath before we eat?"

Custer laughed appreciatively. "Don't tell me that women do not know women, for my own Libbie said you would make just such a request. You'll find a tub of hot water waiting for you in Tom's quarters. Tom, I hope you don't mind—you'll be moving in with Will Benteen."

"No, of course I don't mind," Tom said. "Sergeant Kennedy, detail someone to carry Miss Thomson's trunk to my quarters."

Half a dozen men volunteered, and Kennedy smiled as he chose one. "Lads, why is it you aren't so quick to volunteer for any of the other nice details?"

"If there is a pretty lady involved, Sarge, you can count me in any time," one of the troopers yelled, and the others laughingly agreed.

Emily followed the sergeant and the trooper across the quadrangle to Tom Custer's small house. The room was cozily furnished, and sitting right in the middle of the floor, was a large tub, filled with hot, soapy water.

"Ohh," Emily said happily. "How wonderful!"

"Enjoy, ma'am," Sergeant Kennedy said, touching his brow in a salute as he left.

And enjoy Emily did. She luxuriated in the hot water, feeling the prairie grime wash away. Finally, only because she knew that the others would be waiting on lunch for her, she got out of the tub and dressed.

Tom was waiting on the front porch for her. He had cleaned up and was wearing a parade dress uniform. He offered Emily his arm.

"I'm sorry if I kept you waiting," Emily said.

"You were worth waiting for," Tom said.

"Well, how nice of you to say so," Emily said.

When Emily walked into the Custer home, she was introduced to a half dozen officers and their wives, but there were so many at one time she had trouble keeping the names and faces straight.

She had no trouble with Elizabeth Custer, though. The woman dominated the meal. She was beautiful, true enough, but it was more than her beauty that held sway over everyone, for even the women deferred to her. As wife of the commanding officer, her rank was as indelibly stamped upon her person as the silver leaves on her husband's shoulders.

"To provide you with the privacy I know a young woman needs, I've prevailed upon Dr. Sprague to share his quarters with your father," Libbie explained.

"Thank you," Emily said. "You've all been so nice to us, I don't know how to thank you."

"How far away is the Indian camp, Miss Thomson?" Captain Benteen asked.

"Now, Will, we'll discuss none of that until after we have eaten," Libbie said sharply. "After all, Miss Thomson has been through quite an ordeal. We must give her a chance to relax."

"I don't mind," Emily said.

"Well, I do mind," Libbie said with authority.

"So," Custer said. "I suppose the two of you will be returning to New York on the next train."

"Of course not," Silas said. "What makes you think such a thing?"

"But surely you don't intend to go on with your plans now?" Custer asked.

"Yes," Emily said. "Yes, we do. The Indians have given us permission to return."

Custer laughed. "My dear lady, it is not the Indian's permission you must seek. It is mine."

"But we already have President Grant's permission," Silas said.

"President Grant isn't commanding the fort," Custer said easily. "I am."

"But General, surely you can see the importance of what I am trying to do?"

"Mr. Thomson, please look at this from my point of view," Custer said. "I am charged with protecting the lives and property of the White settlers and travelers in this territory. I am responsible for six thousand square miles. Now you are one of the most famous artists in the world. If something happens to you out there, the responsibility will fall right on my shoulders."

"But surely I can assume the responsibility for my own actions?"

"No, sir, you cannot," Custer said. "Alas, my dear Mr. Thomson, I'm afraid it is neither in your hands nor mine. Back there"—he pointed east—"you have only loyal fans. They will not fix responsibility upon your shoulders should something happen to you. They will fix it upon mine."

"But surely, General, you have fans too?"

"That is true," Custer said. "In fact, I have supporters who have suggested that I might seek political office." Custer coughed. "The highest political office," he went on. "But it is precisely because of this that I also have detractors, political enemies who would stop at nothing to prevent me from achieving my destiny. It is they who would hold me to blame. No, Mr. Thomson, I cannot let you venture back into the Black Hills."

"General, you don't understand..." Emily started, but she was interrupted by Libbie.

"More tea, my dear?" Libbie asked, smiling sweetly.

Emily knew that it was useless to pursue the matter any further now, so she let it drop for the time being.

"Mr. Thomson, perhaps I could engage you to do a portrait of me," Custer said. "It certainly could not harm my cause to have a portrait done by America's greatest painter."

"Perhaps," Silas said noncommittally.

The meal was finished shortly afterward, and then Custer asked Emily and Silas to tell them the location of the village.

"Before I tell you, I must relay a message from Sitting Bull," Emily said.

"You don't have to tell me anything he said, Miss Thomson," Custer said. "You are safe here, now."

"But I want to tell you," Emily said. "I promised that I would."

"Very well."

Emily relayed the message about the Black Hills, and when she was finished, Custer chuckled quietly.

"They're still trying to claim the hills for themselves," he said.

"But...aren't the Black Hills the sacred grounds of the Indians?" Emily asked.

"Miss Thomson, I'll tell you what is sacred about the Black Hills," Custer replied. "Gold."

"Surely, Miss Thomson, you've read my brother's famous comment that the Black Hills are full of gold from the grass roots down?" Tom asked.

"No," Emily said. "No, I don't believe I have."

"Then you are one of the few who haven't," Tom said. "There are ten thousand prospectors out here, and every one of them came because of that statement."

"And each one of them is a potential target," Major Reno said.

"Gentlemen, we have a mission to perform," Custer said, standing. "Ladies, if you will excuse us?"

Libbie held her cheek out for a kiss, and Custer dutifully gave her a peck. The other wives and husbands followed suit, and the officers left.

"Well, ladies, shall we quilt, then? Emily, we would be pleased if you would join us," Libbie said.

# CHAPTER SEVEN

"THEY'RE COMIN' BACK! THE REGIMENT'S COMIN' back!"

The shout outside her window awakened Emily.

She had tried to maintain her end of the conversation during the ladies' quilting circle the night before, but Libbie had noticed her drooping eyelids and bobbing head and finally sent her off to bed. Emily hadn't protested. The moment her head hit the pillow, sleep had taken her.

Now she stirred slowly, still half asleep, when another voice called out below.

The regimental band began to play, the music floating in through the open window. She sat up in bed and blinked, as sunlight spilled across the small room. She got up and began dressing.

*They must've had to move slowly with Sergeant Flynn,* she thought, buttoning her blouse. *They only left late yesterday afternoon. Why did they wait so long to go? Or why not wait until this morning?* It all seemed strange to her. The patrol would've reached the Indian camp well after dark. But she hadn't questioned it at the time. She was too tired. And besides, she didn't pretend to know about such things.

As she dressed, more voices carried up from just beneath her window.

"How's Sergeant Flynn?"

"He's all right," came the answer. "But they was two troopers kilt last night. The general brought their bodies back, though. They're sayin' we'll have a military funeral for 'em tomorrow."

What were they talking about? Emily wondered. How could anyone have been killed?

"How many Indians was kilt?

"I hear tell near on to twenty."

Emily finished dressing and stepped outside quickly. She looked around to see who was talking, but the men were gone, already walking off toward the stables. She looked down the lane toward the main gate, and gasped.

The regiment was riding in.

Dozens of dust-covered cavalrymen rode in beneath the gate. Cheers rose from around the fort as soldiers clapped each other on the back. The band played a triumphant march.

She had not watched them leave yesterday and had no idea how many had gone out. This was no simple rescue mission! This had been a full-scale raid!

"Isn't it wonderful, Emily?" one of the women from the quilting circle asked brightly, stepping up beside her. "What a glorious victory!"

"What is this?" Emily asked. "They weren't supposed to attack the Indians. They were only supposed to bring Sergeant Flynn back."

The woman looked at her kindly, but with something close to pity. "Dear, you didn't really expect them to keep a bargain with savages, did you?"

Emily stared at her, stunned.

"Yes," she said, her voice quiet. "I gave Sitting Bull my word."

The regiment had been dismissed, and the men drifted away in pairs and small groups, now that the excitement had passed.

Tom Custer made his way through the troopers and crossed the parade ground toward Emily.

"Miss Thomson, Emily, may I speak with you?" he asked.

Emily turned her back to him.

"I've nothing to say to you, Captain Custer."

"Please," Tom said. "You must hear me out. Just for a moment."

She started walking, then stopped. Slowly, she turned back to face him.

"What happened?" she asked. "You were supposed to bring back Sergeant Flynn. That was the agreement. Now I hear men were killed on both sides."

Tom's expression changed. "I want you to know, I didn't approve of what happened."

"You went, didn't you?" she snapped. "Then you must have approved."

"That's not true." He shook his head. "I went because I am an officer, and I was ordered to go. I had no choice. But believe me, Emily, I didn't want it to happen this way."

She folded her arms. "Then tell me what did happen."

Tom looked down for a moment, as if ashamed to look her in the eyes.

"We reached the Sioux village just before dusk. The main column stayed away from the village beyond the ridgeline. Autie sent the ambulance in with a two-man escort, under a white flag. They brought Sergeant Flynn out without any trouble."

Emily waited, already dreading what was coming next.

"But while they were in the village," Tom continued, "they were spying, gauging the strength of the Indians, looking at the lay of the land. When they came back they gave all the information to Autie—the number of lodges, the terrain, how the Indians were positioned."

He paused.

"At one o'clock this morning, we attacked."

Emily's face went pale. "Oh no."

"Most of the chiefs escaped," Tom said quietly. "But Sitting Bear was killed."

She inhaled sharply. "And Jacob Two Hearts? Was he...was he killed?"

Tom looked up, surprised by her question.

"No," he said. "He wasn't."

Emily let out a breath.

"He fought a rear-guard action so that the others could get away," Tom went on. "Most of the warriors who stayed with him were killed. But somehow...Jacob Two Hearts wasn't even wounded."

He hesitated.

"But he was captured."

"Captured?"

"Yes," Tom said quietly. "He's in the guardhouse now."

Emily turned toward the squat stone building at the edge of the parade ground, where a small crowd had already gathered. They were trying to look in through the barred window.

"What will happen to him?" she asked.

Tom hesitated. "He is to be hanged. Tomorrow."

Emily's breath caught. "You can't mean it."

"I'm afraid I do."

"But...won't he get a trial?"

Tom rubbed his forehead, clearly weary. "Autie is the military commander of this district. His word is law. He is judge and jury."

Emily stared at him in disbelief. "How convenient for him."

"Emily, don't think too harshly of him," Tom said. "He carries an enormous responsibility. You have no idea the pressure he's under."

She folded her arms across her chest. "Does he hesitate before making a decision that costs a man his life? You, Captain Custer, seem to possess something your brother lacks—compassion."

Tom didn't respond. He looked down for a long moment, then finally said, "You don't understand."

He turned to leave, but after a few steps, he stopped and looked back.

"Oh, there's a dance at the Sutler's store tonight," he said.

Emily crossed her arms. "A dance? To celebrate what? Your brother's betrayal? My own?"

"No, of course not," Tom said. "It's to celebrate your safe return. Your father's. And Sergeant Flynn's. Flynn's already improving. He'll be as good as new in no time."

Emily's shoulders eased slightly. "Thank God for

that. I rather like Sergeant Flynn. And I gather he thinks highly of you."

Tom smiled faintly. "Flynn's been with me since I was a shavetail. He figures I belong to him."

"A shavetail?" she asked.

"A second lieutenant," Tom explained. "When the Army buys new mules, they shave their tails so everyone knows they're green."

Emily allowed herself the smallest of smirks. "And new lieutenants?"

Tom laughed. "You've made the connection."

Then, more seriously, he asked, "Emily, will you allow me to escort you to the dance?"

Emily hesitated. "I don't suppose there's any way to get out of going?"

"Not if you want to remain in my brother's good graces," Tom said.

"And the alternative to staying here as a guest is what?"

"Returning to New York," he said. "Or at the very least, back to Fargo."

Emily exhaled slowly, her eyes once more drifting to the guardhouse.

"Then I have no alternative," she said. "And yes, Captain Custer...you may escort me."

Tom brightened. "You won't regret it, Emily. You'll have a fine time. You'll see."

"Yes," she said, the words barely above a whisper. "I'm certain I shall."

Tom saluted and left. Emily watched him go, unsure of what came next—where she was to take her meals, how she was expected to behave, or even how long she would be staying. After a moment of hesitation, she stepped off the porch and went next door.

Libbie Custer answered the door herself, dressed in a pale morning gown.

"Well, so you are up, I see?" she said, greeting her sweetly but without warmth.

"Yes, Mrs. Custer," Emily replied.

"Please, call me Libbie, dear."

"Thank you...Libbie." Emily cleared her throat. "I wanted to ask—where am I to take my meals? There's no kitchen in Tom's quarters." She felt her face flush as she said Tom's name aloud, though she had no cause to feel embarrassed.

Libbie's smile thinned, though her words were still pleasant. "Captain Custer takes his meals with us. And as the wife of the commanding officer, I'm expected to provide for our honored guests. You and your father shall always be welcome at my table."

"That's very generous of you," Emily said, though she couldn't help noticing how carefully the woman had spoken.

"As Autie was in the field this morning, I didn't serve breakfast," Libbie continued. She turned toward the window, frowning slightly. "Oh, dear. They're building a scaffold. I suppose there's no way to avoid this unpleasantness."

Emily blinked. "Unpleasantness?"

"The hanging, of course," Libbie said, as if discussing the weather. "Autie captured a traitor last night. He will be executed tomorrow. Imagine—a White man living like a savage, fighting against his own kind."

Emily stared at her. "Libbie, a man is going to die tomorrow, and you call it an unpleasantness?"

Libbie's tone grew slightly defensive. "Emily, I understand that you are troubled, but as an Army wife, one must accept these things. My husband bears the burden of command. He is tasked with upholding military law. And this man, Jacob Two Hearts, has been found guilty of treason."

"He's not guilty of anything," Emily said, her voice rising. "That man saved my life. My father's. Sergeant Flynn's. Is that how we repay him?"

Libbie drew a slow breath. "My dear, you must not let your emotions cloud your judgment. This man was raised by the Sioux. He has chosen their way of life. His loyalties are not with us."

"He fought to protect his people from a surprise attack," Emily said. "That isn't treason. That's survival."

Libbie's expression turned pitying. "You are making this far more difficult than it needs to be. Autie knows what he's doing. He is a brilliant military strategist. I'm sure he considered all the factors, including that this...person may have aided you for his own ends."

Emily turned toward the sound of hammering from the quadrangle, the steady rhythm now unmistakably sinister. Each blow drove home the reality.

Libbie smiled again, as if to sweep the subject away with charm. "Come now, let's not dwell on such heavy matters. Tell me, was it a lovely summer in New York?"

Emily could only blink at her.

"What?"

"The summer in New York. Was it lovely?"

Emily struggled to focus. "Yes...yes, I suppose it was."

Libbie nodded, satisfied. "Autie has promised that

we can spend Christmas in New York. Of course, that is months away, but I am already looking forward to it."

Emily seized the opportunity to redirect the conversation. "Will Captain Custer be going with you?"

Libbie's smile faltered, ever so slightly. "Emily, dear, it would not do for you to become too interested in Tom."

There it was. Out in the open.

Until now, Emily hadn't given it much thought. But the moment Libbie tried to forbid it, she found herself suddenly curious. "Any interest thus far has been expressed by Captain Custer, not by me," she said coolly.

Libbie tilted her head. "Of course. And who could blame the poor boy? You are an attractive young woman, and Tom has been long deprived of female company. But I must ask that you do all in your power to discourage it."

"Why should I?" Emily asked.

Libbie folded her hands in front of her. "Because you are not right for him."

"You mean I don't measure up to your standards?" Emily asked angrily.

"That's not it at all," Libbie said, waving a delicate hand in dismissal. "You are a lovely girl with many fine qualities, and I would dearly love to have you as my own sweet sister-in-law. But Emily, think about it for a moment. Tom is a Custer, a United States Army officer, as is his brother. You must understand what that means."

Emily narrowed her eyes slightly. "Meaning what?"

Libbie leaned in, her tone softening without losing force. "Autie will be president one day. After Autie, perhaps Tom. And after Tom, maybe Boston. The Custer name will be written into the fabric of this country's future. To marry a Custer, one must become a Custer. That means more than taking a name...it means bearing a responsibility."

Emily tilted her head. "You became a Custer."

Libbie laughed gently, without modesty. "My dear, I created the Custers."

Emily arched a brow, surprised by her claim.

Libbie's eyes gleamed with pride. "I took an obscure little family from Ohio and made it one of the best-known families in America. There were dozens of war heroes. Do you think Autie was the only one? No, but my lectures, my writing, and my constant presence has generated a whole nation of Custer followers. I made sure George Armstrong Custer rose above all the rest. That legacy is mine to protect. And Tom's future bride, whoever she may be, must add to its brilliance, not cast a shadow."

Emily let out a slow breath. "Don't worry, Mrs. Custer. I have no designs on Captain Custer. And even if I did, I could never be what you want. I couldn't shape my life around preserving the...*Custer luster* you've created."

Libbie gave a soft, amused laugh. "'Custer luster'—that's very good. I may borrow that sometime, if you don't mind."

"Be my guest," Emily said coolly. "Now, if you would, please inform Captain Custer that I will be unable to attend the dance as his guest tonight."

"Oh, heavens no, don't do that," Libbie said. "I think you should go to the dance with him...and see him socially too. Now that we have had our little conversation, I feel much better about things."

Emily hesitated. "I thought you just said—"

Libbie waved the thought away with a flick of her fingers. "I only needed to know where you stood. Now that I do, I see no harm in it."

Emily met her gaze.

Libbie smiled back with a sickeningly serene smile.

She wasn't sure whether she had just been warned or tested—or both. But one thing was now perfectly clear—Libbie Custer always had the upper hand.

General Custer then entered the room, his expression confident, self-assured, and faintly theatrical, as though he were stepping onto a stage. He glanced toward Emily and smiled.

"Well, young lady," he said, striding across the parlor, "we rescued Sergeant Flynn for you, and gained a bonus besides." He turned to Libbie. "News of the battle is already being sent by wire. I spoke with Toby from the *New York Tribune*. He's calling it the *Battle of Two Creeks*, because the village was nestled between two streams. Another victory can't hurt our cause back East now, can it?"

Libbie clasped her hands together as she looked at him with doting eyes. "That's excellent news, Autie. The press will love it."

Emily stood still, her voice tight. "General, is it true you are going to hang Jacob Two Hearts?"

The question hung in the air like a shot fired in a quiet room.

Custer turned toward her, still smiling, though his eyes sharpened. "Yes," he said simply.

He crossed the space between them and took one of

her hands in his, gazing at her with sympathy. "I know the thought of hanging another human being must seem distasteful to you, but such is the harsh reality of war. Discipline must be swift and unquestioned."

Emily's jaw tightened. "Jacob Two Hearts saved my life."

Custer's expression did not change. "I know that. And under different circumstances, that might have warranted some consideration. But he has killed before, Miss Thomson, more than once. He's taken up arms against his own people, betrayed his blood, and brought about many deaths. I cannot overlook that. No commander can."

Emily started to speak again, but before she could say anything, Libbie stepped in with a smooth transition.

"Autie," she said with a bright smile, "Emily is going to the dance with Tom tonight."

Custer's face lit up at once, his focus shifting as though the tension had never come up.

"Well now," he said, chuckling, "isn't my brother Tom the lucky one? And isn't it fitting that we have an occasion to celebrate tonight?"

He turned back to Libbie, running a hand through his long, golden hair. "I was in the saddle all night. If I'm to be fresh for this evening, I'd best get some rest."

He looked back at Emily, his tone gracious. "You'll excuse me?"

Emily gave a curt nod. "Yes, of course, General."

Libbie's tone grew brisk, efficient. "Lunch will be ready promptly at noon."

Emily recognized the dismissal in her voice. "Thank

you," she said, her tone carefully even. "I shall see you then."

She turned and stepped toward the door. Behind her, Libbie resumed her conversation with her husband, but Emily no longer heard the words.

Her mind was already racing. Thoughts of Jacob Two Hearts crowded every corner.

He had saved her life. And by tomorrow, they were going to hang him for it.

# CHAPTER EIGHT

THAT NIGHT, THE RIGORS OF THE CAMPAIGN WERE SET aside as officers, enlisted men, and the handful of their wives gathered in the Sutlers' Store for an evening of music and dance. The scent of lamp oil mingled with pressed wool uniforms and lilac perfume, as the regimental band played familiar waltzes and reels.

It wasn't until that moment that Emily truly realized just how few women lived at Fort Abraham Lincoln. Of the twenty officers stationed at the post, only six were married. Nine of the thirty sergeants had wives, five of whom were laundresses. The laundresses were the only women officially sanctioned by Army regulations. Counting herself, Emily realized there were twenty-one women...and more than three hundred men.

Though Tom Custer had brought Emily to the dance, he generously allowed her to fill her dance card with the other soldiers' names. Like every other lady at the dance, she soon found that every moment of her evening was to be taken.

The band played a fanfare, and General Custer

stepped forward, striking a commanding figure in his parade dress uniform, his long blond hair falling in waves across his shoulders. He was smiling broadly, and when a couple of men near the bandstand called out, "Yellow Hair," he laughed good-naturedly.

"Ladies, officers, men," he said.

"Speech!" someone called, prompting a round of cheers.

Custer grinned. "That's exactly what I'm going to give you, if you'll be quiet and let me."

Again, there was laughter from the men.

"Gentlemen," he said, "I want you to know that *Custer's Own*, as the newspapers are now calling the Seventh Cavalry, is the finest fighting outfit ever to wear the uniform of the United States Army."

A thunder of approval followed, boots stomping the floor in noisy agreement.

"Last night," he continued, "we had a great victory and brought Sergeant Flynn back home alive. We also have two distinguished guests who themselves were held captive by the savages for a short time. We are grateful for their safe return as well."

There was more applause, louder this time—until a voice shouted from the back of the room.

"And don't forget that traitor we're gonna hang tomorrow, General!"

A chorus of cheers rose in response, but Emily felt the knot in her stomach tighten.

Custer's smile faded. He raised his hand and waited for quiet.

"Yes," he said gravely, "though I find little to celebrate in that. Tomorrow will be a somber day. We will bury two of our own, Privates Jenkins and McKean, men who fell in the line of duty and now ride for Fiddler's Green."

Someone raised a mug. "To Jenkins and McKean!"

"Here, here!" echoed others, and the toast was drunk.

Emily turned to Tom as conversation around them started again, and the regimental band struck up an appropriate song.

"What is Fiddler's Green?" she asked quietly.

Tom hesitated, watching a pair of lieutenants lead their wives onto the floor. Then he turned back to her.

"It's a cavalryman's legend," he said, his voice low. "When a trooper dies, he doesn't go to heaven or hell. He goes to a grassy glade under the cool shade of trees, and there he sits and drinks with all the other cavalrymen who have gone there before him, to wait for Judgment Day."

He smiled, but there was something shadowed behind his eyes, a flicker of recognition that death was not some distant notion, but something that was always with him.

"It's just a story," he added, "but it seems to comfort a trooper who knows that the next day, or the day after that, may be his last."

"Do you ever think about dying, Tom?" Emily asked.

He chuckled. "More often than I'd like." Then, as if reconsidering, he added, "And if I know Autie, he'll have some grand and glorious scheme in mind for when we go. Something to create the maximum amount of publicity. My brother has lived by that code, I've no doubt that he will die by it."

"And you'll just go right along with it? Don't you ever question *anything* he does?"

"No."

"Why not?" she asked.

Tom sighed. "Emily, I don't expect you to understand. I'm a soldier. I go where I'm ordered. I follow the chain of command. It's called duty. It's called honor."

"Honor?" she asked. "You'd let a man die tomorrow, call it justice, and hide behind that word? Where was the honor in capturing Jacob Two Hearts?"

For a moment, he said nothing. Then, quietly, he replied, "Sometimes, one must weigh honor in one's soul."

He looked her full in the face.

"It is not difficult to do the right thing," he said. "It is only difficult to *know* what is right."

The music started then, and the first dance began. Tom looked at Emily with a pleading expression on his face, begging her not to ask any more questions about honor or right and wrong. And Emily, because the whole thing was painful to her, held out her hand to him and allowed him to sweep her out onto the floor amid the laughter and music.

As the final notes of the last waltz faded, the atmosphere inside the Sutlers' Store shifted. Dancing gave way to bourbon-fueled bravado. Soldiers clustered in small groups, trading stories of hard campaigns and near brushes with death. Their laughter rang out freely, loud and careless. The women settled into another corner of the room to carry on their own conversations.

———

EMILY SLIPPED, unnoticed, through the door, leaving the party behind her.

The night air hit her like a balm, cool and still beneath a sky littered with stars that were like crystals of ice. Her feet moved quickly, instinctively, across the parade ground. She didn't allow herself to think too hard about what she was going to do.

The guardhouse was dark and silent in front of her. She expected to find a sentry pacing out front, and her mind raced through a dozen half-formed lies she might tell to distract him. But when she rounded the corner, the spot was empty.

No guard.

Whether the soldier had stepped away for warmth or whiskey, or he simply thought there was no need for a guard, or maybe he had deserted his post. Emily didn't know. All that mattered was that the moment had come.

The front of the guardhouse faced the quadrangle, and Emily knew that if she stood under the front window, she undoubtedly would be seen. So she dipped into the shadows alongside the guardhouse and stepped up to the barred window. Pressing herself against the rough timbers, she leaned in close, looking into the blackness that was so dark she could see nothing.

"Jacob," she whispered.

No answer.

"Jacob," she called again, louder this time.

From the darkness, a shape moved.

"I heard you," Jacob finally said, his voice as dry as a broken twig.

Her breath caught in her throat. "Are you all right?"

A pause.

Then his face appeared at the bars, barely visible in the faint light from the moon.

"Why do you ask?" he said. "Do your White friends

want to make sure they have a healthy Indian to hang tomorrow?"

Emily winced. "Jacob, I'm sorry. I didn't want this to happen."

He studied her for a long moment, then exhaled.

"It is not your fault," he said, his tone lower now. "I should have known Custer couldn't be trusted. He lied before. He lied again. I was the fool."

"No," she said softly. "You believed him because you wanted peace."

"I was still the fool."

"I'm going to set you free."

His eyes narrowed slightly. "Can you do this?"

"Yes," she whispered. "The door is held by a bar on the outside. I can lift it."

Jacob stepped back from the window. His voice lost all sarcasm now.

"Then do it, quickly."

Emily stepped to the edge of the shadows and looked across the moonlit quadrangle. At the far end were the enlisted barracks that were dark and still except for a flicker of lamplight behind one set of shuttered windows. To her right were the officers' quarters, the house where she was staying, and the Sutlers' Store. Only the store showed light through the windows, and from inside, she heard a loud guffaw of laughter.

To the left stood the stockade wall, the stables, and the front gate. The two guards at the front gate were facing out, looking for signs of trouble from without. None of them considered the possibility of anything happening from within.

She had a chance.

Moving quickly, Emily slipped to the heavy wooden

bar across the door. Her fingers curled around the thick beam, and she strained to lift it. It resisted at first, but then it gave way. She eased it clear, careful not to let it drop.

"Go," she whispered. "Now."

Jacob moved like a shadow. He passed her without a sound, his figure low and moving fast across the hard-packed earth. In seconds, he reached the rear wall. He climbed quickly, gripping the rough logs like he'd done it a hundred times before. He reached the top, glanced back once, then dropped silently to the other side.

And then he was gone.

Emily stood frozen, her heart pounding so loud she feared someone might hear it. She had done it. Jacob was free. But now she realized that she herself was in danger.

If anyone saw her near the guardhouse, or worse, found the door standing open, there would be no explaining it away. No hiding behind excuses or well-bred manners. They would arrest her without question.

She started across the parade ground, but then stopped short. She was too exposed.

Instead, she slipped along the outer edge of the stockade, keeping to the shadows, as she worked her way around the entire perimeter of the fort. By the time she reached the back door of the Sutlers' Store, her nerves were strung tight.

She paused to compose herself, drew a deep breath, then stepped back into the noise and heat.

Laughter roared again as someone told a story about a river crossing gone wrong. The warmth, the light, the crowded room—everything inside felt impossibly far from what she had just done. Emily tucked a curl behind her ear, and slipped into the group of women as if she'd never left.

She had barely taken her seat when Tom approached.

"Where have you been?" he asked.

Emily's stomach turned over as her mouth went dry.

Had he seen her?

Had someone else?

Before she could answer, Libbie spoke up.

"Tom, for heaven's sake," she said with a teasing lilt, "you don't ask a lady where she's been. There are certain delicate things..."

Tom blinked, then his face flushed.

"Oh. Of course," he stammered. "I—I should've realized. My apologies, Miss Thomson."

Emily forced a soft laugh.

"It's quite all right," she said lightly.

Libbie, ever gracious, turned the conversation toward lighter matters.

"Tell us more about New York, Miss Thomson," she said, smiling. "I've always imagined it as terribly grand."

Emily, grateful for the opportunity to speak about a subject of which she had some knowledge, held forth while the others listened. She spoke of the wide, gas-lit boulevards, the many carriages on the cobblestone streets, and the well-dressed crowds along Fifth Avenue. The other women listened with fascination as she described the towering buildings, the art salons, and the recent exhibition at the Metropolitan Museum.

Emily forced herself to stay composed, though every beat of her heart seemed louder than the last. Jacob's escape was still fresh in her mind, as he went over the stockade wall and disappeared into the night. But she kept her tone light and her smile in place, as she talked on and on about trivial things.

Then the front door of the Sutlers' Store burst open.

"He's gone! The Indian has escaped!" a voice shouted.

The words cracked through the room like a gunshot.

Emily's stomach clenched. Her teacup rattled slightly as she set it down.

"What?" Custer yelled, standing up so quickly that his chair tumbled over.

A breathless corporal stood in the doorway. "General, I was making my regular tour around the post, and when I got back to the guardhouse, the bar was slipped and the door was open. He's gone."

"Damn!" Custer exploded. "An Indian must have sneaked over the walls somehow." He spun to Major Reno. "Turn out the regiment, Major. We're going to bring him back."

Reno stiffened. "Beggin' the general's pardon, sir, but do you intend to take out the entire regiment for *one* Indian?"

"If I had a division, I'd turn it out!" Custer snapped. "Now, hurry it up. I intend to be on the move in no more than fifteen minutes."

"Yes, sir," Reno said quickly. He turned on his heel. "Bugler! Sound *Boots and Saddles!*"

The trumpeter in the band didn't hesitate. He raised the instrument and blew the call that every cavalryman lived for—*Boots and Saddles*, the order for the mounted march.

In an instant, the room was alive with motion.

The celebration was over. Chairs clattered, glasses toppled. Officers called for their sabers, their boots, their horses. In the space of a few minutes, the post transformed from a social gathering into a full-scale military operation.

Only a few men remained in the Sutlers' Store. Frank Blue, the store's proprietor, leaned against the counter as if uncertain whether to pour more drinks or shut the place down altogether. A few rear-guard soldiers stood near the back wall, talking quietly among themselves.

And then there was Silas Thomson.

Emily hadn't seen him approach, but now he was beside her. He stood with his arms folded, watching the excitement outside the windows.

"I have some sketches I'd like you to work on tomorrow," he said without turning his head.

She stared at him, incredulous.

"The Indian sketches?"

"No," Silas said. "Not yet. The sketches I have in mind now are of General Custer and some of his officers. I'd like you to do some preliminary drawings."

Emily turned fully toward him, the turmoil forgotten for the moment. "Father, you can't be serious! You're going to trade in our dream just to feed Custer's ego?"

Silas finally looked at her. His expression didn't change, but there was something in his eyes, something deliberate.

"No, my dear," he said. "I'm going to play on his ego to preserve our dream."

Her mouth went dry. "How?"

He smiled, but his voice remained low and even. "By giving him exactly what he wants. Glorious portraits. Heroic poses. A legacy in charcoal and oil. Let him pose for us, while we get the access we need. To Jacob. To the truth. To the real story behind this war Custer's trying to start."

Emily's gaze dropped for a moment. "And if Custer sees through it?"

"Then we give him more flattery," Silas said. "He's not hard to read. The man's vanity is as loud as a cavalry charge."

Outside, hooves thundered in the courtyard. The sound of shouted commands and jingling tack spilled into the store. The regiment was moving.

Emily drew a breath and let it out slowly. "All right," she said. "I'll draw your officers."

Silas gave a small nod. "We'll start with Custer. In full dress."

He turned and stepped away, disappearing toward the door without another word.

Emily stood alone now, her father's scheme still circling in her mind. She would draw them all, the peacocks in their braids and sashes, the heroes of their own stories. She would give them what they wanted.

And if it meant helping Jacob...then so be it.

———

EMILY and her father stepped out into the night air. The night had cooled since the sounding of *Boots and Saddles*, and the faint scent of wood smoke drifted from the officers' quarters.

She walked beside her father, her shawl drawn tighter over her shoulders. A spark lit in her eyes.

"Libbie's the one to work on, Father," she said. "She's the driving force behind the general."

Silas gave a slight nod. "Really, now? That wouldn't surprise me. They say behind every successful man, there's a woman."

"That's what they say," Emily said, a smile crossing her face.

They walked on in silence, the only sound the rhythm of their steps on the packed ground.

"I'm ready to go to bed," she said after a moment. "Will you walk me to my quarters?"

"Of course," Silas replied.

They crossed the quadrangle at a steady pace, the light from the Sutlers dwindling behind them.

"You took a great chance tonight, you know," Silas said when they reached the midpoint of the quadrangle, well out of earshot from any lingering eyes or ears.

Emily's breath caught. She looked up at him sharply. "What are you talking about?"

"I saw you leave the dance," he said. "At first, I thought you might be unwell. I walked to the door to look after you, and that's when I saw you make your way to the guardhouse. Then I waited...and I saw Jacob Two Hearts climb the wall."

"Oh." Her voice was barely audible. She looked away. "Do you think anyone else saw?"

Silas shook his head, calm as ever. "I don't think so. I was watching carefully."

He smiled faintly. "I even considered creating a diversion if someone came toward the door."

Emily raised a brow. "What kind of diversion?"

He chuckled softly. "I edged the punch bowl to the corner of the table. I was ready to knock it off."

Emily gasped in disbelief, then laughed. "Libbie's Waterford punchbowl?"

"The very one."

"Father, if you'd done that, you might've been hanged yourself! You've no idea how proud she is of that bowl. It was a gift—from Julia."

He blinked. "Julia?"

"Mrs. Grant," Emily said with a smirk. "You're not the only one with friends in the White House."

Silas laughed, shaking his head. "Then I suppose I'm doubly pleased you weren't seen."

When they reached the house, they stepped up onto the porch.

"I hope he gets away," Silas said quietly.

"He will," Emily answered. Her voice was steady now. "I know he will."

He kissed her gently on the forehead, and then watched as she opened the door and stepped inside. Alone, Silas stood a moment longer, his hands behind his back. He looked toward the dark line of the prairie beyond the fort walls. Somewhere, Jacob Two Hearts ran. He prayed he would get away.

# CHAPTER NINE

EMILY DIDN'T KNOW WHAT HAD AWAKENED HER, ONLY that something had. A breath of air that didn't belong. A presence in the room that hadn't been there before.

She sat up slowly in the darkness, the moonlight casting a faint glow across the floor. Her heart thudded in her chest. The fort was still. From beyond the windows came the distant snort of a horse and the footfalls of the night guard. But in her room, it was the silence itself that alarmed her.

"Who's there?" she whispered.

A shadow moved. From the corner near the fireplace, a figure stepped into the moonlight.

"Jacob," she breathed. "What are you doing here?"

He stood quietly, watching her. His chest was bare, and a strand of bear's teeth circled his neck. He looked the same as he had before, calm and composed.

"You shouldn't be here," Emily said. Her voice was soft, urgent. "They're searching for you. If you're caught..."

"They're not searching in your quarters," he interrupted.

She frowned. "No, but—Jacob, this is dangerous."

"I had to see you."

Emily drew the cover closer around her shoulders. "You took a great risk coming here."

"No greater than the one you took for me."

They stared at one another, neither speaking for a long moment. At last, Emily asked, "Why did you come?"

He glanced toward the window, as if listening for the sound of boots on gravel. Then he looked back to her.

"I needed to thank you," he said.

Emily's breath caught. She hadn't expected that.

"I had to help you," she said. "I couldn't let them hang you after what you did...for me, and for the others."

Jacob nodded slowly. "I understand. But it is not something I can easily repay."

"You don't have to repay me."

He stepped closer. Emily could see the weariness in his face now. The hunted look. His body was tense, ready to run. But in his eyes there was something else— something softer.

"I won't stay long," he said. "I only came to tell you that I will not forget you."

She swallowed, unsure how to respond. "Where will you go?"

"South. To the Powder River. I know trails they won't find."

Emily rose from the bed and crossed to the window. She parted the curtain slightly and looked out at the quadrangle.

"You could stay," she said without turning. "You could live among the Whites. Change your name. Dress like them. No one would know."

He didn't answer right away. She heard the floorboard creak as he stepped toward her.

"I would always know," he said.

Emily turned then. The room was quiet. Her thoughts were not. She had so many questions to ask.

"I don't know what's ahead for either of us," she said. "But I do know you saved me twice. And I won't forget that either."

Emily stood motionless in the dim light, watching the spot where she thought Jacob was standing. Her breath was heaving in her chest. Then, like a returning ghost, he stepped back into view, just barely outlined by the moonlight coming through the window.

For a moment, neither of them spoke.

Finally, Jacob's voice broke the silence.

"The Indians have a saying," he said. "A bird and a fish may fall in love and marry. But where will they live?"

Emily looked at him, not sure what he meant. "Jacob, you don't have to go back to the Indians. You could live as a White man anywhere you wanted."

"The White man wants to hang me," he replied simply.

"You could disappear," she said quickly, desperately. "Cut your hair, grow a beard. Put on White man's clothes. No one would recognize you."

Jacob tilted his head slightly. "And this would be good?" he asked.

"Yes," Emily said, stepping closer. "Don't you see?

You could start over. A new name, a new place. I would go with you."

He didn't move. His eyes searched hers for a long, still moment.

"A bird and a fish may fall in love," he said again, softly. "But where will they live?"

Emily's breath caught in her throat. "You don't have to choose," she said. "We could go anywhere...together."

Jacob reached up and brushed a strand of hair from her cheek. His fingers lingered there for a moment.

"I have already chosen," he said.

She didn't want to hear what he had said. Her voice trembled as she answered. "Then go...before it's too late."

Jacob gave a small nod. And then, as quietly as he had arrived, he stepped back through the window. The curtain stirred. A footstep on the porch. Then nothing.

Emily stood frozen, staring at the space he had left behind. She had freed him from the gallows, but he had chosen to return to a life she could never fully understand.

In so many words, he had told her, "*I have a life. I do not wish to start over.*"

And she had tried to tell him, "*You aren't an Indian.*"

Emily pressed her fingers against the wooden frame and closed her eyes.

"I hope you find your place," she whispered into the darkness. "Even if it isn't with me."

And then she turned away, knowing that nothing would ever be the same. In the brief time she had known him, Jacob Two Hearts had touched her heart.

# CHAPTER TEN

JACOB SLIPPED THROUGH THE SHADOWS OF THE FORT, staying close to the wall as he worked his way toward the stables. He caught the scent of burning tobacco and pressed himself flat against the logs, waiting. A moment later, a soldier strolled by, smoking a pipe.

"Bill, you got 'ny idea what time it is?" a voice called from the parapet.

The pipe smoker answered, "I make it nigh on two in the mornin'. We'll be gettin' relieved 'afore too much longer."

"I'll be proud to see that," the parapet guard replied. He shuffled to the edge and sat, legs dangling over the walkway. Jacob could have reached out and yanked him down, but then he'd have the pipe-smoking soldier to contend with. He remained still.

"Hey, Pete, you think the general will catch the half-breed?" Bill asked.

"Pass me up some tobaccy," Pete said. He filled his pipe, then added, "The feller ain't a breed."

"Why you say that? He's half-White, ain't he?"

A match flared. Jacob was afraid that the light would give him away, but Bill was looking up at the sky.

"He's all White," Pete said between audible puffs. "Fact is, I knew his pappy—fella by the name of Marcus Andrews. We was both at Shiloh."

"Shiloh?"

"You Yanks called it Pittsburgh Landing. Bloodiest thing I ever seen. Andrews, he was a capt'n then, rose up to colonel 'fore the war was over. Afterward, he didn't have nothin' to go back to, 'n no Army left to be a colonel in, so he come out to these parts. Me, I'd done paroled myself over to the Yankees, and was posted out here, 'n I run across him in Omaha. Him 'n his wife, 'n a strappin' youngster name of Jacob."

As Jacob listened to the soldier talk, he felt a strange sadness for a time that was, and a future that was never to be

———

"DAD, I've been reading these broadsides about Nebraska," Jacob had once said. "They sound pretty good. I'll bet we could have a farm there as fine as Trailback."

"There will never be another Trailback," his mother had said quietly.

"Martha, I know you have happy memories of Trailback," his father replied. "I do, too. But Jacob's thinking ahead. We can build us a farm as good as Trailback. At least it will be as large and as productive, and in time, why I'll even build you a house as nice as The Glades. But it's going to be in Oregon, and not in Nebraska."

"But Dad, these broadsides..."

"Son, that's just snake oil, put out by the Union Pacific Railroad. Of course, they want people to settle in Nebraska. They've got a vested interest in it. If there are no people in Nebraska, the railroads can't make money. You can understand that, can't you?"

Jacob nodded, unconvinced. "I guess so."

"Don't worry," his father said, tousling his hair. "You'll love Oregon."

————

THE GUARDS' voices brought him back, and Jacob, trapped as he was, could do nothing but listen.

"Him bein' White, how come him to be livin' with the Injuns?"

"Well, sir, ole Marcus signed on with a wagon train, but things went sideways with the wagonmaster. Turned out the man had been in the Ohio Volunteers—fought at Shiloh, and didn't take kindly to ridin' with a Confederate. They butted heads. Marcus figured one of 'em was gonna end up dead."

"What happened then?"

"Half the wagon train split off on their own, I guess. Then, as I heard it, Crow hit the wagon train. Scalped his ma and pa. For some reason, the Injuns didn' take the boy's scalp. I guess they figured it would be even meaner to leave 'im there with his scalped mama and papa, 'n just let 'im starve to death."

"But he got away," Bill said.

"Sort of. Some Sioux, travelin' with Sittin' Bear, come by, 'n they picked the boy up. Sittin' Bear raised the boy like as iffen he was his own."

"Sittin' Bear? Ain't he the chief was kilt the other night?"

"Yep," Pete said. "I guess you might say ole Jacob's done lost two papas in one lifetime. That can't be none too easy."

"You say that like as iffen you feel a mite sorry for him."

"Oh, I don't know if I do," Pete said. "Jacob's a man full growed now, 'n' he could pretty well make up his own mind about what he's a'doin'. Course bein' raised partly by the Injuns I can see where it might be hard for him. But he was White longer'n he was injun."

"Oh, oh," Bill said. "I just seen Sergeant Caine. We best get to walkin', or he'll be havin' our tails for breakfast."

"Right," Pete said, rising. "I don't think they'll catch Jacob. He's been injun long enough to know their ways. My money's on him getting' away clean this time."

The guards continued on their rounds. Jacob waited a few moments longer, then slipped through the shadows toward the stable, where he intended to steal a horse.

———

"BUT STEALING IS WRONG," Jacob had once told Sitting Bear.

"When you are Whites, you do honor to the things which are White," the old man had said. "When you are Indian, you do honor to the things which are Indian. There is great honor for the Indian to steal from his enemy. If you wish to be accepted as a warrior, you must steal a horse from the Crow camp."

"I stole a horse from the Crow last spring," Crazy Wolf had boasted. Though Jacob had made friends with most of the other young men his age, an immediate animosity developed between him and Crazy Wolf. He and Jacob had always been rivals, and the tension only grew. "I made a present of the horse to Aiana."

"Then I'll steal two," Jacob had said calmly. "For Aiana."

Aiana, Sittin' Bear's daughter, had often teased him with her smiles and laughter. Though close in age and raised in the same lodge, she had already let it be known that she regarded him more as a potential suitor than as her brother.

"Brave talk from a White boy who has never proven himself," Crazy Wolf sneered.

"I've proven myself in fights with you," Jacob said. "And I am ready to do it again, anytime you want."

Jacob wasn't just boasting. He and Crazy Wolf had fought several times already, with Jacob usually coming out on top.

Aiana's eyes sparkled. "Will you really get two horses for me?"

"I will," he promised.

It was much easier said than done. The nearest Crow village lay three hours away. If Jacob left just after sundown and rode hard, he would reach the Crow village in the middle of the night. He could take the horses and be back just before sunup—provided he wasn't caught.

Jacob reached the village at about midnight. It was on the banks of a small stream. Jacob could see by the light of the moon, two dozen tipis and a remuda of horses. The remuda was right in the center of the village, so he would have to pass by the tipis in order to reach it.

He tied off his mount and crawled forward. He had practiced crawling great distances for the last several nights. Two nights ago, he had crawled from a long distance outside his village into Crazy Wolf's tipi. There, he had stolen one of Crazy Wolf's most prized feathers, and had worn it proudly the next morning for all to see.

"I took it from your tipi as you slept last night," Jacob said, returning the feather to an angry Crazy Wolf.

Now that stealth would be put to the maximum test, for if one of the sleeping villagers woke up to see him, he would be killed.

A dog barked. The Crow were noted for their dogs, which they kept, not as pets, but as domesticated livestock to be eaten. Jacob had a sack of buffalo bones around his neck. He opened it and scattered the bones. The dogs converged on them, and in a moment's tie, they were completely absorbed in their eating.

As he neared a tipi, a warrior stepped out. Jacob felt a quick stab of fear shoot through him, and he dropped to his stomach and lay very quietly, looking up at the warrior. He held a knife in his hand, watching warily as the man relieved himself, then wandered near the horses before returning to his tipi.

Jacob crawled onward. The horses were skittish, but his voice calmed them.

"Easy, horses," he said in English. He could speak Sioux, but in this moment of stress and tension, he slipped naturally into English, which was less difficult for him. "Easy, horses. We're just going for a little ride. Now, who wants to belong to a beautiful girl?"

He haltered two spotted ponies and led them quietly away.

Jacob had nearly made it back to his own horse when he was jumped by a Crow sentry! The attack caught Jacob completely by surprise, and he was knocked flat. He looked up in terror to see the Crow, grinning from ear to ear, coming toward him with a raised tomahawk. The Crow was going to scalp him alive!

The Crow, who was much older than Jacob, grew overconfident, intent only upon claiming coup on the would-be horse thief. He was not aware of Jacob's amazing agility or terrified strength.

Jacob rolled to one side just as the Crow swung at him, and he lunged with his knife hand, feeling his blade go deep into the Crow's stomach. Jacob twisted the blade and turned the Crow over, as the knife made a fatal tear across his abdomen. The Crow fell to the ground with a death rattle in his throat.

Jacob pulled the knife out, cleaned it, and slipped it back into his scabbard. He looked at the man he had just killed and fought the urge to be sick. He told himself that this was the enemy of his people, and that as a Sioux, he should be proud of his victory. And he reminded himself that it was Crow who had attacked the wagon and killed his mother and father.

And when he thought of his mother and father's scalps now decorating a Crow lodgepole, he was able to steel himself to do what he must do. He dropped down on one knee beside the Crow, grabbed the dead man's hair in one hand, put his knife to the Crow's scalp with the other, then turned his face away as he completed the scalping.

When Jacob returned, the village honored him. Stealing two horses on one raid was, Sitting Bear said, symbolized by his name, Two Hearts. One of the horses the white heart stole, and one the red heart stole. And claiming coup on the Crow warrior entitled Jacob to sit on the war councils from that time on.

His action raised him in the eyes of Aiana and the other villagers. But it created so much jealously in Crazy Wolf that it only deepened Crazy Wolf's resentment.

———

FROM THAT DAY ON, Crazy Wolf had been his enemy. Now, Jacob knew Crazy Wolf would have ammunition to use against him. He would claim that Jacob allowed his white heart to dominate his judgment and had helped the Whites to trick them. Sitting Bear, Aiana's father, and his own stepfather, was killed by the treachery.

And Jacob could not deny it. He had been moved by a White girl. And in doing so, had betrayed those who raised him.

He reached the stable, saddled a horse, and pulled a blanket around his shoulders to keep his naked skin from shining in the moonlight, then climbed on the animal's back and rode it boldly up to the front gate.

"I'm goin' out for Sergeant Caine," he called up to the wall.

One guard leaned over. "Close the gate good, will ya? I don't want to have to come down there."

"I'll get it," Jacob said.

He slipped through, shut the gate behind him, then stayed tight against the wall until he reached the blind corner. With a sharp kick to the flanks, the horse surged forward.

The night air whipped past him as he rode.

And though he felt the thrill of freedom, his thoughts turned to Emily Thomson—and what he had left behind.

*A fish and a bird may fall in love*, he thought...

*But where would they live?*

## CHAPTER ELEVEN

WHILE IN SEARCH OF JACOB, THE REGIMENT ENCOUNTERED a substantial war party led by Rain In The Face, the fierce Lakota warrior whose reputation for cunning and ferocity had preceded him across the plains. Tom Custer led a small unit of men on a daring strike at the rear of Rain In The Face's war party, causing the Sioux chief to break off the fight and retreat into the hills.

But the cost was steep.

Fourteen of Tom's men were killed in the fighting. All but three of the survivors sustained wounds, including Tom himself. A bullet had torn through his shoulder, and though he stayed in the saddle until the fighting ended, he was pale and bloodied when they returned to camp.

Jacob Two Hearts, however, was still missing.

Word of the battle swept through the fort like a prairie fire, fanned by the breathless chatter of officers' wives and camp followers. Emily heard of Tom's injury barely an hour after the first column rode in. She wasted no time hurrying to the infirmary.

Tom sat in a straight-backed wooden chair, stripped to the waist. Dr. Sprague was finishing the dressing on his shoulder. A length of cloth bound Tom's injured arm to his chest. Despite the sharp lines of pain on his face, he had a boyish grin.

"Well," Tom said, as Emily stepped inside, "for a visit from you, I'd gladly take another bullet in the other shoulder."

"Are you badly hurt, Tom?" she asked.

Tom chuckled and winced at the movement. "It's just a scratch."

"And lucky at that," Dr. Sprague said, tying off the bandage. "Miss Thomson, if you have any influence over this reckless hellion, I'd be much obliged if you reminded him he isn't invincible."

"Oh, but I am, Doc," Tom said, his tone dry and faintly mocking. "I'm a Custer—don't you know what that means? My brother wouldn't let anything happen to me."

Tom picked up a whiskey bottle from the table and took a long drink.

"Doc, I've got pains you wouldn't understand," he muttered, then caught himself and let out a short laugh as he took another drink.

Dr. Sprague gave him a pointed look and reached for the bottle. "You were supposed to take a sip to kill the pain—not drain the bottle."

Tom surrendered the bottle with a grin. "I don't need it anyway. One look at this beautiful young lady, and I can take anything."

Emily stood by, her arms loosely crossed. She gave him a knowing smile. "How you do carry on, Captain Custer."

"There is truth in what I say," Tom said. "As you shall see by my improved appetite at the dinner table. Because I am wounded, I was able to persuade Libbie to change the seating arrangement. I am now sitting next to you."

Emily shook her head, amused. "A true warrior's reward, I suppose."

Dr. Sprague cleared his throat. "Miss Thomson, I don't mean to be inhospitable, but if you'd kindly let me finish here, I might manage to keep this man's shoulder in one piece."

Emily laughed lightly. "Of course, Doctor. I do have work to get back to for my father, and I wouldn't dream of interfering with your efforts."

She gave Tom a brief nod and left the infirmary, her thoughts still unsettled by the reports of the skirmish, and by extension, the uncertainty surrounding Jacob's fate.

Back in her quarters, she sat at the small worktable and gathered her sketches. Most were part of the collection she was preparing for her father. But one was not.

Without consciously deciding to, she found herself shading the outline of a figure—long braids, a strong jaw, and piercing eyes.

It was Jacob Two Hearts.

In the three days since Jacob had vanished from the fort, Emily had been working steadily on a drawing of him.

Ordinarily, she needed a live model to produce a faithful likeness, but this time, no model was necessary. Jacob's features were so vivid in her mind that all she had to do was close her eyes, and she could envision him. His high cheekbones, the strong jaw, the quiet intensity in his blue eyes. But she remembered also, the sadness in those eyes.

And she had captured it.

She remembered pleading with him to take another path, one that would return him to a White man's world, but he had turned away. Even when she said she would go with him, it made no difference. He had made his choice, and it didn't include her.

She put her hands together on the edge of the drawing and tried to summon the will to rip it apart.

But she couldn't.

With a cry of frustration, she tossed the drawing under her bed. She told herself she would forget him.

She had to.

———

"I THOUGHT you'd want me to be brave in battle," Tom was saying.

The Custer family had gathered around the long dining table that evening, George, Libbie, Tom, Boston, and their father, Emmanuel. Emily sat beside Tom as he'd promised, with her father across from her. The room was witnessing the rather spirited conversation between Tom and his brother.

"Of course I want you to be brave in battle," Custer replied, setting his knife down with deliberate care. "But, Tom, sometimes you go beyond bravery. You act as if you want—" He stopped himself short.

"What are you saying, Autie?" Libbie asked, her voice sharp with concern.

"Nothing." Custer hesitated, then wiped his mouth with his napkin and looked at Tom. "It just distresses me to see you throw yourself into battle with such reckless abandon."

Tom gave a dry laugh. "Can this be George Armstrong Custer talking? The same man who once declared, 'I shall always go to the sound of battle'?"

"It's not the same thing, Tom, and you know it," Custer said firmly. "There's a difference between bravery...and some insane wish to commit suicide."

"Autie!" Libbie said sharply, placing a hand on his arm. "I'll not have you talking that way about your brother. And certainly not in front of our guests."

For a moment, silence fell over the table.

Custer bowed his head slightly, chastened. "I'm sorry," he said at last. "Tom, forgive me. It was a brave thing you did, and I have no right to question it."

"That's all right," Tom replied quietly. He pushed back from the table, the legs of his chair scraping against the floorboards. "If you'll excuse me, I think I'll go to my quarters."

He didn't look at anyone as he stood and left the room.

The meal continued for a few moments after Tom left, the clinking of silverware against dishes the only sound.

Finally, Libbie spoke, her voice quiet. "Autie...what did you mean? A wish to commit suicide?"

Custer exhaled heavily and rubbed his temple, as if the weight of what he had said was still pressing down on him.

"Sergeant Kennedy told me," he said. "There were three Sioux warriors holed up in a rock outcropping. Tom went right in after them, standing as bold upright as if he had been on parade. No crouch, no cover. I think the only reason he made it through was because he so shocked the Indians."

Libbie folded her hands tightly. "But perhaps that was his plan," she offered. "You've said before that bold action against Indians is the most effective key to success."

"Bold, yes," Custer said, shaking his head. "But not suicidal." He let out another breath and looked down at his napkin, twisting it unconsciously. "It's not just this campaign, Libbie, but all his actions lately. The way he rides into danger. The drinking. The attitude. He's careless...like nothing matters anymore."

He paused, then added grimly, "It reminds me of Colonel Cooper."

Libbie paled. "Oh, Autie, no," she whispered, placing her hand on his arm.

Custer patted his wife's hand, then excused himself from the table.

Libbie hesitated, her eyes following him as he left the room.

After a moment, Emily spoke. "Who is Colonel Cooper?"

Libbie's expression clouded. "He was an unfortunate man who was once Tom's very close friend. He drank to excess, much as Tom does now."

From the adjoining room, Custer's voice drifted back, low and grave. "William Cooper was a fine soldier. A West Pointer. He served under me in the cavalry during the war."

Emily turned toward the sound. "What happened to him?"

"He was one of the bravest men I ever knew," Custer said softly, reentering the room. "But...he had lost too much. His wife and children died of fever back East. The war took everything else."

Libbie lowered her gaze.

"He didn't fight like a man trying to win battles," Custer continued grimly. "He fought like a man who was trying to die."

Emily felt a coldness settle over her like a shadow drawn across her shoulders.

"And Tom reminds you of him?" she asked.

Custer nodded once, his eyes far away. "I can't shake the feeling that my brother is slipping," he admitted. "And I don't know how to stop it."

The room fell into silence again, save for the faint clatter of dishes as a servant cleared the table.

Libbie forced a smile. "Autie, perhaps you're reading too much into this. Tom is young. He is courageous. Maybe he just needs something worth fighting for—besides battle."

Custer didn't answer. He only stared at the place where his brother should have been sitting. Then, abruptly, he left the room.

Emily barely touched her food for the rest of the meal. Her appetite had vanished. Her thoughts circled around Tom—his reckless charm, his laughter, the sadness behind his eyes.

After dinner, Libbie crossed the room to a roll-top desk. She opened it and rummaged through the compartments until she pulled out a leather-bound ledger marked *Campaigns of 1868*.

"Autie is going to write his memoirs someday," she said. "He keeps copious notes from his expeditions. Read this part." She opened the book and passed it to Emily.

Emily took it gently, feeling the weight of it in her hands. She turned the pages slowly, the neat handwriting marching across the paper like soldiers on parade. The words were firm, precise—yet beneath them, she sensed a current of grief.

The passage stood out in bold script, as clear as if it had been printed:

*THE OFFICERS OF THE 7TH—THE entire camp, in fact—is wrapped in deep gloom by the suicide of Col. Cooper while in a fit of delirium tremens.*

Emily looked up, her eyes wide.

"Suicide?" she whispered.

Libbie gave a somber nod. "That's why Autie worries. He sees the same signs in Tom." She paused, then added gently, "And you...you may be the only one who can reach him. Read on."

Emily turned back to the ledger, the pages crackling faintly as she turned them.

Custer's field notes continued in a firm, unflinching hand:

*We reached present camp after a march of seventeen miles over broken country. I had just risen from the dinner table, where I had been discussing Tom Col. Cooper's actions, when Col. Meyers came rushing in. Calling Dr. Sprague, we hastened to Col. Cooper's tent and found him lying on knees and face, right hand grasping a revolver, ground near him covered with blood, body still warm and pulse beating, the act having been committed but three or four minutes before.*

Emily's breath caught. The words were stark. Undisguised. Like a bullet through the heart.

*Placing him on his back, we saw how well the shot had been aimed. Only the eyes wore the ghastly look of death. Conversation with other officers revealed he had contem-*

*plated the act under the influence of rum, and suffering some misguided guilt from his part in the recent battle of Washita. One by one, all came to gaze on one who but a few minutes before had been companion of our march.*

Emily glanced up at Libbie, but the general's wife merely gave a solemn nod, urging her on.

*Actuated by what I deemed my duty to the living, I warned the officers of the regiment of the fate of their comrade. I hope the example will not be lost on them. But for intemperance, Col. Cooper would have been a useful and accomplished officer, a brilliant and most companionable gentleman.*

Emily closed the ledger gently and returned it to Libbie, her fingers lingering for a moment on the worn leather cover.

She sat still, the silence between them stretching long.

The words weighed on her—not just for what they said, but for what they did not. A man lost not to bullets or war, but to sorrow and the bottle. And another—Tom —possibly drifting toward that same dark edge.

She looked toward the window, where the sky had faded toward dusk, and for the first time that day, she felt truly cold.

"You can see," Libbie murmured, "why Autie might be disturbed by Tom's actions when he compares them to Colonel Cooper's."

"Yes, of course I can," Emily said, her voice low. Then, after a moment's hesitation: "Libbie...what happened at Washita?"

Libbie offered a smile. "Washita was one of Autie's greatest victories."

Emily frowned. "Then why did the general write

that Colonel Cooper was suffering from misguided guilt over it? And what did Sergeant Flynn mean when he said that Tom lived with the devils of Washita?"

Libbie stiffened slightly, her posture still composed. "I'm sure I don't know," she said. "The general's notes on the battle are in this same ledger. Here—read for yourself."

She returned the book to Emily, and as Emily accepted it, she noticed the subtle shift. Libbie had not called him *Autie* this time. She had said *the general*.

Even Libbie, loyal to the bone, seemed guarded when it came to Washita.

Emily turned the pages slowly, carefully. The entries had the same firm hand, the same military precision, but the tone here was different, as though each word had been weighed before being written.

Orders. Movements. Formations. A battle well-fought.

*November 1868, the Washita Valley, Indian Territory.*

*Recorded by G.A. Custer, Commanding.*

*I rode with the scouts so as to be as near as possible in the advance. The cavalry followed from a quarter to a half mile back, lest the crunching of the crusted snow signal our whereabouts.*

*Orders prohibited a word above a whisper, a match struck, or a pipe lighted—great deprivation to a soldier. Thus, silently, mile after mile we went until the guides rode back and reported that we were within two or three miles of the Indian village.*

*The command resumed the march with guides, who were afoot, in the lead. At the crest of the hill, the Osage guide shielded his eyes with his hand and peered into the valley below.*

*"Heap Injuns down there."*

The scout's words lingered in Emily's mind. *Heap Injuns down there.*

She could picture it—the stillness of a sleeping village blanketed in snow. The hush of trees in the predawn dark. Then, the sudden shatter of gunfire. The screams. The confusion.

*It was after midnight. Complete silence was to be observed. I ordered the officers to remove their sabers so the clank of metal would not be heard. Then I divided the command into four detachments of equal strength. One was to move to the woods bordering the village, another down-river to the timber below, a third to occupy the crest north of the village, and the fourth, my own, to remain at the point of the discovery. The attacks would be simultaneous, and the enemy, being surrounded, would have little chance to escape. Everything depended on accurate timing and the element of surprise.*

*We waited until two hours before dawn. The moon had gone down and the night was perfectly black. A brilliant light, the morning star, appeared—but even that soon disappeared with the morning fog, which limited visibility to only twenty yards.*

*Then came the moment to advance. I gave the signal, and the band broke into "Garry Owen". Cheers resounded from the other detachments. The entire command rushed into action, four units as one. The Battle of the Washita was enjoined and carried on by my brave men to a successful conclusion—103 Indians killed, 53 captured.*

*The sad side of the story is our killed and wounded. Captain Hamilton and Major Elliott led their men after a small band of Indians and pursued them too far... Nineteen*

*enlisted men, with these gallant officers, were killed. Three*
*officers and eleven enlisted men were wounded.*

Emily read the final line again.

*103 Indians killed. 53 captured. A successful conclusion.*

She looked up, her fingers tightening on the edge of
the book.

But what wasn't written?

What was left unsaid?

Libbie sat across from her, upright and composed,
her chin held high.

"Those who regard Washita as anything less than a
glorious victory simply wish Autie ill will," she said evenly.

Emily frowned. "Then what devils does Tom face?"

Libbie sighed, folding her hands neatly in her lap.
"Tom is a sensitive young man. He was very close to
Colonel Cooper, and when Colonel Cooper committed
suicide—no doubt because Washita was his first experience with the horrors of battle—Tom assumed the
colonel's burden of guilt. That burden has plagued him
all this time."

Emily exhaled slowly, the pieces falling into place.
"Oh, how terrible for him," she murmured.

"But Tom is also an honorable man," Libbie continued. "And he would do nothing to bring dishonor to the
Custer name. I have no doubt that the excitement of
command will bring him out of his despair."

She paused, then offered a faint, hopeful smile.
"Autie intends to leave Tom in command of the Seventh
while we are in New York, you know."

Emily blinked. "No. I hadn't heard."

Libbie's expression grew more solemn. "Emily, you
do recall the talk we had about Tom's destiny?"

"I do."

"Good." Libbie's smile never wavered, but there was a warning behind her words. "I hope you will bear that in mind while we are gone. I should not like to see Tom suffer because of some ill-considered act."

Emily bristled at the implication.

"I assure you, madam," she said evenly, "I am not the person you need to fear on that score."

Libbie's smile widened, though her eyes remained sharp. "I find that comforting," she said sweetly. "Now, if you will excuse me, I shall see to Autie."

Emily watched her leave, barely concealing her irritation. Even her father, who normally retreated into introspection during *women talk*, commented on his daughter's vexation. He looked up from his plate and raised an eyebrow.

"Shall we retire as well, daughter?"

"Yes, father," Emily said, as she rose from her chair. "Please, will you see to my wrap?"

When the Thomsons were out of the Custer home, Silas turned to Emily, his tone amused. "Why are you angry with Mrs. Custer?"

"No reason, Father," Emily replied tersely.

Silas chuckled. "Am I to believe that you are angry simply because it is in your nature?"

She sighed, some of the tension leaving her shoulders at the familiar sound of his dry humor.

"Mrs. Custer is afraid that I will show undue affection for Tom."

"I see," he said, tilting his head in thought.

"Of course," Emily continued. "I explained that such a thing is unlikely, but she persists in her fear. Perhaps I should go to her again and put her mind at ease."

Silas studied her for a long moment before asking quietly, "Why?"

"Why?" Emily blinked, surprised by her father's question. "Don't you think I should?"

Silas smiled faintly. "Do you like the young man?"

She hesitated. "Well...I must admit he has all of his brother's charm—but none of his conceit. And there's a kind of sweetness about him, too."

Silas nodded thoughtfully. "Then pay no attention to Mrs. Custer."

Emily narrowed her eyes. "Father...are you encouraging a friendship with Tom?"

"Yes," he said simply.

Emily studied him with suspicion.

"Didn't she just say that he'll be in command while they're gone?"

"Yes," she admitted.

"Then perhaps he could be made to see the validity of our request to go into the Indian lands and paint."

Emily sighed knowingly. "Oh. I see. In other words... you want me to use him."

Silas shrugged, unapologetic. "Yes. But only if you can do so without hurting him."

"I don't think that can be done."

Silas gave her a wry smile. "Oh, I don't agree with you at all. In fact, your attention may be just what he needs to rid himself of these devils that plague him."

# CHAPTER TWELVE

IF JACOB HAD ANY DOUBTS THAT HE MIGHT NOT BE accepted back into the village, it was because even now he did not understand the depth of the Hunkpapa commitment to him. He had become one of them through sacred ceremony, his body consecrated, his spirit accepted. And as far as they were concerned, he was as Sioux as any who had been born to the tribe.

The joyful acceptance of his return and the celebration of his escape made him realize more than ever that he had done the right thing by returning. His loyalty had been tested and proven. He had chosen his people.

And in choosing them, he had turned away from the White world and Emily Thomson.

Shortly after his return, he announced his intention to enter the sweat lodge, which was a sacred act among the Sioux, where they joined in communion with the Great Spirit. The lodge itself was a small, tightly sealed dome of willow and hides. In its center, rocks were piled, then a fire was built, and the rocks were heated until they glowed red. Then water would be poured on the rocks, releasing steam that choked the air and burned the skin.

To withstand such heat was more than a test of physical strength. It was considered the single most spiritual act a Sioux could perform. It was in the sweat lodge that those individuals blessed with great spirituality received messages from the Great Spirit. And though Jacob had never seen a vision, he never left a sweat lodge without an uplifted feeling and a sense of purpose.

He was gathering stones for the fire when a voice startled him.

"Perhaps you would not mind sharing your sweat lodge with me?"

Jacob turned sharply.

Sitting Bull stood before him.

A hushed murmur rippled through the nearby warriors. The great chief, Tatanka Iyotake, was the most respected of all the Lakota leaders. Greater even than Gall, or Rain In The Face, or Crazy Horse. His visions were legend. He had never shared a sweat lodge with another man.

To request such a thing now was the highest honor Jacob could imagine.

He bowed his head with humility. "It would be my honor, Tatanka Iyotake."

Sitting Bull gave a small nod.

Jacob took great care in building the sweat lodge, and when it was ready, he walked proudly through the village to Sitting Bull's wickiup to inform him.

Without a word, Sitting Bull rose from his mat of soft furs and followed Jacob.

Inside the lodge, the sacred fire burned low and hot.

Jacob scattered wet cedar and sweetgrass over the stones, and steam hissed into the dark space. Sitting Bull stepped inside and settled onto the ground with the ease of a man at peace with the world, and with himself.

They sat in silence for a long while. The air was thick with heat and steam, as their skin glistened with sweat. Jacob thought this would be how it would be. Silence, stillness, communion through just being together.

But then Sitting Bull spoke.

"Do you know how I got my name?"

Jacob shook his head. "No."

"It was my father's name," the chief said, his voice calm. "And he gave it to me for an act of bravery. I was the same age then as you were when you counted coup against the Crow warrior."

He paused, letting his words sink in.

"The name was a great gift from my father," he went on. "For he was given it by the Great Spirit. And that is the story I will tell you...if you wish to hear it."

Jacob bowed his head slightly. "I would very much like to hear," he replied.

Sitting Bull leaned back slightly, letting the heat surround him even more.

"One night, when my father was on a hunting party, a great buffalo bull came slowly toward the camp. The bull made strange sounds deep in its throat, and the other hunters grew afraid, but my father did not.

"His name then was Returns Again. And he believed the bull had been sent by the Great Spirit to speak to him.

"He did not run. He stepped forward...to listen."

Jacob closed his eyes, picturing the scene clearly, a lone bull moving toward the camp, its breath rising in thick clouds into the frozen air.

"What do you wish, messenger of the Great Spirit?" my father asked.

"The bull moved his head from side to side, slowly, solemnly, and continued speaking in the language of buffalo. None of the hunters could understand, until the Great Spirit granted my father the gift to hear the words.

"The bull spoke four names, again and again. Four, as you know, is a sacred number to our people.

"And one of those names...was Sitting Bull.

"My father took that as the name given him by *Wakȟáŋ Tȟáŋka*, the Great Spirit. And when the time came, he gave it to me.

"*Tatanka Iyotake.*

"That is the name the White men now speak."

Jacob followed every word, knowing that such a name was never claimed lightly. It had passed from a vision to a father, and now to a son.

"That is a great gift, *Tatanka Iyotake*," Jacob said. "I am honored you have shared it."

Sitting Bull tilted his head, studying the younger man through the rising steam. Then his voice returned, quiet but firm.

"And now...shall I tell you of a vision I have seen?"

Jacob sat up taller.

"I would be honored."

Sitting Bull's eyes seemed to grow darker, even in the dim light from the fire.

"There will be a great battle," he said quietly, "between the Lakota and the soldiers."

Jacob's hands clenched.

"All the Indian nations will fight under me," Sitting Bull continued. "And all the soldiers will fight under Yellow Hair."

*Yellow Hair.*

*Custer.*

A cold shiver crept down Jacob's spine, despite the overwhelming heat.

"The Indians will win," Sitting Bull said. His voice remained calm. "A great victory. There will be much crying and wailing in the homes of the soldiers, for all will be killed."

Jacob exhaled slowly. "That is a great vision," he said, his voice barely above a whisper.

Sitting Bull turned to look at him.

"You are a man of two hearts," the chief said. "After that battle, one of your hearts will die, and one will live. But I do not know which one."

Jacob felt the pounding in his chest of his own heartbeat.

"My Indian heart will live," he said steadily.

Sitting Bull watched him for a long moment.

"This may be so," he said. "But for now, I cannot say."

"Tatanka Iyotake, do you fear that I will betray you?" Jacob wanted to know.

Sitting Bull did not answer right away. His gaze drifted to the glowing stones at the center of the lodge before returning to Jacob.

"No," he said finally. "For if it is to be your Indian heart that dies, it will die a brave death and will not betray its people. But neither will your white heart allow you to betray the Whites."

He paused, and when he spoke again, his voice was solemn.

"There will be a battle between your two hearts, as great as that I will fight with Yellow Hair."

"The Indian will win the battle you fight with Yellow Hair," Jacob said. "And the Indian will win the battle between my two hearts. I will not bring dishonor to myself."

Sitting Bull nodded.

"You would bring dishonor," he said, "only if you disobeyed the heart that wins the battle. If your Indian heart is victorious, it would be dishonorable to deny it. But if your white heart wins, it would be dishonorable to deny that as well."

Jacob's throat tightened. "How will I know which is right?"

Sitting Bull gave a faint smile, as if he had been waiting for that question all along.

"You will know."

And with that, he closed his eyes.

Jacob, out of respect for Sitting Bull's meditations, was silent also. The heat pressed in around him, but he barely noticed it. Sitting Bull's words turned over and over in his mind.

*You would bring dishonor only if you deny the heart that wins.*

He had vowed not to betray his Indian heart. He believed that vow still. And yet...something about Sitting Bull's vision struck deeper than he wanted to admit.

For the first time, Jacob sensed that his fate was no longer in his hands alone. The path had already begun to form beneath his feet. And no matter which direction he followed, no matter which heart won, a part of him would not survive.

Sitting Bull exhaled deeply, then spoke once more.

"I have a song for you," he said. "It has come to me as I sit here. I will sing it for you now."

His voice rose softly into the dim, steaming air of the sweat lodge, a two-note chant, repeated again and again. The melody was simple, but there was power in it, like something ancient being awakened. The words of the song, though delivered in Teton Sioux, rang clear in Jacob's mind:

> *Like the empty sky, it has no boundaries,*
> *Yet it is right in this place.*
> *When you seek to know it, you cannot see it,*
> *You cannot take hold of it,*
> *But you cannot lose it.*
> *If you do not understand,*
> *Then you can understand.*
> *When you are silent, it speaks,*
> *When you speak, it is silent.*

Jacob did not try to decipher the meaning of the words but instead let the phrases soothe his mind.

He closed his eyes, and when he opened them again, Sitting Bull was gone. Songs were chanted outside the tent, but he did not hear. Jacob had glimpsed the truth.

———

AIANA TRIED NOT to think about the soldiers who had come in the night to kill her family, but she couldn't help it. Sometimes the memories came back to chill her like a cold wind blowing from the winter mountains. Often, the memories came while Aiana was asleep, and she would cry out in terror and wake up shaking with fear.

And yet...not all the nights were like that.

There were times when Aiana would wake up and it would still be night and she could see the moon, hanging cold and quiet in the early morning darkness. At that moment, just between sleep and wake, she would think of the man she loved.

And in those rare moments, she felt something like peace.

As the stepson of her father, Jacob had become the head of her family, and he provided for her and made the decisions for her, and treated her as a father would his daughter, or a brother would his sister. This was as it should be for a woman with no husband.

But Aiana did not want to be a woman without a husband. There was nothing in tribal law that forbade her from marrying the stepson of her father, which was just what she wanted to do. She wanted to be Jacob's wife.

One night in late autumn, as Aiana lay thinking of Jacob, she heard the murmur of voices. The shamans were leaving for the mountains to seek visions, to pray in solitude beneath the stars.

She closed her eyes, listening until she could no longer hear their footsteps. Then, she rose quietly and stepped to the entrance of her wickiup.

The night air was cold and clean.

Above her, the moon hung bright and full, casting the village in a pale, silvery glow. The stars blinked through the drifting clouds.

She folded her arms and stood still, her breath rising in the chill.

And she prayed.

Not aloud. Not even in words.

She simply opened her heart.

Would Jacob ever look at her as a woman, and not just as a sister or as an obligation?

Would he always be caught between the world he left behind and the one he now called his own? Or would the time come when he would choose?

As she stood in the stillness, Aiana sensed movement from across the camp, and then she saw Jacob.

He was walking away from the central fire, his silhouette framed by moonlight as he moved toward the ridge beyond the village.

She watched him go, the wind stirring gently through the tall grass.

*Perhaps,* she thought, *she should not wait for him to choose.*

*Perhaps the Great Spirit had already answered her prayer.*

She returned to her lodge, but she couldn't sleep. Instead, she sat beside the fire pit, the coals glowing low, as she wrestled with her thoughts.

Some time later, she heard footsteps outside.

Jacob entered the lodge and stopped when he saw her.

Their eyes met, and for a long moment, neither of them spoke.

Then Jacob knelt beside her, and there was no need for words.

They lay together in silence, listening to the crackle of the fire and the gently blowing wind. Whatever had once stood between them no longer seemed to matter.

Aiana moved closer to him, and Jacob wrapped a blanket around them both. He held her gently, and she rested her head on his shoulder.

In that quiet moment, beneath the pale moon and the watchful stars, something unspoken passed between them...something understood. Not claimed. Not taken. Only accepted.

And when sleep finally came, it came to both of them.

Jacob awoke in the early morning darkness.

The moon still hung high in the sky, casting a silvery glow through the opening of the lodge. A soft pool of light spilled across the floor and over the bedding where Aiana slept, her face calm, her breathing deep and steady.

She was wrapped in buffalo robes, her body still and at peace.

Jacob watched her in silence, his thoughts drifting. The warmth between them, the quiet understanding—they had not spoken of it, but it had become something real.

He reached over and gently rested his hand on her shoulder, a simple gesture of comfort of presence. She stirred only slightly, then settled once more.

He did not move for a long time. When he finally fell asleep again, he felt at peace.

———

AFTER THAT NIGHT, Aiana was Jacob's woman.

At first, they told no one of the growing bond

between them. But as the nights grew longer and the winds grew colder, all that changed.

Their lodges were joined. Their days began and ended together.

And by the time the first snow came, Jacob knew it was time to tell the others of his decision.

One evening, as the gathered elders sat before the council fire in the center of the village, Jacob stepped forward.

"I have made my decision," he said with a calm voice. "I will take Aiana as my wife."

There was a murmur among the elders. Not all agreed, but none questioned his right.

Jacob had made his choice. His Indian heart had spoken.

Crazy Wolf vehemently disapproved. He muttered something under his breath before turning and disappearing into the darkness beyond the circle of firelight.

No one followed him.

Sitting Bull remained silent.

Jacob met his gaze, and after a long moment, the great chief gave a single nod.

Without a word, he motioned for the shaman to step forward.

Under the open sky, with the stars watching from above and the embers of the council fire glowing between them, Jacob and Aiana were joined in the sacred bond of marriage.

The shaman spoke few words, but they were enough.

When the ceremony ended, the people offered quiet approval.

By the time the first snow covered the valley, Jacob

sat in his own wickiup, wrapped in buffalo hides, his new wife resting peacefully in his arms.

Outside, the wind howled across the frozen plains, but inside, the fire burned warm.

And so did something deeper.

Jacob held Aiana close, listening to the rhythm of her breathing, the pulse of her life beside his.

*And now,* he thought, *my Indian heart has made its choice.*

He had never known such happiness. For the first time since he was a boy, he felt truly at home.

# CHAPTER THIRTEEN

New York
December 31, 1875

Dear Tom,

As I write, it is New Year's Eve, so you will receive this in the New Year. I trust all is well with you and with our military family at Fort Lincoln. Please extend my kindest regards to Silas Thomson and his daughter.

Autie and I have met with Paul Gideon, their agent here, who reports that some of the earlier works from Fort Lincoln, particularly the portraits of Autie, have attracted considerable attention. He agrees with us, incidentally, that Silas Thomson is far too gifted an artist to be allowed to venture into Indian territories.

The holidays here have been rainy and rather gloomy. I did not have the fun I had anticipated looking at the shop windows, but the gray skies dampened both the streets and my spirits. On Christmas morning, I went to church, Episcopal, of course, but came back, weary and disgruntled from the ritual prayers and processions. Autie, as always, finds the day something of a bore and is glad when it passes. I missed the home atmosphere, and all of you.

Autie gave me a lovely black silk dress, which I am sewing myself as there is no one here to help me. I gave him a solid silver table-spoon and teaspoon. Maggie completed the set with a fork and dessert spoon to match. It made a fine presentation, if I may say so.

Autie has so many invitations, I have to drive him to accept them, as it is a privilege to meet such interesting people. One evening, he dined at three different events! There was a dinner at the Lotus Club, another at the Stoughtons, where he met Sir Rose Price, a noted sportsman, and perhaps the greatest treat of all, a luncheon at Mr. Bierstadt's studio, where we were introduced to Earl Sunracen. We also dined twice with the Barretts.

Mr. Lawrence Barrett is enjoying enormous success in Julius Caesar at Booth's Theatre. The staging is unbelievable. Sometimes as many as three hundred people crowd the stage, and the final tableau is astonishing. Brutus is burned on a funeral pyre. It makes you want to scream to see the blazing funeral pyre and Brutus rising above it. It is something that would make even you, dear Tom, want to leap to your feet and cheer. It is quite the spectacle.

We also saw Oakey Hall, the former mayor, performing in a play of his own writing. It was...unusual. Imagine a man of fifty launching an acting career. Sensational, certainly, and unmistakably lawyer-like in delivery. Still, it was worth the price of admission just to say we had seen it.

Autie and I have a room opposite the Hotel Brunswick where we take our meals and collect the mail. Oddly enough, life here is less expensive than it is at Fort Lincoln. Still, I confess I am looking forward to hearing about our return journey. I enjoy New York, but I find myself missing the simplicity and the loyalty of our military family.

Now, Tom, a word of advice, as always, given in affection. Don't spend more money than you can help at the Sutlers', drinking, and card-playing. Don't be influenced by the badness around you. And most important of all, guard your heart. Loneliness has led many a good man into poor judgment.

Oh, if only I could find a companionable wife for you...one who would understand her role as a Custer, one who would forsake all her own *ambitions and desires for the fulfillment of yours. That's the kind of wife you need, Tom. That is the kind of woman you need. Do not be misled by a pretty face, or soft words, or kindness that comes from the wrong place.*

*You will know what I mean.*

*Choose wisely, Tom.*

*Affectionately,*

*Libbie*

"What do you suppose she means?" Tom asked.

He had been reading Libbie's letter aloud to Emily. The two of them were seated on the floor of the commandant's house, eating popcorn from a shared bowl and sipping warm apple cider while the wind howled outside.

Emily raised her eyebrows in feigned innocence. "Well, Captain Custer, I'm sure I don't know. She couldn't mean *me*, could she? Surely she doesn't think I would fool you by loneliness, or kindness."

"No," Tom said in a mocking tone. "It couldn't be you. Libbie said this person had a pretty face."

"Tom Custer!" Emily cried, laughing as she tossed a handful of popcorn at him.

"Here now!" Tom retorted. "We'll have none of that. I'm the commanding officer of the Seventh Cavalry. How would it look if some of my officers came in and saw popcorn all over the floor?"

"Better them than Libbie," Emily said.

"You've a point there," Tom agreed, glancing toward the window. "But there's little chance that she'll show up unexpectedly tonight. The snow is already knee deep and still coming down strong. I've known folks to get turned around twenty-five yards from their own front door in this kind of storm."

"I know, it's awful," Emily said, as she picked up the scattered popcorn. "But let her come, if she wants. There's not a trace of our unmilitary frivolity left behind."

Tom reached into his coat pocket and pulled out a second envelope. "There was a letter from Autie, too. Want to hear it?"

"Of course," Emily said as she settled back onto the floor. "I'm always curious what a future president has to say."

Tom grinned, unfolded the letter, and began to read:

New York
December 31, 1875

Dear Tom,

We have been here over a month now. We have delightful rooms at the back, quiet, opposite the Brunswick. We are having the most delightful and interesting time possible. I have entry to all the theaters in the city. At a reception at the Historical Society, its president and a group of other men all over eighty flocked around Libbie. At a reception of the Palatte Club, the president took her in to supper. Dancing followed, which was an amusing affair, as the ladies insisted on dancing in their hats.

Silas Thomson's paintings of life at Fort Lincoln were recently exhibited and received with great enthusiasm. One portrait in particular—of yours truly, of course—caused a modest stir. I was told that a young lady claimed to have fallen in love with me solely from Mr. Thomson's painting. Libbie showed admirable restraint at the news.

The latest in regard to Army reduction is that the house will not interfere with the cavalry, but will cut off five regiments of infantry, and one of artillery. I imagine there will be much debate, but at least the cavalry is safe.

Regarding promotion, I have no expectations this spring or summer. Instead, I anticipate we'll be in the field with the Seventh, and I believe we stand on the edge of our greatest campaign yet. Several congressmen and senators have told me privately that my best method of advancing into the political arena would be by producing a sterling victory over the hostiles this summer, possibly even over Sitting Bull himself. I will seek that scoundrel out and ride him down to the tune of "Garry Owen", you may count on that.

Get plenty of rest this winter, brother, for come summer, I shall cover us all with glory.

Autie

"WELL," Emily said, as Tom finished reading the letter. "You certainly have your life all planned out for you, don't you, Tom?"

Tom exhaled slowly, staring into the fire. "It would seem that way, wouldn't it?"

She studied him for a moment. "Is it what you want?"

He didn't answer right away. Instead, he stood, walked to the fireplace, and grabbed the poker. With slow, deliberate motions, he stirred the logs, sending sparks dancing up the chimney. The fire crackled and hissed, filling the silence between them.

"Excuse me," Emily said, letting out a short breath. "I should have known better. It's a question of honor, right?"

Tom's shoulders stiffened. He turned to face her, with a pained expression on his face.

"Oh, don't bother explaining," Emily said, waving him off. She lowered herself onto the bearskin rug in front of the hearth and stretched out, her eyes fixed on the fire. "I've learned much of honor since I have been out here. You aren't alone in your slavish devotion to it."

"You mean Jacob Two Hearts?"

Tom's offhand comment caught Emily totally unawares. She felt as if she had been hit in the stomach with a club, and she stared at Tom in absolute shock.

"What?" she asked in a very small voice. "What did you say?"

Tom moved to the mantel and leaned against it, his face unreadable. "I found the drawing you did of him. And I know you're the one who set him free."

Emily's mouth went dry. "How...do you...know that?"

Tom's voice was quiet, not accusing. "A drawing isn't like a photograph. A drawing shows the artist's emotions. The drawing you made of Jacob? I would give anything if you would make such a drawing of me."

Emily looked away. "I see."

Tom didn't press her. He only continued, his voice gentler now. "And when you found out he'd married Sitting Bear's daughter...I saw it in your eyes."

There was a long pause.

"You loved him, didn't you?"

Emily shook her head. "No."

Tom raised an eyebrow. "Oh?"

She ran a hand through her hair, avoiding his gaze. "Maybe once. But not now."

Tom studied her carefully. Then, after a quiet moment, he reached out and placed a hand gently on her arm.

"Then could there be a chance for me?"

Emily turned her head sharply. "Tom, do you even know what you're saying?"

His voice was steady. "I love you, Emily. I want to marry you."

She stared at him, taken aback, her mouth slightly parted in surprise.

"But what about Libbie?" she asked.

"Libbie is already married," Tom said, allowing a faint smile to touch his lips.

"You know what I mean," Emily replied. "She doesn't approve of me."

"She thinks you wouldn't make a proper Custer wife. That's all."

"Well, she's right," Emily said. "I could never be the kind of woman she wants me to be."

Tom straightened, the humor gone from his face. "I don't care what Libbie wants. I care about what I want."

Emily looked at him carefully. "And what about your honor?"

"To hell with honor," Tom said quietly.

He stepped closer, his arm moving gently around her shoulders.

For a moment, Emily didn't move. Her heart pounded with something that wasn't fear—but wasn't certainty either.

Tom leaned in and kissed her softly on the temple, a touch more comforting than bold.

"I'll fit my life to yours," he whispered. "I love you, Emily."

Emily hesitated, then turned to face him. For a moment, they simply stood there, eyes locked in the warm glow of the fire.

And then, without planning, without words, they kissed.

There was no urgency, no heat, just a quiet exchange, as if each was testing the shape of the future.

When it ended, neither spoke.

Emily wasn't sure how they had gotten to this point. One moment, they were throwing popcorn in front of the fire. The next, she found herself leaning toward Tom, drawn by something she hadn't let herself say.

She had been drawn to him from the beginning, from the first time she had seen him running toward the coach in Bismarck, though she had never admitted it. Theirs had always been a strange, almost melancholy connection. Tom had never crossed a line and never spoke or acted in a way that could be called improper. And yet, there had always been something smoldering beneath his careful reserve.

Emily leaned into him, resting her head against his chest.

He whispered her name once, and she closed her eyes.

For a long time, they stayed that way—no rank between them, no past, no future. Just warmth. Stillness.

Then, in the hush of the moment, Tom spoke.

"Marry me," he said quietly.

Emily lifted her head to look at him.

"Tom..." She faltered, her heart thudding inside her chest. "You don't know what you're asking."

"Yes, I do," he said. "I've known from the first time I saw you."

She searched his face. This wasn't a question asked on impulse. It was something he had wanted to ask for some time. He had been waiting for just the right moment.

Emily swallowed. "Yes, Tom," she said, her voice barely audible.

Neither of them spoke again. The wind howled outside. The fire crackled and snapped in the hearth.

And for the first time in a long time, they both felt something like peace.

# CHAPTER FOURTEEN

GENERAL CUSTER'S LEAVE WAS OFFICIALLY OVER BY THE first week of February. But instead of returning to Fort Lincoln, he was ordered to Washington to testify before Congress on the matter of building new posts and forts across the Western Territories.

General Terry petitioned for Custer to be relieved of this duty so that he could take charge of the spring campaigns, but his entreaty went unheeded. The result was that while the Custers were attending gala balls and glittering receptions in the capital, sandwiched in between Custer's appearances before various congressional committees, Tom was left in command of the Seventh.

Though Emily continued her work from her quarters, many evenings were now spent in the commandant's house with Tom.

One morning, while Emily and Silas were working together, the subject turned unexpectedly.

"Are you in love with him?" Silas asked.

Emily looked up, startled. They had been discussing light and color, and the abrupt question surprised her.

"What?"

Silas dabbed a bit of color onto his canvas and worked it in, as if it were much more important than the discussion he had initiated by his question.

"I asked," Silas said mildly, continuing to work paint into the corner of his canvas, "if you love Tom Custer."

Emily was cleaning a brush with turpentine, and she studied it closely before answering.

"I think I do," she said quietly.

"Well, I should hope so," Silas replied, not looking up. "If you plan to spend your life with him."

"That's funny," Emily said. "I would've thought you'd say, 'I hope you want to marry him,' and leave it at that. That's what most fathers would say."

"I'm not most fathers," Silas said. "And you're certainly not most daughters. You know I spent years in Paris. The French view these matters differently. Perhaps that's rubbed off on me. Besides, we are artists, you and I. Artists feel things much more deeply, and it is only natural that our emotional sensitivity would carry over into our physical feelings."

He turned and met her eyes.

"I don't judge you for caring deeply about someone. I would only caution you not to marry out of obligation. Marry for the right reason, or not at all."

Emily walked over and wrapped her arms gently around his shoulders.

"Father, I don't want to do anything that would hurt you."

"Then don't do anything that will hurt yourself," he said.

She paused. "I can't promise that."

She walked away from her father and looked out the window. In the quadrangle below, a troop of mounted soldiers were preparing to leave on detail. The sound of hooves and shouted orders drifted up faintly.

"What is it?" Silas asked.

"It's Tom," Emily said, still staring through the window. "His dreams. Or rather, his nightmares."

She turned back to face her father.

"Father, have you ever heard what really happened at Washita? I mean, really?"

"I read General Custer's report," Silas said. "Same as you did."

"The one that said one hundred and three Indians were killed," Emily said. "But did you know that only eleven of them were warriors? The rest were women and children. Even babies."

Silas said nothing.

"And the fifty-three captured? They were all women and children, too," she continued. "They slaughtered over six hundred horses. Did you know that?"

"No," he said quietly. "No, I didn't. Did Tom tell you this?"

"No," Emily said. "He couldn't. That would be disloyal to his brother. Tom could never tell me all that. He just has nightmares, and drinks too much, and keeps it all bottled up inside him."

She paused, her voice low now.

"It's eating him alive."

"I can see how something like that would," Silas said quietly. "So that was what drove Colonel Cooper to take his own life."

Emily nodded. "Yes. I learned of it through Sergeant Flynn."

Silas hesitated. "You don't think...I mean, there's no chance that..."

"That Tom might do the same thing?" she asked, finishing the thought.

He didn't answer, but the concern in his eyes was plain.

"It's a possibility," Emily admitted. "But not in the same way. Tom would find a way to accomplish the same thing. If he were to fall, it would be in the line of duty. He would find a way to make it look like honor."

She turned from the window, her voice more anxious.

"That's why I worry about this upcoming campaign. General Custer hasn't returned, and the Seventh has to go out and round up a group of warriors who won't stay on the reservations."

"And Tom is going to lead the expedition?"

"Yes."

"But surely," Silas said, trying to find reassurance in his own words, "the prospect of marrying you, of building a life together, will deter him from any foolhardy action?"

"I hope so," Emily replied softly. "But I can't be sure, Father. I just...can't be sure."

As Emily and her father were discussing him, Tom was at the moment sitting behind his desk reading Libbie's latest letter. He had not shown it to Emily, nor even told her of its existence.

There was no need to. It would only upset her. And he had no desire to do that—not now. The last part was particularly venomous, and Tom had read it many times over:

*I do not blame you, Tom, for supposing you have fallen in love with Emily Thomson. She is a most beautiful woman, and you, so long denied the joys a wife might have suffered what any man in your position would suffer, a loss of good judgment.*

*But Emily is not for you. She will do nothing to further your career, nor will she even have your best interests at heart. She is an artist, ambitious only in her own chosen endeavor. I will not allow this proposed marriage to take place, and neither will Autie. When at long last this Washington business has ended, and we are allowed to return, Autie will invoke his right as military commander of the district to require Miss Thomson and her father to leave Fort Lincoln.*

*I know this may sound unnecessarily harsh to you, Tom, but believe me, it is done in love. We are doing this for your own good, and for your future.*

Tom rose from his chair, picking up the letter. He walked to the fireplace, staring into the flames for a long moment.

Then he tossed the paper into the fire.

He watched it turn gold, then brown, then finally blacken and crumble as it burned. When it was gone, he took the poker and spread the remains evenly across the grate, until nothing remained but fine black dust.

"Tom, the detail is ready to go," Captain Benteen said, stepping inside the commandant's quarters with a quick knock. He had been seeing to the preparations for the expedition to return the hostiles to the reservation.

"Thanks, Will," Tom said, rising and slipping into his coat. "I guess I'd better get started."

"Are you sure you want to lead this detail yourself?"

Tom paused. "Why do you ask?"

"It's just that...well...as acting commander, you have every right to stay back at the post and let Reno or me handle this. After all, the majority of the regiment will still be here at the fort."

"I'll take it," Tom said. "Look, I've got enough trouble with Major Reno now. He outranks me, and by all rights, he should have command while Autie's gone. But Autie gave it to me. I didn't ask for it, mind you...I didn't even want it."

"The general made the right choice," Will Benteen said.

"The general chose his brother," Tom replied. "Anyway, what's done is done. But if I send Reno out with this detail, I'm afraid it would be rubbing salt into the wound. No, I'll take the detail out... Reno will stay here, in command of the fort."

"You're the boss," Benteen said with a shrug.

Tom followed him to the porch and buttoned his coat. The snow had melted into the thick, gooey mud of early spring. It was the brown time, between the white of winter and the green of spring, a dismal, ugly day.

"Have someone bring my horse around," Tom said. "I want to say goodbye to Emily."

"All right," Benteen said. Then he added with a grin, "If I had someone like Emily waiting on me, I'd be saying goodbye to the troop, not to her."

Tom smiled faintly and walked down the wooden walkway to Silas Thomson's quarters. He knocked lightly.

Silas opened the door. "Well, hello, Tom."

"Hello, Silas. I came to say goodbye to Emily."

"Come in," Silas said. "If you'll excuse me, I need to fetch a few brushes."

He left the room quietly, giving them a moment alone.

"I'm going to be gone for a few days," Tom said when Emily appeared from the back room.

"I know," she said. "Tom, please, for my sake if not your own, be careful. Don't do anything foolish."

"I promise you I won't," he said. He smiled. "Besides, I've got reason to be careful now." He stepped forward, putting his arms around Emily. "I don't want to wait any longer. I want us to be married as soon as I get back."

Emily blinked. "Tom, are you sure that's a good—?"

"As soon as I get back," he said.

"Tom, I thought we were going to wait."

"I want us to already be married by the time Autie gets back. I want to surprise him."

"I see," Emily said. She turned and walked out of his arms. "It isn't really Autie, is it? It's Libbie. And you don't want to surprise her, you want to defy her. Only you can't do it in front of her."

"Libbie has nothing to do with it," Tom said. "She isn't leading my life. I am."

"Then have the courage to wait until she returns," Emily said.

Tom gave a long, quiet sigh, then managed a faint smile. "Very well. If that's the way it must be...then that's the way it shall be. But I won't lie, it would have helped, thinking of us getting married as soon as I get back. It's going to be a long two weeks in the field."

Emily stepped closer, resting her hand briefly on his

arm. "Then think of this moment, Tom. Let this carry you through." And with that, she kissed him.

He smiled a wide boyish grin. "With that, I could march forty miles through snowbanks."

He gave her one last hug and stepped out the door.

Emily wrapped herself in a blanket and stepped out onto the front porch to watch Tom form the column, then ride through the front gate. The entire post had turned out to see them off. The band was playing and flags were flying, and as the detail passed by the other troops, they came to attention and saluted.

Even Emily was affected by the scene, and for a few moments, she contemplated a life of being the kind of wife Libbie wanted for Tom. But even as she was thinking about it, she knew she could never do it. And if she couldn't be the right kind of wife for Tom...she shouldn't marry him at all. Oh, why did she agree to do it? And why didn't she have the courage to refuse him?

After the gates closed behind the departing column, Emily turned and went back inside. She reached for her brushes and accidentally knocked the entire tray to the floor. Muttering under her breath, she dropped to her knees to collect them.

As she was crawling around on her hands and knees to retrieve them, she saw in a stack of old drawings and sketches, the drawing she had done of Jacob Two Hearts last summer. She hadn't seen it in months, but the image was striking. His face, his eyes...they stared back at her with silent intensity.

Emily hesitated, her hand reaching for the drawing. Then she buried it deeper into the stack. Out of sight. Out of mind.

———

THE BLANKETS WERE STAINED with blood from Aiana's lungs, and her fever was so high that her hand radiated heat as Jacob held it in his. Several totems had been placed on the ground beside her, and outside, a shaman danced and chanted a song, but the sickness showed no mercy.

The tent flap stirred, and Sitting Bull stepped inside. Without speaking, he seated himself beside Jacob and looked at Aiana's face. For a long time, the two men sat in silence, broken only by the uneven sound of her breathing.

At last, Sitting Bull spoke.

"When you were White, did their doctors have medicine for this sickness?"

"I don't know," Jacob replied. "I think not. I remember a cousin who had this illness once. The doctors tried what they knew, but it made no difference."

Sitting Bull nodded slowly. "She is going to die."

"Yes," Jacob said. "I know."

The chief placed a hand lightly over Jacob's and gave it two brief pats. Then, without another word, he rose and left.

Jacob sat motionless. He looked at his wife's face and tried to choke back the lump in his throat. Why had she gotten sick? Was it God's punishment against him for becoming a heathen?

———

A MEMORY CAME to him as he recalled his mother's voice.

"Why do they call Indians heathens, Ma?" he had once asked.

"Because they are Godless, son," she'd answered. "Indians are lost children in the Kingdom of God."

"Why? Doesn't God love everybody?"

"Yes. But you must love God too, and you must love His son, Jesus Christ. If you don't, you are a heathen."

"Don't the Indians love God?"

"Some Indians do. Those who have been civilized. But most have their pagan gods, and they are lost."

"What does it mean if you're lost?"

"You know what it means, Jacob. You've heard the preachers."

"I've heard them talk about saving souls."

"And you know what that means."

"It means going to heaven."

"That's right. And if someone is lost, it means they aren't saved."

"And they're going to hell?" he'd asked.

"Yes," his mother said. "Unless someone saves them. Sometimes they can be reached, if they hear the Word. But there are some who are worse than heathens."

"Who?"

"A person who knows about God and Jesus, and yet turns his back on the Lord. That's the worst kind of sin."

———

JACOB REMEMBERED the conversation with his mother as clearly as if it had happened yesterday.

He bowed his head. From somewhere deep within,

he tried to remember how to pray. How to speak to the God of his childhood. To ask for mercy. To beg forgiveness. To plead for Aiana's life.

But the words wouldn't come.

He sat in silence, the firelight flickering across Aiana's face, and he felt the weight of two worlds pressing down on him.

# CHAPTER FIFTEEN

THEY HAD BEEN ON PATROL FOR FIFTEEN DAYS. SO FAR, the search had yielded nothing. Twice, they had seen small mounted bands of warriors, but the warriors were traveling light on fast ponies, and they easily outdistanced the soldiers, then returned to laugh and mock them. It was, thus far, a most frustrating expedition.

That afternoon, the Ree scouts had found signs that they may be close to a large party. Tom halted his troop and ordered camp made while the scouts fanned out again, hoping to verify what they had seen.

That evening, a cook fire crackled while Tom sat cross-legged near the flames with Captain Benteen and Lieutenant Godfrey. Sergeants Flynn and Kennedy were passing around tin cups of coffee. The heat was welcome against the chilly spring night that came with sundown.

"If the scouts find nothing more tonight, we'll turn back in the morning," Tom said, staring into the fire.

"Oh, Tom, we're so close," Benteen said. "Give it one

more day. If we just press on a little farther, I've got a feeling we'll find them."

Tom gave a tired nod. "Maybe so. But Autie will be back shortly. By rights, he should be doing this."

"Wouldn't you like to surprise him with a successful mission?" Benteen asked.

Tom smiled faintly. "I'm not all that sure he would want to be surprised like that. Especially not from me."

Benteen frowned. "Tom, you stand in his shadow too much. It isn't fair."

"You sound like Emily," Tom said. "I don't mind standing in my brother's shadow. There's no jealousy between us, and I have no ambition, beyond serving my brother."

"Even when you don't always agree with him?" Benteen asked.

"And when have I disagreed?"

Benteen hesitated. "Washita, maybe?"

Everyone at the fire grew quiet. They all knew about Tom's troubles with Washita. They'd seen the aftermath, the twisted bodies, the scorched lodges. And yet none of them had ever heard him speak one word about it.

Tom sucked the coffee noisily from his cup before he spoke. Then, quietly, he said, "It was not my place to agree or disagree. It was only my place to follow orders. And it is not your place to question me now."

There was nothing more to say.

"The scouts are returning," Sergeant Flynn said, grateful for the change in subject. The men stood and watched as the riders approached. Flynn handed two cups of coffee to the scouts as they dismounted.

"Good, good," Bloody Hand said, wrapping his

hands around the cup, enjoying the warmth as much as the coffee's bracing effect.

They drank in silence for a moment, warming themselves. Then Bloody Hand looked up.

"I have found the village," he said.

"Where?" Tom asked.

"There," the scout said, pointing west into the dark hills.

"How far?"

"Three-hour march," Bloody Hand replied.

"What's the village like?"

"Good village for us," the scout said, raising both hands and flashing his fingers twice.

"Twenty lodges," Benteen repeated, calculating quickly. "How many warriors?"

"Same," Bloody Hand said. "Twenty."

Benteen turned to Tom, with excitement in his eyes. "Well? What do you think? Shall we hit it?"

Tom rubbed his chin and looked into the distance. "I know what my brother would do, and without the slightest hesitation."

He paused, considering.

"And as I am serving in my brother's place, I know what I should do. But..." he looked back at Bloody Hand. "Are you sure there are warriors in the village? I don't want to attack if no one is there but women and children."

"Warriors," Bloody Hand said without flinching. "I am sure."

Tom folded his arms across his chest, then turned and walked out beyond the ring of firelight. He stood there in the darkness for several moments while the others waited by the fire for his decision. Finally, he spoke.

"Will, get the men mounted," he said. "We'll move now and get in position to strike at dawn."

"Yes, sir," Benteen said. He didn't hide his approval.

Sergeants Flynn and Kennedy returned to their companies and began hurrying the men, instructing them to check their equipment. They were to use rags or leather to lash down mess kits, canteens, and sabers to prevent the clanking of metal from announcing their arrival and ruining the element of surprise.

Soon, the fires were extinguished and the column formed up. With the scouts out front, the detachment of the Seventh Cavalry was underway.

As the column rode through the night, Tom rode at the front, his mind elsewhere. He prayed that this would not be a repeat of Washita. Better he would be killed in battle than lead his men into another morning like that.

———

HE COULD STILL HEAR the gunfire echoing through the valley. The confusion. The shouts. The crying. That one moment, seared into memory—a boy, no more than four, wandering through the smoke, dazed, alone.

A voice beside him: *"What are you shooting at that kid for?"*

Another voice: *"Hell, his mama's dead—I'm doing the kid a favor."*

Tom closed his eyes.

The report of the rifle. The boy collapsing in the snow. The red spreading across white.

A different voice: *"Got 'im. And he never even flopped once."*

---

"TROOP, HALT," Tom suddenly said, holding up his arm. The memory of the incident at Washita was with him so strongly at this moment that he couldn't go on.

The line came to a stop. Horses snorted in the stillness, and men shifted uneasily in their saddles.

Benteen rode up beside him. "What is it, Tom? Have you seen something?"

"What?" Tom answered. "Oh...uh, no," he said. He looked around at the soldiers as if surprised that they were stopped. "Why did you ask me that?"

"You halted the column."

"Oh, I thought I heard someone's gear clanking," he lied. "Have Godfrey ride along the line to double-check their tack."

"All right," Benteen said, no questions asked.

Tom turned in the saddle, looking back along the long dark snake of the column. He said nothing more. After a moment, he gave the signal. "Move out."

Back among the ranks, some of the privates who had come into the Army after Washita, didn't know of the devils riding with them. They may have wondered at the reason for being stopped and then ordered on again with no explanation. But they thought, such things were to be expected in the Army. The cavalry had a saying, *Ours is not to reason why, ours is but to do or die.* And tonight, they would do.

Down in the village, Crazy Wolf moved from rock to rock, checking each warrior's position. He crouched beside them, ensuring their rifles were loaded and ready. The warriors were waiting on the sides of the two hills that overlooked the approach to the village. They all had buffalo hides draped over their shoulders to keep them warm as they waited for the soldiers.

"Crazy Wolf, I think that it is not good that we use the village as bait," one of the warriors whispered. "Suppose the soldiers attack the village before we attack them? Then squaws and children will be killed."

"That will not be," Crazy Wolf replied. "I will signal when to open fire. Then we will kill every soldier, and their horses, too, so they cannot escape from us."

"But shouldn't we tell the ones in the village of your plan?" the first warrior asked. "If they do not know what is happening, they will grow frightened and try to run, and then some will surely be killed."

"If we tell them, someone may give it away," Crazy Wolf said flatly. "A glance, a word, even a signal. I will not take the risk."

"But they are Sioux," the warrior said. "They won't give away the plan."

"I said no," Crazy Wolf snapped. He turned his eyes back to the trail, glowing faintly in the early light. "The soldiers are coming. I will have a great victory when the sun comes again. For many days, the people will sing of this victory in the lodges and tipis. Now, say no more, for the soldiers may have scouts riding ahead."

Crazy Wolf returned to his position behind one of the rocks and settled down, wrapped in his robes, to wait for the soldiers and contemplate the glorious victory that was before him. He had defied orders, but when he won the battle, no one would dare challenge him at the councils.

Sitting Bull had taken the main body of Sioux many miles away, back toward the territory of Montana. But there were many, including Aiana, who were much too ill to travel with the main party, and they were coming more slowly, with Jacob Two Hearts in charge.

To protect them, Sitting Bull had sent Crazy Wolf south with orders to draw the soldiers away from the trail. But Crazy Wolf had twisted the order into something else, a trap. And now word from his scouts confirmed the bait had worked.

Tom's men were nearly in position. As dawn was just beginning to touch the horizon, a small boy from the village came down to the stream with a wooden bucket swinging from his hand. He saw the soldiers, and knowing nothing of Crazy Wolf's plan, cried out a warning to the village, then threw the water bucket and started running back.

One of the troopers drew a bead on the boy, but Tom saw him.

"Don't shoot the boy!" Tom snapped.

"But he's gonna give us away!"

"He already has," Tom said grimly. "Dismount, but hold your fire. Horses to the rear."

Up on the ridge, Crazy Wolf saw the boy's warning and realized his moment had slipped away. He had no choice now. If he didn't open fire now, the situation would only get worse. His signal shot was followed by a volley of rifle fire as the hills erupted with fire and smoke.

"It's an ambush!" Tom shouted. "Spread out! Skirmish formation! Return fire!"

Within moments, the well-trained and disciplined

soldiers were sending a return fire into the hills on both sides, picking the Indians off one by one.

Crazy Wolf saw the battle turning. He fired one last shot, then shouted for retreat. He was the first to the ponies, leaping into the saddle and kicking his mount hard. The rest followed, unwilling to risk capture or death.

"Lieutenant Godfrey!" Tom called, when he saw the Indians fleeing. "Go after them!"

"Yes, sir! B Troop, mount up!"

Tom raised a hand. "Be careful, Godfrey," he warned, remembering the plight of Hamilton and Elliot, who had followed fleeing Indians from Washita only to run into a large ambush. "Go no more than a mile after them. No farther."

Godfrey nodded. "Understood, sir!" The thunder of the hooves of his troops' horses nearly drowned out his reply.

Tom watched as Godfrey and his men pursued the fleeing warriors. The horses kicked up mud in thick sprays, and the sound of hooves and hoarse shouting filled the valley. The men were caught up in the lust for battle now, intoxicated by the chase. He wished that he, and not Godfrey, was leading the pursuit, but as commander, his duty was to remain with the column.

"Captain Custer," Benteen said, pointing toward the village below, "white flags are flying from a couple of the tipis. Shall we ride down?"

"No," Tom said, his voice sharp.

Benteen looked at him, puzzled. "Then what do you have in mind?"

"I'll go down," Tom said. "Alone."

"What if it's a trick?" Benteen asked. "It could be another trap like the one we just rode into."

"If it is, I don't think they will be willing to close in on just one person," Tom said. "You stay back here. If you don't hear from me in fifteen minutes, attack the village."

"Yes, sir," Benteen said, with obvious reluctance.

Tom mounted his horse and rode slowly toward the village. As he drew near, figures began to come out of the tipis, mainly women, children, and old men. Some stumbled, some leaned on sticks or each other. Many looked feverish and gaunt. He was surprised that the warriors had set up their ambush this close to the village. He would never have guessed it was full of the sick and dying.

As he reached the center of the camp, more than twenty Indians surrounded his horse. Tom looked at them with sympathy. It was clear—these people were no threat. Some were so obviously ill that he didn't even know how they were still on their feet.

"Does anyone here speak English?" Tom asked.

"I speak English, Captain Custer."

Tom looked toward the sound of the voice and saw Jacob Two Hearts standing by the opening of one of the tipis. He was tall and strong, not at all like the others. He was wrapped in a blanket, but he appeared to be unarmed.

"What is this place?" Tom asked, sweeping his arm toward the worn tipis and ragged people.

"It is a village of the dying," Jacob said. "Most here are ill. Many will not see another sunrise."

"And you?" Tom asked. "Are you sick?"

"No," Jacob said quietly. "But my wife is. She is among those who will die."

Tom shifted in the saddle, the leather creaking as he turned to take in the camp again. "I'm sorry, Jacob. I truly am."

Jacob nodded but said nothing.

"Why did you attack us?" he asked.

"I didn't," Tom said calmly. "We were attacked by your warriors from the hills."

The young boy who had given the first warning said something in Sioux. Jacob glanced at him, then spat angrily at the ground.

"Crazy Wolf," he said. "The fool let you follow him here. He used the village as bait."

"Your friend Crazy Wolf sounds like a real smart fella," Tom said.

"He is not my friend," Jacob replied.

"What are you doing here, Jacob?" Tom asked. "Don't you know it is beyond the limitations set by my brother?"

"Yes," Jacob said. "We came to follow the buffalo, and the women and children came to follow the men. Now, Sitting Bull and the others have gone back, but these people are too sick to keep up, so I am leading them home."

"And Crazy Wolf?"

"His orders were to lead your soldiers away from the village. Instead, he brought you to it."

Tom pulled his watch out and looked at it. "Jacob, I need to fire three rounds to signal my men that I am all right. If I don't, they'll assume I have been trapped, and they will attack."

"Go ahead," Jacob said. "I'll explain to the people what you are doing."

Tom drew his service revolver and fired three shots into the air.

After explaining the situation, Jacob stood quietly, the echo of the last shot fading over the hills.

"So," he said, "I have been recaptured. I suppose now you'll take me back to hang."

Tom crossed his arms and looked at Jacob and the others. He saw not a prisoner, but a man, worn down by loss and yet still standing.

He knew how pleased his brother would be if Jacob was recaptured. But he also knew that he couldn't do it. Emily's face came to him unbidden. He knew what this would mean to her.

"No," he said at last. "I'm not going to take you in. I'm going to let you lead these people back to the reservation."

Typically, Jacob didn't thank Tom for sparing his life. He rarely said what wasn't necessary.

"Send a soldier escort with us," he said instead.

"Why?" Tom asked.

"General Crook also has soldiers out," Jacob said. "If we have an escort, Crook won't bother us."

Tom considered that. "You may have a point."

When the rest of the column arrived, the reaction was the same—quiet disbelief. No one had expected to find a village ravaged by sickness, filled with shivering children, fevered women, and old men too weak to stand.

Tom spoke to the sergeant, urging him to do what he could. Several troopers stepped forward, offering to help carry water, pass out rations, or tend the sick. Even the veterans of the Plains Campaign had their limits when it came to what they were willing to shoot at.

Godfrey returned a short while later.

"Crazy Wolf and his bunch scattered, sir," he reported. "We chased them for about a mile, like you ordered. We picked off a couple more, but most of them got away. There aren't enough of them left to be a real threat."

Tom nodded. "Good. I'm sorry they got away, especially Crazy Wolf, but I'm glad we inflicted enough damage on them to teach them a lesson."

"What are you going to do with all these people?" Benteen asked, gesturing toward the village.

"I'm sending them back to the reservation," Tom said.

"You should take them to the fort," Benteen countered.

"Why?" Tom asked, glancing sideways at him.

"Look at them, Tom. There's over thirty people here."

"What difference does that make?" Tom asked.

Benteen folded his arms. "If you took them back, you'd have thirty captives to go with the twelve warriors we killed this morning. That'd look pretty good in a report to General Terry's headquarters."

Tom gave a tired smile. "I'm not interested in looking good in a report. Besides, as soon as we got them to the fort, we would just let them go anyway. Only, by then, many would be dead. I don't intend to subject these dying people to that ordeal."

Benteen exhaled and looked off toward the foothills. "All right, Tom. Whatever you say." Then, after a pause: "I guess we'll take Jacob back with us, at least."

"No," Tom said.

Benteen turned sharply. "What? Tom, you can't be serious! Your brother has sentenced Jacob to die, you know that! He's an escaped prisoner!"

"I know," Tom said quietly. "I also know he's a husband with a dying wife. And right now, he's the best chance the rest of these people have of getting back alive. I'll not trade his one life for twenty-nine others."

Benteen frowned. "I hope you know what you're doing."

"I'm the military commander right now," Tom said. "It's my decision."

Tom turned toward the troops.

"Now, I'll need an escort detail to go with them. That's to prevent General Crook's men from making a mistake if they run across this group."

"With the Cap'n's permission," Sergeant Flynn spoke up from behind the ranks, "that's a job I'd be up to takin'."

Tom turned in the saddle. "Are you sure, Sergeant? That'll mean two more weeks in the field."

Flynn gave a slight shrug. "Aye, sir. 'Tis somethin' I need to do."

Tom nodded, understanding more than the man said. "All right. Pick two men. The detail is yours."

Flynn saluted, then turned and began walking through the column to pick his men.

Well, old friend, Tom thought as he watched Flynn. *Perhaps this will help you pay back the debt you feel you owe to these people*, he thought. *And I hope it helps with mine, too.*

# CHAPTER SIXTEEN

Jacob walked alongside the travois, bending over frequently to adjust the blankets and furs that he had put over Aiana. As he did so, he could feel the burning heat of her fever and see the flecks of blood she had coughed up.

"Jacob," she said weakly.

Jacob stopped the horse and leaned down.

"Yes, Aiana, I am here."

"Jacob, I do not want to die in a travois," she said.

"You aren't going to die," Jacob said, and he knew that it was his white heart speaking, for, like a White, he was unable to accept the death of someone he loved.

Aiana smiled in understanding. "I am dying and you know this," she said. "But I don't want to die in a travois. I want to die in a wickiup. I want to be in our bed in our wickiup. Jacob, please, do this for me. Build a wickiup here."

"All right," Jacob said. "I will."

Jacob cut the travois loose, then leaving Aiana lying

by the trail, he rode quickly to the head of the column to find Sergeant Flynn.

"Flynn," he called. "My wife wants to die in a wickiup."

"A wickiup?" Sergeant Flynn said. "Damn, boy, it takes a little effort to build one of those things, don't it?"

"Yes," Jacob said. "They are only built at a village where you intend to stay."

"Maybe a tipi would be all right for her," Sergeant Flynn suggested.

"She wants a wickiup, and she shall have one," Jacob said resolutely.

"All right, lad," Flynn said easily. "I'll not try'n stop you, if you've your mind set on doin' it. But I'll not be able to halt the column, you understand?"

"Yes."

"Would there be anythin' I could be gettin' for you, Jacob? Another blanket, mebbe, or a mite more food?"

"No," Jacob said.

Flynn stuck out his hand in a White man's handshake. Jacob took it without a moment's hesitation—how easily the action had come to him.

"'Tis awfully sorry I am about your wife," Flynn said. "I wish there was somethin' I could do."

"Thank you," Jacob said. He turned to leave and had gone but a short distance when he stopped and called back to Flynn.

"Yes?" Flynn answered.

"Flynn, do you know how to pray to God and Jesus?"

Flynn smiled. "Sure'n you'd be askin' a Catholic the likes? 'Tis not a good Catholic I am, mind you, but I've never forgot the teachin's o' the Church."

"Would you say a prayer for Aiana?"

"Bless you, lad, 'n I'd be more'n honored to," Flynn said. "Though not knowin' how good a standin' I am in with the Lord, I'm not promisin' 'nythin', you understand."

"I already know she will die," Jacob said. "Just ask God and Jesus to make her dying easy."

"I'll do that, lad," Flynn said earnestly. "I'll do that."

Jacob worked with near Herculean effort, and finally, just before nightfall, he had finished the wickiup. He stepped back and looked at it with satisfaction. It was the best one he had ever built.

"It is beautiful, my husband," Aiana said, her voice strangely clear and alert. Shocked, Jacob looked back toward her.

But Aiana's appearance put a lie to the sound of her voice, for she was pale and drawn.

"It's ready for us to move in," Jacob said. "I can even start a fire, see? I've built a fire hole for the smoke to escape."

"Oh, yes, build a nice fire," Aiana said. "It will be good to be in a wickiup with a fire."

Jacob carried Aiana into the wickiup and lay her on soft furs, then he built a fire, and they watched the wood burn. From his position on the bed, he could see the edges of color that the sand in the wood made in the flame as it burned.

He looked over at Aiana and saw a look of contentment on her face—that look was worth all the work and more. Silently, he thanked Sergeant Flynn for saying the prayer that helped Aiana, and he wished he could say a prayer to God to thank Him as well.

Aiana was composing her own prayer. It was a song,

and the rhythm and melody in her mind were as real as at a tribal ceremony:

> *This happy site of fields and hills in*
> *A land of grassy plains and colored flowers,*
> *With stands of trees dancing in the wind...*
> *I know joy in the light of the Spirit*
> *At the ways it appears*
> *In many varieties.*

Aiana was most happy now, with her husband and her favorite furs and rugs in her very own wickiup. She would be dying soon, this she knew. But all the rest of her life left to her would be spent in happiness.

She thought of a wise old Indian saying: *The flower which blooms but a single night differs not at heart from the mighty tree which lives a thousand years.* She was like that flower. She had but a single night...but her heart was crowded with a lifetime of joy.

———

JACOB CRAWLED into bed with Aiana, and he put his arms around her and pulled her to him, cradling her head on his shoulder. He felt the burning fever of her body, and he wished he could pull it out of her, absorb it with his own body.

She had been his wife for but seven months. It had been a happy seven months, and she had come with him as he followed the buffalo, and she had cooked for him and warmed him at night, and he felt that it would never end.

But then Aiana contracted pneumonia. Though

Jacob didn't know the name of the disease, he did know its symptoms, for it had been quite common among the Indians the last few years, and it was almost always fatal.

Aiana felt the deep breathing of Jacob in her arms and knew that he was asleep. She wanted to stay awake, to be aware for all the time she had remaining. And now, with the moon shining brightly in the darkness of predawn, she waited to die.

Soon, the line between reality and hallucination began to disintegrate. She could hear music, and she could see people...her father, her brother who had died in the time before Jacob, and many others. She knew that they were all people from the world beyond life, and they were all beautiful and glowing with some inner light.

The wickiup was filled with color—reds, blues, yellows, greens—and the colors seemed to be alive. Then Aiana became part of the color and at one with everything in the wickiup. She drifted about the wickiup like smoke, and she could look down upon the bed and see herself and Jacob, sleeping in close embrace. She didn't know how she could do this, but strangely, she didn't wonder about it. It seemed, some-how, quite natural to her.

She drifted a bit longer, seeing a living montage of herself and Jacob on the bed, and the two of them as healthy children, bathing in the streams, riding horses, dancing to the music of the drums and the songs. Then, she began collecting the pieces of herself and returning to her body. She felt herself falling into the fur of the buffalo robes. She tried to stop herself, but she couldn't. Soon, all the colors, the music, and the people were gone. She was in a forest of great trees. She looked up to see the sky, but there was none. There was only the shaded roof provided by the trees.

Aiana closed her eyes and lay on a dust mote. She drifted without mind, without body, slowly and unseeing for a time that had no beginning and no end.

———

SERGEANT FLYNN WAS FINDING it more difficult to escort the Indians than he thought. Without Jacob, he had only the two other soldiers who were able-bodied enough to work. The Indians who were less ill than the others helped, but Flynn's abilities were being taxed to the utmost.

The rivers and streams were flooded with the melting snows, and routes that were easily passable in the summer were now fraught with swirling freshets. They reached one particularly swollen river, and the little band of Indians, with their pitifully small herd of ponies and horses, wondered how they would manage.

Miraculously, Sergeant Flynn managed to get the women and children across on buffalo-hide rafts without any serious accidents. But many of the horses and ponies were lost to the swiftly flowing current, and when they regrouped on the other side, some of the Indians who had been riding were forced to walk.

"Build more travois," Flynn ordered.

"Sarge, you ain't plannin' on puttin' a travois behind our horses, are you?" one of the other soldiers asked.

"Yes," Flynn said.

"Sarge, you ain't serious?"

"Aye, lad, I've never been more serious. 'N you tell me why I shouldn't be."

"These here is cavalry horses, Sarge," the soldier protested.

"How, these animals don't even know they are horses, let alone cavalry horses," Flynn said. "Sure'n it'd make no difference to a horse whether he be pullin' a travois across the plains, or the grandest Drag down Park Avenue in New York."

"It just don't seem fittin', somehow, that we gotta turn cavalry horses into injun ponies," the soldier complained, but he and the other soldier began constructing the travois.

As Sergeant Flynn and the others worked on the travois, White Ghost, who was not as ill as many, but who was too ill to travel with the other chiefs, sneaked away from the band. He had been seeing Crazy Wolf trailing them for most of the day, and he wanted to talk to him.

White Ghost followed the bank of the stream upstream until it curved behind the ridge where he had seen Crazy Wolf. He climbed the ridge to the top and looked down on the banks of the stream, where he saw the Indians, Sergeant Flynn, and the other two soldiers busily constructing travois.

"Crazy Wolf," he called quietly.

"I am here," Crazy Wolf answered.

White Ghost looked around and saw Crazy Wolf and five warriors coming out from behind rocks. They were on the other side of the hill and could not be seen by anyone down on the bank of the stream.

"I have watched you following us," White Ghost said.

"Have the others seen?"

"Some have seen," White Ghost said.

"The soldiers?"

"I think not," White Ghost said.

"What are the soldiers doing?"

"They are helping us," White Ghost said.

Crazy Wolf laughed. "Do you expect me to believe that the soldiers are helping you back to the others?"

"Yes," White Ghost said. "They come with us so that General Crook's soldiers do not attack us."

"General Crook is a long distance from here," Crazy Wolf said.

"Perhaps. But Jacob Two Hearts feared that he was close."

"Jacob is a squaw," Crazy Wolf said. "Where is he?"

"He remained behind," White Ghost said. "Aiana is dying, and Jacob is with her."

"Aiana is dying because the Great Spirit is angry with her for marrying a White."

"Jacob is Indian," White Ghost said.

"And the white stone turned to red," Crazy Wolf said sarcastically.

Crazy Wolf crept up to a rock and peered down at the work party. "How many soldiers?" he asked.

"Only what you see," White Ghost said. He looked at the five warriors with Crazy Wolf—there had been nearly twenty when Crazy Wolf started out. "Where are the other warriors?"

"Dead," Crazy Wolf said flatly. "White Ghost, you go back now so the soldiers do not miss you."

"You must ride to Sitting Bull," White Ghost said. "Tell him the soldiers with us must travel in peace. I would not want them to be killed for helping us."

"I am chief of the war party," Crazy Wolf said. "I will do as I decide."

"If I do not like what you do, I will take it to the council," White Ghost said.

Crazy Wolf laughed. "You are an old man, White Ghost. The council listens to your age, not to your bravery. Go now. Return to the others as I have said."

White Ghost looked at the young chief, and his heart was sad for the hate and cruelty he saw. He knew it was useless to speak more, so he turned and worked his way back to the others, arriving just as the last travois was finished.

"All right, let's move 'em out," Sergeant Flynn called, smiling at his resolution to the problem of transportation.

Ahead, in the rocks on the ridge, Crazy Wolf and his warriors waited. There were only three soldiers, and they were not suspecting anything. It would be an easy victory.

# CHAPTER SEVENTEEN

JACOB TWO HEARTS RODE INTO THE VILLAGE WITH HIS head bowed sadly. He was greeted by White Ghost and the five other survivors of the march of the sick, and they expressed their sorrow to him over Aiana's death.

"How many survived the march?" Jacob asked.

"Only those of us you see," White Ghost said.

"You mean the others died on the trail?" Jacob asked. "But many were not that sick."

"They did not die of the sickness," White Ghost said. "We were attacked by a soldier patrol of General Crook. There were few in the patrol, or all would have been killed."

"But I don't understand," Jacob said. "How could that be? Didn't Sergeant Flynn explain to General Crook's soldiers that Custer had given us free passage?"

White Ghost looked down at the ground.

"What is it?" Jacob said. "White Ghost, what is wrong?"

"Perhaps you should see the lodge pole of Crazy Wolf," White Ghost said.

Jacob looked at White Ghost a moment longer, then swung down from his horse and walked quickly through the camp toward the tipi of Crazy Wolf.

Crazy Wolf's tipi was painted red, and red streamers were flying from the top of the tipi around the smoke hole. Jacob looked at the lodgepole and saw among the old, dried scalps, a new one. It was fresh...and sandy colored. The color of Sergeant Flynn's hair.

"Crazy Wolf!" Jacob called angrily.

Crazy Wolf stepped out of his tipi, and seeing Jacob, grinned broadly.

"Ah. So you have come to admire my trophies, have you?" Crazy Wolf asked. He was eating a piece of meat, and he stood there, chewing insolently, while he talked.

"Why did you attack Flynn?" Jacob asked.

"Because he was my enemy," Crazy Wolf said. "He is White...I am Indian."

"But he was helping us," Jacob said. "I promised him safe passage."

"One White man does not speak to another for me," Crazy Wolf said. "All White men are my enemies, and I will attack them wherever I see them."

"Where were you when General Crook's soldiers came?" Jacob asked. "Why were you not there to fight them and protect the others?"

"After I defeated Flynn, I returned to the village to tell the council of my victory," Crazy Wolf said. "I did not know that General Crook's soldiers attacked the sick march, or I would have fought them, too, and had an even greater victory."

"You didn't stay to protect them?" Jacob asked. "After you killed their escort, you abandoned them?"

"I told you. I wanted to tell the council of my victory."

"No," Jacob said. "You left because you were afraid. You are a coward, Crazy Wolf."

Jacob spoke slowly and distinctly so there could be no chance that Crazy Wolf would misunderstand. Crazy Wolf did understand, but he wasn't alone. Others heard the words too, and they spread through the village like wildfire. This would mean a fight...and death for one of them.

Crazy Wolf's eyes narrowed, and he tossed the meat aside and wiped his hands in his hair. Then he walked into his tipi and reappeared a moment later with his war lance in his hand. He hurled the spear into the ground by Jacob's feet.

Jacob smiled. "I accept your challenge to a duel, Crazy Wolf," he said.

Young boys who were standing nearby left quickly to tell the others in the village. "Come," they called in great excitement. "Jacob has called Crazy Wolf a coward, and they will fight."

"It will be a grand and exciting fight," one of the others said. "They will fight to the death!"

Despite the inherent horror of such a spectacle, it was just that—a spectacle—and in the village, the prospect of the thrill and excitement was so much greater than the anticipation of horror that the news was welcomed.

The news was welcomed, for other reasons as well. Both Crazy Wolf and Jacob Two Hearts were natural leaders, and both had their own following. Each group saw this as the opportunity to eliminate their enemy, and around each warrior assembled his followers to wish him luck.

One hour after the challenge was issued, the entire population of the village was assembled in a grassy field alongside the adjacent stream. A large circle had been laid out on the grass, marked with small, white stones taken from the streambed.

Neither combatant would be allowed to leave the circle, and only they would be allowed to enter it.

Jacob was on one side of the circle, and across from him stood Crazy Wolf. Crazy Wolf's friends were gathered around him, giving him last-minute instructions, while, around Jacob, his own friends were equally encouraging.

Two braves were massaging Jacob's arms and shoulders. Jacob, who had stripped to the waist, stared across the circle at his adversary as White Ghost spoke to him.

"Crazy Wolf has chosen the war club," White Ghost said. "It is his best weapon, and he feels it is your worst."

"I know," Jacob said.

"I can appeal to the council to choose a different weapon," White Ghost said. "One in which each of you have an equal skill. It is your right."

"No," Jacob said. "The war club will be fine."

"He is very clever with it," White Ghost cautioned. "Be careful of a trick."

"I will be careful," Jacob promised.

Sitting Bull stood with the council, and he gave the signal for the two combatants to begin.

"Aiiyeeee!!" Crazy Wolf yelled, and he jumped into the circle and danced around in a crouch, holding the club loosely and confidently in his right hand. "Now,

White man," he called. "Feel terror in your heart, for I am going to kill you."

"Save your threats for the children of the village," Jacob said. "I do not tremble before the boasting of a coward."

Crazy Wolf yelled again and leaped toward Jacob. His sudden move surprised Jacob. Crazy Wolf swung at him, and he managed to parry the swing slightly so that the club caught him, not on the head, as Crazy Wolf intended, but on the shoulder. A numbing pain shot through the left side of his body, and suddenly his left arm seemed to weigh so much that he couldn't lift it.

Crazy Wolf knew that he had scored, and he leaped back into position and swung again. He had correctly reasoned that his best chance lay in advancing quickly to eliminate Jacob. But Jacob was ready for him this time, and Crazy Wolf's club whistled past without touching him.

Jacob wasn't in position to counterthrust with his club, but he was able to swing his left hand, landing a resounding slap on Crazy Wolf's face. Crazy Wolf's face turned red from the stinging blow, and the villagers laughed uproariously. Their ridicule only added to Crazy Wolf's fury. He swung again, this time more wildly than before, and Jacob slapped him again.

Now the onlookers roared with laughter, and Crazy Wolf became so furious that he lost control. The grace and agility with which he had launched his first, telling blow had given way to blind rage, and Jacob realized the advantage in keeping him off balance, and at the first opportunity, he slapped him again.

Finally, like a charging bull, Crazy Wolf lunged toward Jacob, holding his club out before him, thinking only of scoring one crushing, killing blow. But Jacob sidestepped him neatly, then brought his own club crashing down on Crazy Wolf's arms.

Crazy Wolf dropped his club and went down. Quickly, Jacob was on him. He pinned Crazy Wolf's arms, then raised his club for the kill. One quick blow, and Crazy Wolf would be dead. The crowd held its breath in expectation of the gruesome, morbidly fascinating scene.

Jacob held his club poised for a moment, looking into the face, and terror-filled eyes of the helpless victim pinned below him. Finally, Jacob lowered his club.

"No," he said. "There is no honor in killing a coward."

"Kill me!" Crazy Wolf shouted, realizing then that Jacob was condemning him to ridicule—a fate, in his eyes, even worse than death.

"No," Jacob said. He stood up and gazed down at the defeated and disgraced warrior. "Only the brave die in combat. You do not deserve an honorable death."

Jacob tossed his war club to one side and turned his back on Crazy Wolf, leaving him lying in the dirt.

"No!" Crazy Wolf leaped to his feet and shouted at the council. "This was a duel to the death! He cannot do this! He must kill me!"

"Your life belongs to him," Sitting Bull said. "He may take it or let you live as he wishes."

"Aiyeee!" Crazy Wolf shouted, and there, before all the villagers, he began pulling his hair out in large chunks, screaming in rage as he plucked himself bald.

———

"IT'S THEM, CAP'N," Sergeant Kennedy said. "Flynn, Howe, 'n Peters. They've all three been scalped."

Tom Custer looked toward the three bloated forms, but he could get no closer. He couldn't bear to look at the men he had killed. And he felt he had killed them, as surely as if he had wielded the war clubs that struck them down, because he had trusted Jacob Two Hearts.

"Wrap them in canvas and take them back," Tom said. "We'll see that they get a decent burial at the fort."

"Are we going after Jacob Two Hearts now?" Benteen asked.

"No," Tom said. "Not until Autie gets back. Then we'll take the entire Seventh out, and we'll clean out all the renegades. This time, I shall go along as a willing and eager participant. I want to be there when we finally catch up with Mr. Two Hearts. And I especially want to be there when we hang him."

One of the privates from the detail rode up to Tom and Sergeant Kennedy.

"Sir, the bodies is all sewed up good 'n proper," he reported.

"Load them on the ammunition wagon," Tom said. "Sergeant Kennedy, we'll return to the fort now."

"Yes, sir," Kennedy said. "Troop, prepare to mount!" he commanded.

As Tom watched the soldiers moving in well-disciplined drill, he thought of Sergeant Flynn. The Army had been Flynn's life. It had provided him with a home, a family, a purpose—it was his religion. Once, during an engagement, when Tom Custer's horse had been shot from under him, Sergeant Flynn had ridden back into the fray and handed his reins to Tom.

"By your leave, sir. Take my mount."

Tom shouted at Flynn to remount and leave him when a riderless horse happened by. Flynn caught it, and with a big grin, jumped on its back. "Now, sir, we're both mounted," he shouted.

Sergeant Flynn, who had saved his life more than once, had been killed...betrayed by the one man who owed him the most.

Tom thought of the court-martial that would come. He would offer nothing in his own defense.

"I, Thomas Custer, captain, US Cavalry, did willfully disobey the standing orders of my commanding officer, in that I failed to return Jacob Two Hearts to Fort Lincoln to stand execution."

Tom said the words quietly, weighing their impact. Yes, he thought, they alone should be sufficient in themselves to convict him and force him out of the Army. He would draw up the charges against himself as soon as he returned to the fort.

Mercifully, Sergeant Kennedy didn't speak much as they rode back to the fort. That left Tom alone with his thoughts, his own guilt, his own hates. He had only one wish remaining. He would request—beg, if need be—that he be permitted to remain on active duty long enough to capture Jacob Two Hearts. In fact, if he had to, he would remain as a private, if that was the only way he could be in on the capture of Jacob Two Hearts.

———

IT WAS early evening as the troop returned to the fort. The sun was dying in a brilliant display of golds and reds, and the detail was one long silhouette as Tom led it through the gate. Tired and dispirited, the troop proceeded to the flagpole in the center of the parade ground. There, Tom called for them to halt, then released them to Sergeant Kennedy. He dismounted and gave his reins over to an orderly, then walked slowly across the quadrangle toward Emily, who, with others of the fort, had turned out to greet the returning patrol.

"We found them," Tom said quietly.

"I know," Emily replied. "The messenger told us. Tom, I'm so sorry."

Tom took off his hat and ran his hand through his hair, then pulled at the small goatee he had grown during his brother's absence. "I was such a fool," he said. "I should have known better than to trust Jacob Two Hearts. I should have brought him back to hang."

"No," Emily said. "Tom, I don't believe Jacob did this. He couldn't have done it."

"He did it, Emily," Tom said. "He was in charge of the Indian sick march."

"But he couldn't have. I just know he couldn't have."

Tom uttered a small, bitter laugh. "Emily, my dear, we were both taken in by him. Only Autie saw him for the scoundrel he is. It's too bad he wasn't here when I let Two Hearts go. He would have prevented me from making such a mistake." Tom put his hat back on. "I shall have to face up to him as soon as he returns."

Emily sighed broadly. "That will not be too long, I'm afraid," she said.

"What? Why, what do you mean?"

"They are back. At least, they are as far as Bismarck. Captain Benteen went into town to fetch them. They should be here by supper."

# CHAPTER EIGHTEEN

"UNACCEPTABLE. TOTALLY UNACCEPTABLE!"

George Custer was sitting behind his desk, holding the warrant in which Tom had charged himself with disobeying a standing order by not arresting Jacob Two Hearts and with permitting a band of hostiles to trespass unmolested on restricted territory, a dereliction of duty that resulted in the deaths of Sergeant Flynn and privates Howe and Peters.

Custer tossed the papers into the wastebasket by his desk.

"What are you doing, General?" Tom asked.

"What does it look like I'm doing?" Custer asked. "I'm throwing this nonsense away."

Tom started to reach for the wastebasket to recover the papers, but Custer kicked the basket, sending its contents scattering across the room.

"Leave it alone!" Custer roared.

"I don't want preferential treatment," Tom said angrily.

"Dammit, Tom," Custer said. "Everything you did,

you did as the commanding officer. All right, maybe your judgment was wrong—but it was a judgment, not dereliction of duty. If every commander who had ever made a mistake in judgment was court-martialed, there would be very few commanders left."

"But my judgment was colored by personal considerations," Tom protested.

"All judgment is colored by personal consideration," Custer said. "You remember the stink when I returned to Fort Riley during the epidemic to check on Libbie? It was my judgment as commander that I could go. That judgment was colored by personal considerations."

"It also resulted in a court-martial and a year's suspension from active duty," Tom said. "I deserve no less punishment."

"No," Custer said. "It isn't the same thing at all. I merely used that as an example. Tom…I'll not approve this list of charges, and I'll not prefer charges myself. As far as I am concerned, this incident is over."

"All right, Autie," Tom said, contritely. "But it isn't quite over."

"What do you mean?"

"Jacob Two Hearts," Tom said. "He's coming back to Fort Lincoln, and he's going to hang."

Custer smiled. "On that point, I agree with you," he said. "And that brings me to the news."

"What news?"

"Glorious news, Tom. The War Department has authorized one all-out campaign. We are going to sweep through the Indian territories and clean them up once and for all. Any Indians who oppose us will be crushed. Those who won't go back to their reservations here will be shipped to Florida. And Tom, the vanguard of the entire operation, is to be the Seventh Cavalry."

"What does General Terry say to all that?" Tom asked.

"General Terry has already given it his blessing," Custer said. He hopped up and rubbed his hands together excitedly, then walked over to the window and looked out at the troopers drilling on the quadrangle. He turned to look back at Tom, a big smile on his face.

"The truth is, Tom," he went on, "Terry doesn't know a damned thing about fighting Indians, and he's admitted as much to the War Department. That leaves me in charge out here."

"Autie, after this campaign, you'll get your generalcy back," Tom suggested.

"Generalcy, hell," Custer said. He tugged at his beard. "After this summer campaign, Tom, I will be nominated for president of the United States."

"Autie, are you certain?" Tom asked.

"I was told that by no less a figure than the Honorable James G. Blaine," Custer said. "For he himself will make the nominating speech."

Tom smiled broadly and reached out to take his brother's hand.

"Autie," he said, "you, *President* of the United States. What a staggering thought."

"You can see then, can't you, how unwise it would be to have the suggestion of a scandal now among any of the Custers. We must all unite, Tom. You, Boston, Libbie, Maggie, and me. All of us. And this is no time to be bringing in outsiders...if you know what I mean."

"No," Tom said. "No, I'm not sure I do know what you mean."

"Tom, Tom." Custer smiled, putting his hand on his brother's shoulder. "I know you got lonesome here while Libbie and I were back East. And I know that there was someone here who was interesting and pretty to help keep the lonesomeness from overtaking you."

"You are talking about Emily, aren't you?"

"Emily is a pretty girl, Tom. She's more than that... she's a beautiful girl. Under other circumstances, I might be giving you a run for your money in vying for her attention. But Tom, we must close now. Emily Thomson doesn't fit into the Custer plans."

"I see," Tom said.

"I hope you do."

"Autie...I've asked her to marry me."

"Have you now? Well, then, you shall just have to get out of it."

"I don't want to get out of it. I love her."

"Tom, do you love her more than honor, duty, and country?"

"Well, I—"

"Think about it, Tom. Think about the great destiny that waits for me...for all of us. Could you throw that away for this woman?"

"Autie, you don't know what you are asking of me," Tom cried.

"Yes, I do know," Autie said. "I'm asking the supreme sacrifice, and I know that isn't fair. But I am asking it, Tom."

"What...what do you want me to do?"

"I want you to sever all relations with Emily Thomson. If you'd like, I can send you out on a mission tonight, and by the time you return, she will be gone."

"No," Tom said. "No, that wouldn't be right. I'll take care of it myself."

"Good man, Tom," Custer said. He smiled broadly. "Someday, a historian will write a book about the Custer legacy, and there will be a special place in it for the sacrifice you are making today."

———

"Do you like it?" Libbie asked, twisting and turning before the mirror, admiring her new dress. "I made it from material Autie bought me for Christmas."

"It's beautiful," Emily said. "It's as lovely a reception toilette as I have ever seen."

"I saw it in Harper's Bazaar," Libbie said. "Oh, I brought the magazine back with me in case you wanted to look through it." Libbie handed the magazine to Emily.

"Why, thank you, Libbie," Emily said, surprised by Libbie's generosity.

"My dress is on page three-seventeen," Libbie said. "Read the description aloud as I look in the mirror, would you, please?"

"Of course," Emily said. She found the place in the magazine and cleared her throat. "Are you ready?"

"Of course," Libbie said, laughing. "I'm told that in Paris they do this very thing. Models parade around in dresses before prospective buyers while the dresses are described aloud."

"Yes," Emily said. "It is called a fashion show. I have seen such things, even in New York."

"Well, now we shall have one in Fort Lincoln. Please go on."

Emily began to read the description of Libbie's dress.

"This stylish dress is of black faille. The trained skirt is trimmed high up with alternate wide and narrow gathered flounces, surmounted by a ruche. The polonaise is in the princesse design, that is, one piece in front, and the back separates about five inches below the waist and falls square on the sides. The intervening space is filled with large loops of faille ribbon, which form a cascade of trimming. The bottom of the polonaise, the sleeves, and large double pockets are trimmed with several rows of jet galloon, which also form a square bertha on the waist. The front of the polonaise is edged with fringe."

Emily finished reading and looked up at Libbie, who had been turning and flouncing with the description, and was now smiling broadly.

For the moment, Emily forgot the circumstances that had made Libbie her antagonist. She saw Libbie only as a rather remarkable woman who lived a life of hardship and deprivation on the wild frontier, yet by the sheer force of her personality, brought some semblance of civilization to a remote military post. There was much about Libbie Custer to admire, Emily had to admit.

"I am so looking forward to the dinner tonight," Libbie said. "It has been a long time since Autie and I entertained our little Fort Lincoln family. All the senior officers and their wives will be here tonight."

"It has been dull here without you," Emily said. "And speaking for myself as well as the others, I can say this is an event we have been looking forward to for a long, long time."

THE TABLE WAS SET for sixteen. The combined treasures of the Custer family and the other officers' families yielded enough silver, crystal, and china to do credit to any formal dinner, anywhere. Adorning the menu were delicacies recently brought back by the Custers: champagne, German chocolates, and tinned brandied peaches. For dinner, they were served French onion soup and curried lamb. The meal and the conversations were undertaken with great relish. Then Tom stood up and cleared his throat, holding his glass high in a toast.

Emily reached over and squeezed her father's hand. She knew that Tom was about to make the announcement of their engagement. But she wished that they had spoken of it again beforehand, for the truth was...she wasn't certain she wanted to go through with it.

Tom tapped lightly on his crystal goblet, and the clear, melodious ring summoned everyone's attention. He looked at his brother and sister-in-law, then at Emily. But his eyes, instead of glowing with pride, were shadowed by shame. Why? Emily wondered. What was going on?

"Ladies and officers of the Seventh," Tom said. "First of all, let me say how glad I am to have General Custer back, and to relinquish command of the Seventh to its rightful commander."

After the respectful applause subsided, Tom cleared his throat and went on.

"My brother has returned with glorious news, which he has allowed me the privilege of passing on to you. Commencing next month, the Seventh Cavalry will return to the field for an all-out campaign to rid the

Black Hills once and for all of the dangers posed by hostiles. Ladies and gentlemen, we will take to the field with the greatest army since the Civil War, and the Seventh Cavalry will be the vanguard of that army."

"Hear, hear," Reno said, applauding heartily, and the others quickly joined in.

"I am pleased also to say that my brother has given me the special task of finding Jacob Two Hearts and returning him here to hang. That is one task I am undertaking with the greatest of pleasure."

"Oh," Emily said, and the others at the table glanced toward her. She looked quickly at her plate, her cheeks flaming in embarrassment.

"I'm sorry, Miss Thomson," Tom went on. "I know you and your father feel you owe your life to him. But Sergeant Flynn felt the same way, and it cost him his life. Jacob Two Hearts is a traitor and a murderer. And we will bring him here and hang him."

"Tom, I...I can't watch such a thing," Emily said.

"I know," Tom said. He swallowed and looked down toward his plate for a moment, as if summoning the courage to go on. "That's why special arrangements are being made for you and your father."

"Special arrangements? What are you talking about?" Emily asked. "What do you mean?"

"Emily, dear, this is no place to talk about it," Libbie said. "Such things would be better discussed in privacy, don't you think?"

"Tom Custer, I want to know what you are talking about!" Emily demanded. "What special arrangements have you made which can only be discussed in privacy?"

"Emily, I..." Tom began, then looked at Libbie with a helpless expression.

"Emily, dear," Libbie said. "The general and I feel, and Tom concurs, that it is selfish of us to keep you here any longer. A remote military post is no place for a young, vivacious, talented girl such as you. And the world is being denied your father's talent. We're sending you back to New York, and oh, how I envy you! I would give anything to return to New York...words can't describe how lovely it was this winter."

"But no!" Emily said. She looked first at Libbie, and then at Tom, in absolute shock.

"Emily, be reasonable," Tom said. "I will be in the field for the entire summer. I can't expect you to wait here, can I?"

"Of course you can't, Tom," Libbie said, answering for Emily. "It would be extremely selfish of you to even consider it."

Emily stood up quickly and pushed her chair back, her napkin clutched in her hand. Tears welled in her eyes, and she threw the napkin at Tom.

"I hate you, Tom Custer!"

# CHAPTER NINETEEN

"Be honest with me, darling," Silas said to his daughter. "Is your heart truly broken...or is your pride merely wounded?"

Silas was comforting his daughter in her quarters shortly after the disagreeable scene that had taken place in the dining room. Emily, who was patting her eyes lightly with a perfumed handkerchief, looked at her father with a surge of appreciation for his understanding.

"What a fool I must have appeared," she said.

"No, dear, not at all," Silas assured her. "The fool is Tom Custer. Fool and coward as well."

"Coward? Father, whatever Tom Custer is, he isn't a coward. Why, he's been mentioned in the dispatches even more than the general."

"Coward, I said, and coward I meant," Silas said. "He lacks the courage to stand up to his brother for the one thing he wants most in the world."

"Perhaps so," Emily said with a sigh. She smiled through her tears. "But I am an even bigger coward, for I lacked the courage to tell Tom Custer that I didn't want to marry him. I would have gone through with it."

"Then your heart isn't broken," Silas said.

"No, Father," Emily said.

Silas smiled broadly and rubbed his hands together. "Then perhaps you will take heart at the news I have for you."

"What news?"

"Tomorrow, we are to be escorted into Bismarck, where we are supposed to catch the train East."

"I know," Emily said. "But why should I take heart over such information?"

"Because we aren't going back East," Silas said.

"We aren't?"

"No. Yesterday I spoke with Mr. Bell of the Bismarck Livery Barn. He has agreed to sell us a team of horses, a wagon, and all the supplies we will need to travel through the Indian territories. Now I ask you, do you still want to go?"

"Father, I don't know," Emily said. "You heard them at dinner tonight. They are planning a major operation against the Indians."

"All the more reason, it seems to me, why we should go while we have the opportunity. Daughter, this may very well be the last year the Indians will follow their old ways. Don't you see? If we don't go now, the chance will be forever lost. Their culture will have disappeared." Silas looked at Emily, and his eyes narrowed. "Unless you believe, as does Tom Custer, that Jacob Two Hearts murdered Sergeant Flynn."

"No," Emily said. "I could never believe that."

"Then our assurance of safe passage by Sitting Bull should still protect us."

"You're right," Emily said. "You're right. If we don't go now, we will lose the opportunity. And we do have Sitting Bull's promise of safety. All right, Father, we'll go."

Silas smiled broadly, then kissed his daughter on the forehead. "Then get your things in order, dear," he said. "And get a good night's sleep. For tomorrow, at long last, we shall begin our adventure."

After Silas left, Emily packed her pencils, brushes, paints, and some of her drawings in progress. She packaged the finished work to send to Gideon in New York. She started to destroy several drawings of Tom, Libbie, and Autie, which were not intended for public viewing, then decided instead to leave them. It will be my parting gesture to the Custers, she thought as she spread them out on the table.

Emily had expected Tom to come by to offer some apology, or at least an explanation. But he didn't, and Emily, rather than being upset, was glad. For in truth, she had no wish to face him again tonight.

———

DESPITE THE TRAUMA of the evening, Emily slept well that night and awakened the next morning, fresh and ready for a new adventure. One of the soldiers from the detail came to help her with her belongings.

"Ma'am, this here pitcher, it's one o' Sarn't Flynn, ain't it?" the soldier asked.

"Yes," Emily said.

The soldier picked up the drawing and looked at it. "You know, Sarn't Flynn always wanted to be in a pitcher. He tole' me about it once, when we was lookin' at that big paintin' over to the Sutlers' Store."

"Would you like to have that sketch?" Emily asked.

The soldier broke into a large smile, and his eyes gleamed excitedly. "Yes'm, I truly would," he said.

"Then it's yours."

"Thank you, ma'am." The soldier stuck the drawing under his tunic, then picked up Emily's trunk and swung it onto his shoulder. "Thanks a lot."

Emily followed the soldier outside and saw Libbie standing on the boardwalk in front of her own house next door.

"Soldier, you go on and load Miss Thomson's trunk," Libbie said. "I wish to speak to her alone."

"Yes, ma'am," the soldier said, and trudged on toward the carriage, which was hitched up and ready to go.

"You didn't stop by for breakfast this morning," Libbie said.

"I wasn't hungry," Emily replied.

Libbie looked at Emily, and for just a moment, Emily saw a hint of sadness in her eyes.

"Emily, my dear, I hope one day you will find it in your heart to forgive me."

"I'm sure you did what you felt was right," Emily said.

"Yes," Libbie replied. She walked over and put her hand lightly on Emily's arm. "One day you will thank me," she said. "For truly, dear, you were not meant for the life of a Custer wife."

"Perhaps not," Emily said. "But it should have been my decision to make."

"Did you have the courage?" Libbie asked, and the

truth of her remark caused Emily to look down in quick shame.

"No," Libbie said. "I didn't think so."

"Goodbye," Emily said and started toward the carriage.

"Please, Emily, write to us from New York," Libbie said. "You've been here long enough now to know how lonely it gets, and how we hunger for some news from the East. Promise me when you get to New York, you will write."

Emily wanted to tell her that she wasn't going to New York, but she was afraid that if she did, Libbie would tell her husband, and he would find some way to stop them. Instead, she said, "I'll write when I get to New York," enjoying at least the satisfaction of knowing that would not be for some time, yet.

"Daughter, we must be going," Silas called from inside the coach.

"I must be going," Emily said.

"Godspeed," Libbie said and spontaneously threw her arms around Emily.

Emily felt Libbie against her, and suddenly she realized the woman's terrible vulnerability. Despite her dominating personality, despite her position as the commanding officer's wife, despite her self-appointed role as queen of the Custer Dynasty, she was still a small, frail woman, pitted against the harsh vastness of the West. And despite everything, Emily felt a sudden surge of pity for the woman who at all costs had to maintain a brave front.

"Libbie, I really will keep in touch," Emily said, and a lump came to her throat as she saw that Libbie's own eyes were sheened with tears.

Emily hurried across the quadrangle and climbed into the coach. She heard the detail sergeant order his men to mount, the coach driver whistled at his horses, and the coach started to move.

"Hold it!" someone shouted. "Driver, hold that team!"

Emily looked out the window to see Tom Custer running toward her.

"Whoa," the driver said, and the coach stopped.

Tom ran to the coach and opened the door.

"Emily, I can't let you go like this," he said, his face reflecting his anguish. "I don't care what Autie says. I love you, and I want to marry you."

"Tom, dear Tom," Emily said. She put her hands in his. "So you've found your courage at last, have you?"

"Yes," Tom said. "Emily, I don't care if I'm court-martialed, or even kicked out of the service. I won't let you go. I can't let you go. Autie can go hang for all I care. He wants to be president? Let him, if he can. But not if it means I have to give you up."

And now, buoyed by Tom's courage, Emily found her own, for at last she had the strength to tell him that she didn't want to marry him.

"Tom, you are a dear, dear man, and I shall never forget you," she said.

"Never forget me?" Tom replied, puzzled by her words. "Emily, that sounds like you are planning on leaving anyway."

"I am leaving, Tom."

"But why? I told you I don't care what Autie or Libbie or anyone has to say. Don't you understand, Emily? I'm asking you to stay here and marry me, now."

"I know you are, Tom," Emily said. "But I can't marry you."

Tom started to speak, but Emily held her hand up gently to his lips.

"It has nothing to do with Autie or Libbie," she said. "Or perhaps it does. But not because she is forcing it, but because she is right. Tom, we simply are not right for each other. I could never lead the life of an Army officer's wife."

"I'll resign my commission," Tom said.

"And do what?"

"Anything," Tom said desperately. "I could be an engineer, I'm trained for that. Or I could get a job as an administrator somewhere. I've experience in directing men."

"No," Emily said.

"But why? I love you, Emily. Don't you believe that?"

"Yes, I do believe that," Emily said. "But there is something you love even more, Tom Custer. You love honor, and if I married you, you would forever feel your honor stained. We couldn't be happy with that hanging over us."

Tom opened his mouth, but no words came out. Finally, he sighed and looked into Emily's eyes. At that moment, a chill ran through her, for in his eyes she saw sadness, not just over the termination of their relationship, but over the hand which fate had dealt him. And for some inexplicable reason, she saw a suggestion of tragedy. She couldn't understand it, it wasn't even a conscious thought—but subconsciously, she saw a hollow glimpse of doom.

"Goodbye," Tom finally said. He stepped back and looked up at the driver. "You may go," he said.

The driver whistled at the team, and the coach jerked forward again.

"Open the gates!" the driver called, and as the coach rolled through the gates, Emily leaned out the window to look back at the little fort that had been her home for the last seven months. She felt a small pang of remorse over leaving. She saw Tom standing there, watching the coach pull away, and she also saw several dozen other soldiers busy at their details, a soldier ballet in blue.

And she saw General George Armstrong Custer standing on the front porch of his quarters with his arm around his wife's shoulders, waving goodbye.

Then the gates were closed and the scene was blotted out forever.

———

To the east of town, the train was beginning to build up speed. A long smear of black smoke stretched up into the crystal clear blue sky, visible for miles across the plains. Even the soldiers in the lookout towers at the fort could see the thin stream of smoke, and most thought of the beautiful young girl and her father, who had been so much a part of the fort life through the winter and were now returning to New York.

What they didn't know was that at that very moment, Emily and her father were not on the train but were closing their deal with Gibson Bell at the Livery Barn.

"Now mind, if the soldiers catch you, you'll not be telling them I know'd where you was a'goin'," Bell was saying. "General Custer'd boil me in oil iffen he know'd what I was doin'."

"Your secret is safe with us," Silas assured him, "Just be sure we get good animals and a sound wagon."

"You're gettin' the best I got 'n' that's a fact," Bell said. "Why this rig could pull you all the way back to St. Louis if you was of a mind to go." Bell took them behind the barn, and there, as Bell had promised, were two fine-looking horses and a sturdy wagon.

"I got all the provisions you asked for, too," Bell said. "Flour, bacon, coffee, beans, a rifle, and bullets."

"I didn't ask for a gun," Silas said.

"I know you didn't," Bell said. "But I figured as maybe you'd just forgot, so I threw it on in."

"I didn't forget," Silas said. "I just don't want one. I'm going out there to paint the Indians, not to shoot them."

Bell, grumbling, took the rifle out of the wagon. "It's your funeral," he said. "But you'd never catch me out there without a gun, that's for sure."

"It is likely, Mr. Bell, that we'll never catch you out there at all," Silas said laconically, as he paid the money over to the liveryman for the rig.

"You're mighty right on that, sir," Bell said without embarrassment. "You're right as rain. I ain't in no hurry to get myself kilt, or my scalp lifted, and that's for sure 'n certain."

"Well," Silas said. "Climb aboard, Emily, and we'll get underway."

# CHAPTER TWENTY

THE INDIAN TERRITORY WAS GREEN WITH SPRING AND running with streams swollen and sparkling with the melted snows. To the west, a ridge of purple mountains thrust into the sky.

Emily and her father watched as the first pink fingers of dawn spread over their camp. The last morning star made a bright pinpoint of light in the southern sky, and the coals from the campfire of the night before were still glowing. Silas threw chunks of dried wood onto the fire, and soon tongues of flame were licking against the bottom of the coffee pot. A rustle of feathers caused Silas and Emily to look up just in time to see a golden hawk diving on its prey. The hawk soared back into the air, carrying a tiny scrub mouse, which was kicking fearfully in the hawk's claws. A prairie dog scurried quickly from one hole to another, alert against the fate that had befallen the mouse.

Silas poured them both a cup of steaming black coffee, and they had to blow on it before they could drink it. They watched the sun turn from gold to white, then stream brightly down onto the plains.

Though Silas and Emily didn't realize it, they had been watched since before dawn. An Indian, his face lined with age and experience, sat quietly behind a rock outcropping, studying them. Finally, he stood up and walked into the camp. His sudden appearance startled Emily, and she gasped.

"I am White Ghost," the Indian said.

"I am Silas Thomson, and this is my daughter, Emily."

"I know," White Ghost said. "I was in the camp when Crazy Wolf brought you to us."

"Then you know that Sitting Bull promised us safe passage," Silas said.

"That was before the snows came," White Ghost said. "Much has happened since then."

"Yes," Silas said.

"The soldiers have killed many of my people," White Ghost said.

"I know," Silas said. "But we are not soldiers."

"Do you have gun?"

"No."

"I will see."

White Ghost began to poke through the wagon. He came across several drawings and held them out admiringly.

"You have many pictures of soldiers," White Ghost said.

"Yes. We were held at the fort by the soldiers and couldn't come to the Indian territories to paint Indians, as we had told Sitting Bull. But now we have left the soldiers."

White Ghost, who was looking through the pictures, came across one of Sergeant Flynn and studied it for a moment.

"Flynn was good man," he said.

"Then why was he killed?" Emily asked. "He was trying to help you."

"Indians have bad men, same like Whites," White Ghost said. He put the pictures down and walked over to sit on a rock. He folded his arms across his chest and looked straight at Silas. "Now you make picture of White Ghost," he said.

Silas smiled broadly. "White Ghost, we would be delighted to."

"Wait," White Ghost said. He pulled a pistol from his belt and held it in front of him.

"Do you want me to do the preliminary sketch, Father?" Emily asked, when she saw Silas wince with pain as he began drawing.

"Yes," Silas said, rubbing his hand.

"Can woman do this?" White Ghost asked, pointing at Emily.

"Yes," Silas said.

White Ghost looked at Emily with an awed expression.

"I did not know women could do such things," he said.

Emily's strokes were quick and sure, and within a few moments, she had created a picture of White Ghost, a proud, dignified warrior. She had even managed to capture the expression of wonder in his eyes as he watched her work.

"This is good," White Ghost said. "I keep."

"White Ghost, will you tell the other Indians to let us travel in peace?" Silas asked.

"Yes," White Ghost said.

"Thank you."

"It does not matter," White Ghost said. "The good Indians will let you travel in peace even if I say nothing. The bad Indians will be bad, even if Sitting Bull asks them to be good. So it does not matter what I say."

"Thanks, anyway," Silas said.

———

So, Jacob thought, Emily is still here, and now she is in the Black Hills.

He recalled that night in the fort when Emily had come to set him free. Her willingness to take such a chance for him had evoked strange feelings in him. Thinking about it now, he felt guilty, as if he had betrayed his people...as if he had betrayed Aiana.

Jacob looked again at the drawing of White Ghost, who told him that the girl had done it. That meant that he was holding the very paper she had only recently held. He wanted to go out on the prairie and find her, to tell her he hadn't forgotten how she had saved him from certain death.

"Jacob," Fool Dog called, snapping Jacob out of his thoughts. "Sitting Bull is holding a council now, and he asked you to come."

"I will come," Jacob said.

Several Indians were squatting around the campfire when Jacob arrived, many of whom he had never seen before. He was surprised to see so many strangers.

"Is he White?" one of the strange Indians asked of Sitting Bull, pointing to Jacob.

"He was White," Sitting Bull said. "Now he is Red."

The simple explanation was enough to satisfy the Indian and the others, and no one expressed any hostility toward Jacob as Sitting Bull began the conference.

"I will tell you a story," Sitting Bull said simply.

"During the geese flying time, Crook's soldiers made war on the camp of Two Moon, the Cheyenne chief, and Low Dog, the Oglala chief. They came in the night while the people slept, and they killed many and set fire to the tipis and burned food and blankets. They also stole many horses, but Two Moon, who is a very brave chief, stole them back." Sitting Bull pointed to Two Moon as he spoke, and the others smiled and congratulated him for his cleverness and bravery in recovering the horses.

"Now, Two Moon has something he wishes to speak about."

Two Moon stood up and looked over the assembled faces.

"Soon, I think, there will be many more soldiers and more war," Two Moon said. "I have sent scouts to watch the soldier camp at Fort Lincoln. There, Yellow Hair has stored much feed for horses and loaded many wagons. Soon, I think, he will come into the Black Hills to make war against all Indian people."

"But are we not safe here?" one of the Indians asked. "We are beyond the Powder River, and Yellow Hair said the soldiers would not come here."

"That was before," Two Moon said. "But there have

been many raids by Indians against the Whites who look for gold, and now no place is safe."

"But we have not made such raids," the protesting Indian said. "The soldiers should find those who make the raids, not us."

"Who is making the raids?" another asked.

"It is Crazy Wolf," Sitting Bull said. "He seeks a way to rid himself of shame."

"He is causing us much trouble," Two Moon said. "You should tell him to stop."

"I have told him," Sitting Bull said. "But my words mean nothing to him."

"But you are a chief," Two Moon protested. "Can you not stop him by saying so?"

"Can I stop the rain just because I am a chief?" Sitting Bull asked.

"No."

"Neither can I stop Crazy Wolf. He has plucked the hair from his head and does not know reason now. Evil spirits have stolen his senses."

"Then surely he will anger the soldiers enough so that they will come for us," Two Moon said. "I think we should not wait. I think we should attack the soldier fort now."

"We cannot," another said. "There are too many soldiers there, and they have thick walls and large guns which shoot twice—one time in the gun and again when the great bullet hits the ground."

"Then, if we do not attack the soldier fort, what can we do?"

"We can attack all Whites who are in the Black Hills," another said. "All miners, travelers, and farmers who are in the Black Hills will feel fear of us."

"No," Jacob said, speaking for the first time.

"Oh, the one who was once White will speak now," one of the strangers said. "And will you ask us not to attack Whites?"

"Not all Whites," Jacob said. "There are two, a father and daughter, and they are doing no harm."

"Do you speak of the two who draw pictures?" Two Moon asked.

"Yes," Jacob said. "They are no harm to us. We should not harm them."

"I say all Whites," another said.

"Sitting Bull, did you not tell them they could travel and draw their pictures in peace?" Jacob appealed.

"White Ghost, you spoke with them," Sitting Bull said. "What are your words?"

"I looked for a gun but found none," White Ghost said. "They travel only to draw pictures. They do not bring the road, they do not dig for yellow metal, they do not kill the buffalo, they do not put up fence. They capture only the way things seem to the eye. They will not harm us, and we should not harm them."

"Then we shall not," Sitting Bull said. "For now, I say we shall not harm any Whites. Perhaps if we show the soldiers we can live in peace, they will allow us to do so."

"But they are readying for war," Two Moon insisted. "I know this. I say, let them make war. I have fought already. My people have been killed, my horses stolen. I am satisfied to fight."

"Perhaps they will make war only against Crazy Wolf," Sitting Bull said. "I have a plan which will keep them from making war against us."

"What is your plan?" Two Moon asked.

"The Cheyennes, the Oglalas, the Minneconjous, and the Hunkpapas will camp together. Also, the Brules, the Sans Arcs, and the Blackfoot. All nations will come together as one great nation. We will be as many as the blades of grass, and then the soldiers will dare not attack."

"We will try your plan," Two Moon said. "But I think the soldiers will attack anyway."

"If they do, they will see the strength of many," Sitting Bull said.

The Indians began to discuss how so many Indians would share the water and grass and buffalo, and deer, but Jacob didn't listen. He had heard enough to know that Emily would be safe, and that was all he cared about for the moment.

# CHAPTER TWENTY-ONE

IT COULDN'T BE GOING BETTER, EMILY THOUGHT. FOR nearly a month, she and her father had traveled unmolested through Indian country, stopping at scattered Lakota, Cheyenne, and Arapaho settlements. In each one, it was as if they had been expected. The people turned out willingly to pose for them, sitting patiently as Silas and Emily carefully drew their likenesses on paper.

They were offered food, shelter, and sometimes stories to go with the faces.

The generosity astounded Emily. They were so cooperative and friendly that it didn't seem possible to Emily that there was any danger. She couldn't understand how the Army thought the Indians were hostile.

But though she and her father's relationship with the Indians was peaceful, the war between the Indians and the soldiers had already begun. Cavalry patrols and Indian parties stumbled across each other, and the result was always clash. The land between the Powder

River and the Black Hills was charged with a tension that neither side could ignore.

In one such clash, three Lakota warriors were killed. The soldiers stripped the bodies of anything of interest and carried their spoils back to Fort Lincoln. One item, in particular, was placed directly on General Custer's desk.

"You sent for me, Autie?" Tom asked. He had been at drill when word came that his brother wanted to see him in his headquarters right away.

The general sat behind his desk, one arm folded across his chest, the other stroking his beard. Without comment, he slid a sheet of paper across the desk.

"Do you recognize this, Tom?"

Tom picked it up. His expression changed to an easy smile. "Sure, I recognize it. It's a drawing by Emily. Where did you get it?"

Custer gestured toward a young officer standing rigidly at attention. "Tell my brother where you got it, Lieutenant Ward."

The lieutenant cleared his throat nervously before speaking. "I took it off the body of a Sioux warrior, sir. In fact, it's a drawing of that warrior."

Tom looked at the drawing again. "It must have been one she did while she was in the village before she came to the fort."

"Look at the bottom of the drawing," Autie said evenly.

Tom looked where Custer had indicated. There, printed in neat, deliberate letters, was the notation: *Thomson, Black Hills, 1876.* His stomach turned.

"Oh, my God." He looked up sharply. "Emily is out there! Autie, we have to go get her!"

"Why?"

"Because she could be killed!"

"She and her father knew the risks," Autie said coldly. "I will not risk a patrol on a rescue mission, particularly when the people my soldiers would be risking their lives for, don't even want to be rescued."

"You don't have to send a patrol," Tom said, stepping closer to the desk. "I'll go. I'll take some volunteers and—"

"No," Custer cut in. "I can't allow that."

"Autie..." Tom's gaze shifted to Lieutenant Ward, who was standing rigidly at attention but listening with open ears. "Lieutenant Ward, would you excuse us, please? I'd like to speak to the general in private."

Ward snapped a salute. "Yes, sir." He executed a sharp about-face and left the room, the door closing behind him.

After the lieutenant was gone, Tom turned back to face his brother. He took a breath, as if composing himself, then spoke, not angrily but with quiet conviction. "Autie, because of you, I didn't marry Emily. You called it a supreme sacrifice. You were right—it was. I haven't forgiven myself, or you, either. But that was partly my own fault, for it was my cowardice that allowed you to force such an unhappy decision upon me."

He stepped closer, voice low but unshaken. "But I'll be damned if I let Emily wander through hostile country, in danger of being killed, because I am too much of a coward to act. I will go after her whether I have your permission or not."

"You would go despite my orders to the contrary?"

"Yes."

"If you do, I will court-martial you, Captain. That is a promise."

A slow, ironic smile spread across Tom's face. "General, do you really think you can scare me with that? Don't you think I know you wouldn't dare do such a thing and jeopardize your political future? How would it look if you court-martialed your own brother because he went into the Black Hills to try and save America's most famous artist and his daughter?"

Custer exhaled sharply, raking a hand through his golden hair. He was defeated and he knew it.

"Fine. You may take two companies and go after them. But I want you back at this fort within two weeks. Do you understand me, mister?"

Tom grinned, clasping his brother's hand. "Thank you, Autie. But I don't want two companies—or even one. I want five good men. That's all."

Custer's brows shot up. "Five men? That's preposterous."

"Five men," Tom said again. "And I'll pick them myself. We can travel fast, light, and most of all, unobserved. There's no way I could conceal two companies."

Custer clenched his jaw, exasperated that Tom had won every point. "All right. But remember what I said about two weeks, Tom. I want you back by then."

"I'll be back." Tom promised. He turned and started toward the door, then paused and looked back over his shoulder. "And when I do get back, Autie, I intend to marry Emily immediately, if she'll have me. Nothing you or Libbie can say will change that."

Custer's lips pressed into a thin line. "We won't try to interfere."

Tom nodded, then stepped out.

He left headquarters sick at heart and frightened at the thought of Emily and her father alone in the Black Hills, but elated even, that for the first time in his life, he had bested his brother. He crossed the quadrangle, wasting no time in finding Sergeant Kennedy.

"I'm riding out on a rescue expedition," Tom told him. "I need five volunteers. Tell them to meet me at the stables in thirty minutes."

"Yes, sir."

That settled, Tom went to his quarters to ready his field gear. He paused just inside the door. His room had been Emily's when she was at the post, and for a moment, he could almost feel her presence.

How often he had wished he had never listened to Autie. If he had stood up to him earlier, Emily wouldn't be in danger now. And what's more, she would be his wife. He had tried to make it right, riding to her that morning and asking her to stay, to marry him, but she had refused.

And why wouldn't she? He had broken her heart and humiliated her at dinner the night before. What else could he expect?

Tom shook his head, angered at himself. He was a fool, and he had let his one chance slip by him. But if he got another chance, he wouldn't let it go by again.

When Tom walked into the stables, he expected to see five men waiting. Instead, nearly five hundred stood shoulder to shoulder, rifles slung, sabers at their sides, faces set with determination.

"Sergeant Kennedy," Tom said, struggling to find his voice. "What is this? I said five men."

"Everyone in your battalion volunteered, sir. If word

had spread to the regiment, I reckon they'd have volunteered, too."

Tom looked at the men, all eager and dressed out in full field gear. Never in his life had he felt greater pride in the Seventh Cavalry than at this moment. He stood there, unable to speak.

"I can't choose them, Sergeant Kennedy," he said quietly. "I would be honored if you would select five men for me."

"Four men, sir," Kennedy said.

Tom raised an eyebrow.

"I'll be going with you," Kennedy added simply.

"Very well, I'll wait outside the gate," Tom said as he swung up on his horse.

Moments later, Kennedy rode out with four handpicked troopers. Tom gave them a single nod, and without another word, they turned their mounts toward the hills.

———

"YOU KNOW, DAUGHTER," Silas was saying, "a couple more weeks and I think we shall have everything we need."

"I know," Emily said. "It has been wonderful. The Indians have cooperated so well, and we have drawings of the villages, of the hunt, oh, and I just love this series on the children," she said, holding up a couple of the sketches. The other drawings were propped up against the side of the wagon that served not only as their transportation but as their living quarters and working area as well.

"Here come some more," Silas said, pointing to a

group of horsemen who were approaching the wagon. "They'll be wanting their pictures drawn."

Emily laughed. "You can't say we haven't been getting cooperation from the Indians, can you? In fact, quite the opposite. They are so anxious to have their pictures drawn that they keep coming to us, so that we have a difficult time showing them in their villages."

"Well, we can't turn them down," Silas said. He looked around. "Now, what happened to those charcoal sticks?"

"Oh, I put them in the wagon," Emily said. "I'll get them."

Emily climbed up onto the wagon, opened the canvas cover, and went inside. The canvas allowed only shaded light so that searching for the charcoal drawing sticks was difficult. She began looking through the blankets, papers, baskets, boxes, and other paraphernalia.

"I said I put them in here," she called out to her father. "But I tell you, I can't find them."

She felt the wagon tip as someone climbed on. "You don't have to come up here, Father. I'll find them."

The curtain parted and Emily looked around. There, grinning obscenely was the painted face and bald head of Crazy Wolf!

Emily felt a knife of fear stab into her heart, and she gasped. But she fought the urge to scream and finally managed to regain some measure of composure.

"Crazy Wolf," she said. "Have you come to have your drawing made?"

"Come see," Crazy Wolf said, still grinning hideously. He jumped back down onto the ground, and Emily, puzzled by his strange behavior, followed him.

"What is it, Crazy Wolf?" Emily asked. "Why are you acting like this?"

Crazy Wolf made a proud, sweeping gesture with his hand. And then Emily saw the handiwork of which Crazy Wolf was so proud. Her father, with an arrow in his heart, lay sprawled on the ground, his eyes open but unseeing. His face wore a look of surprise and disbelief.

Emily felt the world spinning, then everything went black.

---

"CAP'N, THESE ARE WAGON TRACKS," Sergeant Kennedy said. "What would wagon tracks be doin' out here?"

"It has to be them," Tom said. "Let's follow."

"It could be miners."

"Not likely," Tom said. "Miners would use pack animals, and I don't think any settlers would be fool enough to come in here alone."

Sergeant Kennedy saw a pile of horse dung between the wheel tracks, and he poked at it with a stick.

"Whoever it is can't be far away," he said. "They was through here no more'n twelve hours ago."

"Let's go," Tom said, urging his horse into a lope.

They covered over ten miles in an hour. Then, as they crested a ridge, they saw an object in the valley below.

"Cap'n!" Kennedy called.

"I see it," Tom answered, yanking his horse to a halt. Below, in the valley, a wagon stood motionless. A few Indians were standing around it, but from this distance he couldn't tell what they were doing.

The horses, excited from their long run, stamped and tossed their heads.

"Dismount," Tom said quietly. "Campbell, you take the reins."

"Yes, sir." The private gathered all the horses and led them below the crest so they wouldn't show up against the sky.

Kennedy's eyes stayed on the wagon. "What do you reckon we've got here, Cap'n?"

"I don't know. But I don't want them seeing us before we find out. Come on, we'll follow the gulley around until we're even with them, then creep up for a closer look."

"Right," Kennedy said.

"Take off anything that might rattle," Tom ordered.

The men removed canteens, spurs, and cartridge belts.

"Anyone carrying coins? I don't want them jingling."

"Empty your pockets, men," Kennedy said. "Pass it to Campbell."

"Hey, if I don't make it back, does that mean Campbell gets to keep it?" one of the soldiers asked.

"If you don't make it back, what the hell do you need with it?" Kennedy asked dryly. "Drinks are free in Fiddler's Green."

The soldier grinned faintly. "Aye, that they are." He emptied his pockets without further comment.

When they were ready, Tom nodded. "Follow me."

He ran in a low crouch, moving quickly and silently through the gulley, his men following close behind. They followed it around the valley until Tom judged they were even with the wagon. Then silently he crawled up to the top of the ridge and looked down at the wagon.

"Oh, my God!" he said. For an instant, he couldn't breathe. Then he turned his head in revulsion. For there before him, the Indians were systematically mutilating Silas Thomson's body.

Suddenly, all planning and military discipline went by the wayside. Tom Custer felt only one thing—a blind, killing rage. He gave no orders, formed no plan of attack. He just stood up and ran toward the Indians. "You butchering bastards!" he roared.

The soldiers hesitated only a second before following.

The sudden appearance of the four soldiers caught the five Indians around the wagon totally by surprise. Tom shot the nearest warrior through the chest, dropping him in a heap. The others started for their horses.

"Kill the horses!" Tom bellowed. "Don't let the butchering bastards get away!"

The soldiers dropped to one knee and aimed their carbines at the horses as carefully as if they were shooting at fixed targets. Their carbines cracked as one, and three of the horses fell dead. Tom fired twice more, killing the last two mounts.

The remaining warriors realized now that they had nowhere to go, so they were forced to fight. They turned to face their charging adversaries, holding their lances and war clubs at the ready. The soldiers were unarmed, having expended their lone cartridges on the horses.

One warrior threw his lance at Tom. It struck the ground inches from his feet. Tom ripped it up and charged with it, driving it through the man's throat. The warrior collapsed, choking.

Tom turned then and saw that one of his men was down, a warrior standing over him with a raised war club. Tom leaped at the Indian, knocking him over, then, wrenching the war club from him, brought it crashing down on his head, killing him instantly.

Now it was four soldiers against two warriors. The last pair tried to run away. Tom pulled his pistol and dropped to the dirt. He steadied his revolver with both hands, and fired twice. Both men fell.

Silence.

The battlefield reeked of blood and dust. Five warriors lay dead. Tom had killed them all.

From where he lay, chest heaving, Tom rasped, "Look in the wagon. I can't."

Kennedy hurried to the wagon, climbed up, and peered inside. When he turned back, relief was on his face. "It's all right, sir. She ain't in there. They must've took her alive."

Tom closed his eyes briefly, then his jaw tightened. "All right?" His voice was hoarse. "She'd be better off dead."

# CHAPTER TWENTY-TWO

CRAZY WOLF STOOD JUST INSIDE THE TIPI, THE flickering gold light of two burning torches throwing shadows across the hide walls. The air was thick with the smell of smoke, damp earth, and unwashed hides.

In the center, Emily Thomson lay bound at the wrists and ankles, staked to the packed dirt floor. Her clothing was torn and streaked with dried blood and dirt. She had fought this madman with every ounce of strength, but the rawhide cords were now holding her down.

He had grabbed her when she fainted after seeing her father lying dead. Throwing her across his horse, he had left the others to plunder the wagon. Whatever they took—blankets, drawings, clothing—none of it mattered to him. This prisoner was all he needed to settle the debt.

Revenge. That was what he wanted. Jacob Two Hearts had humiliated him before his people, when he spared his life instead of killing him. And even worse, the story had spread throughout the bands of Indians. Now, his bald scalp which he had stripped by his own hand in a fit of anger was a constant reminder of his disgrace. He had sworn to keep it that way until he could redeem himself.

When the people found out that it was Emily who had set Jacob Two Hearts free, they respected her even more. Many had shared the story of the fight between Jacob and Crazy Wolf. Now, when she was fully awake, she was afraid. She would have been a fool not to be, but her hatred for Crazy Wolf, for what he had done to her father, burned hotter than fear.

When she saw Crazy Wolf, her chin lifted. "So, the coward has returned."

His painted face twisted into a grimace that was half grin, half snarl. "Woman," he said slowly, "you will know pain."

That was when she saw what was in his hand, a whip made from a long, thin strip of rawhide. He dipped it into a gourd of water, letting it soak before running it through his fingers.

Emily knew what wet rawhide could do as it dried— shrinking until it crushed whatever it bound. She took a deep breath in anticipation of what she knew was about to come.

The whip hissed through the air and cracked against her shoulder. The blow felt like a hot brand pressed to her skin. She gasped but kept her eyes locked on Crazy Wolf. Again and again he swung the whip hitting her arms, her back, her legs, until the sting of each lash all seemed like one single burn.

Despite the welts coming up on her skin, Crazy Wolf seemed to be holding off on the intensity of the strikes.

It was as if he wanted her humiliated and defeated, but he did not want to kill her.

At last he stepped back, breathing hard. "That is a lesson," he said. "You will do as I say."

When she didn't answer, he continued. He cut two short pieces from the whip, and dropped them into the gourd. Pulling them out dripping wet, he crouched before her.

He tied one strip tightly around her right thumb, the other around her left. At first, the bindings weren't tight, but as time passed, the rawhide began to shrink. A dull ache turned to a sharp throb, and then to a crushing tingling that spread up her hands.

She clenched her teeth, refusing to speak, as sweat formed on her brow, and her breath became more and more ragged.

"You can stop this," he said at last. "Just beg me."

"For what?" Emily whispered.

His eyes narrowed. He swung the whip again, each strike landing where the welts had already risen. She bit back a sob until one blow caught her across the ribs, forcing the air from her lungs, and she could not control the cry that rang out.

When he heard her cry, he stopped the beating, and cut the rawhide off her thumbs. For a moment, he stood over her, torchlight catching the streaks of paint on his bald head, his eyes demonic.

"Woman, you now belong to me."

Emily's lips curled into a thin smile. "Never."

Something in her defiance snapped his control. He lunged, knife in hand, and reached for her.

Emily twisted her shoulders, rolled toward the fire pit with such strength that she pulled up two of the stakes. Before he could stop her, she snatched up a torch with her free hand. She swung it at Crazy Wolf, igniting his pants.

Crazy Wolf began beating out the flames, dropping his knife in the process.

She used the moment to grab the knife and cut the cord at her other wrist and ankle. With unsteady hands, she shoved the knife in her pocket, and then picked up the torch again, This time she used it to sweep embers from the fire pit onto his feet causing him to dance around to stop the burning.

In that moment, she saw her chance to escape. She bolted through the tipi flap into the night. Barefoot and running hard, she headed into the darkness beyond the dying campfires that marked the sleeping lodges. When she reached the tall grass, she knew she was in the open prairie.

She kept running, until her lungs burned and her feet were swollen. In the moonlight, she found a low bluff where she felt safe enough to stop. Dropping to her knees, she took in great gulps of air until her breathing returned to normal. Then she listened—no hoofbeats, no voices—only the whisper of wind through dry grass and a far off howl of a coyote.

Emily pressed herself into the shelter of the rocks, as she closed her eyes to offer a prayer of thanks to God that she had escaped.

But had she really escaped? She had no food, no water, and no horse. She had no idea where she was and whether there was another person anywhere within walking distance. But for this minute, she was away from Crazy Wolf, and the degradation she was sure would have happened, had she not gotten away.

She pulled her torn dress into place as best she could, and closed her eyes in exhaustion. When daylight came, she would decide what to do next.

----

ONE WORD KEPT POUNDING through Tom Custer's mind as he rode back toward Fort Lincoln—

Betrayal.

Betrayal. Betrayal. Betrayal.

Sergeant Flynn had been betrayed—cut down while trying to lead the Indians to safety.

Emily and her father had been betrayed—slaughtered when all they had done was sketch what they saw.

And he himself had been betrayed—by his own damn guilt. For eight long years, Washita had haunted him. He had told himself it was war, that it had been necessary. But now? Now he wished there had been a hundred Washitas. A thousand.

He remembered overhearing a plan once—cold, calculated, spoken in all seriousness. Smallpox. Infect the blankets with disease and send them into the lodges. Ten thousand dead before they knew what had struck them. At the time, he had turned away in disgust, thinking it monstrous.

Now?

Now he wished the plan had been carried out.

His hands clenched the reins until the leather creaked. They should have burned every village to the ground, salted the earth so nothing could grow, left nothing but ash and silence.

The column clattered across the drawbridge. The gates swung wide, and inside the quadrangle the

Seventh Cavalry stood in parade formation, rows of blue uniforms in perfect alignment, sunlight glancing off polished brass and the mirror-bright edges of sabers.

A hero's welcome.

Tom barely saw it.

At the center of the formation, General Custer pivoted sharply, his hand snapping up in a perfect military salute.

Tom ignored it. He didn't return the salute, didn't acknowledge the men at attention, didn't dismiss his own command, didn't even turn matters over to Sergeant Kennedy. He swung down from his saddle, shoved the reins into a trooper's hands, and strode toward his quarters.

"Dismiss your battalions!" Custer's voice cracked across the parade ground, sharp as a rifle shot, his anger plain.

Tom didn't care. Nothing could erase what he had seen, what he had lost.

He kicked the door to his quarters open, crossed to the shelf, and yanked down the whiskey bottle. Pulling the cork with his teeth, he drank in deep, burning gulps. The liquor scorched his throat, blazed into his gut, but he kept drinking until the heat dulled the edge of his thoughts.

When he finally lowered the bottle, his head spinning, he saw Custer in the doorway, arms on his hips, framed by the lantern glow. The light caught in his golden hair and beard, casting a halo that seemed almost unreal.

"They're dead," Tom said flatly, tossing the bottle toward his brother.

Custer caught it with one hand. The anger in his

face softened. "I'm sorry, Tom. If there's anything I can do..."

"There is."

"What? Just tell me."

"Help me to kill the Indians."

Custer's brows lifted. This was not the same Tom who had once agonized over every campaign, who had carried Washita's guilt for years. Slowly, Custer's mouth curled into a smile. He pulled the cork from the bottle, drank, and wiped his mouth with the back of his hand.

"You want to kill Indians, do you, Tom-boy?"

"Yes."

"That I can promise you. Within the week, we will embark on the campaign that will go down in history as *Custer's Triumph*."

Tom took the bottle back, draining the last swallow. "I've got a better name for it."

Custer tilted his head. "What would that be?"

"A name that says exactly what I want to do to all of them," Tom said. "I think it should be called *Custer's Massacre*."

# CHAPTER TWENTY-THREE

IT WAS EARLY JUNE, THE SEASON THE SIOUX CALL THE Moon of Making Fat, and the Hunkpapa were holding their annual Sun Dance. For three days, Sitting Bull danced, cut himself in sacrifice, and endured the suffocating heat of the sweat lodge. On the third day, he collapsed into a trance.

When he emerged, the camp was already gathering. Warriors and chiefs from many bands, Hunkpapa, Oglala, Minneconjou, Sans Arc, Blackfeet, and Cheyenne, all came to hear him speak.

"Hear me," Sitting Bull said. "Voices came to me in my vision, and the words I speak are words of truth."

The drums fell silent, the chanting stopped, and warriors and chiefs gathered around to listen.

"A voice cried out: 'I give you this because they have no ears.' And when I looked into the sky, I saw soldiers falling like grasshoppers, their heads down, their hats falling off. They fell into our camp. Because the White men would not listen, Wakantanka, the Great Spirit, gave them to us to be killed. Their leader is Yellow Hair."

A warrior gave a long cry, and others took it up until the camp roared with their shouts of excitement and challenge. The drums started up again, and a hundred warriors took up the dance.

"Jacob," Sitting Bull said, as Jacob Two Hearts walked by. He patted the ground beside him. "Come, sit with me, and we will talk."

Jacob came to him and sat down.

"Once I told you, that after the great battle, one of your hearts would be dead and one would live," Sitting Bull said.

"Yes," Jacob replied. "My Indian heart chose Aiana."

"But now Aiana is dead. I was wrong before. I told you only one heart would win. Now I see both hearts will live."

"I don't understand," Jacob said.

"When Aiana lived, your Indian heart lived. Aiana is dead, and I think your Indian heart will die."

"No," Jacob said. "I will never betray my people."

"You say you will not betray your people, yet you would betray the heart which yet lives?"

"Sitting Bull, why do you think only my white heart lives?"

"I saw you in my vision," Sitting Bull said, "and I saw a White woman who makes pictures with a stick."

"Emily Thomson," Jacob said quickly. "She and her father are traveling through the Black Hills, making pictures. But I have not gone to see them."

Sitting Bull's expression grew grave. "Evil has struck them. I saw the girl's father struck down, and the girl taken prisoner."

"Emily is a prisoner? Where? Who has her?"

"It is Crazy Wolf."

Jacob's jaw hardened. "I should have killed him when I had the chance."

"And now your blood runs hot because he has the White woman," Sitting Bull said.

"Yes," Jacob admitted.

"That is good. I saw your anger in my vision. You should find her."

"I will," Jacob said, "and I'll be back in time for the battle to come."

"No," Sitting Bull said firmly.

"What? Why do you say no?"

"You will not fight in this battle," Sitting Bull said.

"Of course I will fight in this battle," Jacob said. "I am a war chief. I have earned the right to fight in this battle."

"Hear me, Jacob. If you fight, against whom will you fight?"

"The soldiers," Jacob said.

"And against your heart?"

He hesitated. "Yes. No...I don't know."

"I would feel great sorrow if you fought on the side of the soldier against your people," Sitting Bull said.

"I couldn't do that," Jacob said.

"But I would also feel great sorrow if you fought against your white heart. It would be best if you did not fight in this battle at all."

"But what will I do? Where will I go?"

"You will go find your White woman, and with her, make a new life. You will become White again."

Jacob shook his head. "Sitting Bull, I couldn't abandon—"

"I have spoken," the chief said. "From this day, you will not be one of us. You may travel in our lands in peace, but you will not live in our villages."

Jacob stood up and looked down at Sitting Bull. He wanted to argue further, but the chief had closed his eyes and was drifting back into another trance. There was nothing left for him to do but leave the village and look for Emily.

———

EMILY WAS SO exhausted that she had slept better than she could have thought possible. When dawn came, she found a shallow draw with a few scrub willows for cover. Her body was so weak, she couldn't go any farther. She was thankful that she found a stream with reasonably clean water, and she scooped up water to try to soothe her battered body as well as to quench her thirst. She tried to think when she had last eaten, but she couldn't recall.

When darkness fell again, she moved on, guided by the stars and the distant line of hills. She hoped she might find a trail that would lead to some sort of civilization, whether it be another Indian village, a miner, or even a patrol of soldiers.

But before midnight, her luck turned. She had just crossed a dry wash when a shadow rose from behind a boulder. Her heart dropped when she saw the bald head of Crazy Wolf. She could make out that he had a coil of rope in his hand.

She tried to run, but exhaustion and hunger took over. In moments, she stumbled and fell, hitting the ground so hard that the breath was knocked from her.

Crazy Wolf's rough hands jerked her upright, and he slipped the rope around her shoulders. He pulled her along behind him until they reached his camp where his horse was tethered.

By the time the moon was high, she was seated near a small fire, her hands bound in front of her while Crazy Wolf turned a spit with a rabbit skewered over the flames. Dirt and dust clung to her skin. Her hair hung in matted strands, her dress was torn, and her fingernails were cracked.

She thought bitterly of a reception in New York—the elegant gowns, the polished floors of the gallery, the way she had once fretted over whether to choose pheasant under glass or leg of lamb. Now she sat, hoping for scraps of rabbit.

For some strange, inexplicable reason, the contrast struck Emily as amazingly funny, and she began to laugh.

Crazy Wolf's head came up sharply. He was holding a part of the rabbit in both hands, and a piece of it was hanging from his lips, and his face was shining with the rabbit's grease.

Emily laughed harder.

"Why do you laugh?" he demanded

"I was remembering a time long ago," Emily said, still laughing, "when I couldn't decide which food to choose. And now I sit here like a stray dog, waiting for your leftovers."

Emily continued to laugh, and tears started coming down her face. She had no idea why she was laughing. She knew that only she could appreciate the irony of her situation, and its tragedy was greater than any humor. But she couldn't help it. Her laughter was wild, uncontrollable.

"You stop laughing," Crazy Wolf growled.

"I can't," she said, her voice breaking.

He stood, hand curling into a fist. "I make you stop—"

The first shot cracked from the darkness. Crazy Wolf jerked, blood soaking his shirt. A second shot rang out, and he collapsed beside the fire.

Emily screamed, then looked toward the shadows. Two men stepped into the firelight. One was tall and thin, with a prominent Adam's apple and large eyes. The other was shorter and stocky, with a thick black beard.

The short man's eyes slid over her, cold and assessing. "Well now, Harley...looks like this injun was keepin' somethin' for himself."

Harley's lip curled. "She's still breathin', Luke. Means she ain't the kind of lady you bring home."

Luke's laugh was short and mean. "No, she's the kind you keep."

With a sinking heart, Emily realized she had not been rescued, only delivered into another kind of danger.

———

IT WAS the next day before Jacob found the camp. He spotted a makeshift skin shelter from a ridge and dropped into a gully to circle closer. He dismounted and crawled up to the top of the ridge on his hands and knees, then crept on his stomach for the last few yards.

Finally, he reached the summit and peered down toward the camp.

It was strangely quiet. He knew it was Crazy Wolf's camp, because he had tracked him. And he knew from the bloodied footprints, he had Emily with him. But Crazy Wolf should have been making preparations to move on. And where was his horse?

Jacob studied the campsite for a few minutes longer, then, looking all around to make certain that no one was watching him, he rolled over the top of the ridgeline, keeping low, and darted quickly and silently down into the camp.

Just as he reached the campsite, he saw the body of Crazy Wolf, shielded by the shelter.

He looked around for Emily's body, but he found nothing. She was gone. He sighed, then looked back toward Crazy Wolf's body, wondering who had murdered him.

Jacob knelt to examine the body more closely. He had been shot twice in the chest. Crazy Wolf's medicine bag still hung around his neck. Whoever killed him had no special hatred for Crazy Wolf, or the medicine bag would have been removed to prevent Crazy Wolf from entering the Happy Hunting Ground.

A warrior's medicine bag was a special totem, a magic amulet that without, no warrior would feel secure. Its contents were secret, known only to the warrior who carried it, and seen by no other until after his death.

Jacob opened the bag. Inside were a tuft of feathers, a bear claw, a polished rock, an arrowhead, and a small pile of dirt. The bear claw he recognized—it had been stolen from Sitting Bear's rug. A warrior who carried a claw from an animal he had not killed possessed no real power.

Shaking his head, Jacob replaced the items, set the bag back around Crazy Wolf's neck, and using rocks and the skin of the shelter, made a grave.

Then he picked up the trail of the two horsemen who had evidently killed Crazy Wolf. They were White men, he knew, because the horses were shod. They had left the camp with an unshod pony. The pony wasn't carrying quite as much weight as it had been earlier on the trail, and Jacob figured that Emily had replaced Crazy Wolf.

For a moment, he considered following. But she was with two White men. Surely she was safe now. They were probably taking her back to civilization and the life she knew before coming out here. If he followed them and saw her, she might not even want to see him.

Jacob also realized that he was an Army fugitive and that a reward might be out for him. If that were the case, he certainly would not be allowed to talk to her, and the moment her rescuers spotted him, they would likely shoot before hearing him out.

No, he thought. She is safe now, and she would probably not want to see me.

Jacob turned away from the trail and rode in the opposite direction.

# CHAPTER TWENTY-FOUR

On June 3rd, 1876, the Seventh Cavalry Regiment set out to join forces with General Terry's expedition against the Sioux. It was the beginning of the grand and glorious campaign that General Custer had been promising Tom and the other officers of the regiment for several months now.

Custer's Seventh was augmented by artillery, infantry, laden ponies, pack mules, scouts, civilian employees, wagons, and reporters. There were seventeen hundred animals and twelve hundred men, and the column stretched for two miles. George Armstrong Custer, Lieutenant Colonel, US Army, Brevet Major General Volunteers, commanded. Beside him rode his wife.

In the mists of early morning, the troops saw a mirage. They saw themselves riding in the sky. The Indian scouts, upon seeing this vision, let out a wailing chant of fear. The soldiers, too, were frightened. Many swore that they saw Sergeant Flynn, as well as Howe and Peters, Hamilton and Elliot, and all the other soldiers of the Seventh who had been killed.

It was as if the portals to Fiddler's Green had opened and those cavalrymen who had gone on before were calling to their earthbound comrades, inviting them up to join them.

"It's just a mirage brought on by the early morning mist," General Custer assured his men.

"Sure, it's a good-luck sign," Colonel Keough said.

Young Autie Reed, General Custer's nephew, rode next to his father, Captain Jim Reed, and Boston, Custer's youngest brother, was along as well. Autie and Boston were greatly taken with the mirage, and they asked Mr. Ingersoll, the photographer, if he could get a picture of it, but Ingersoll told them that mirages didn't photograph.

Tom was less enthusiastic than his younger brother and his nephew. Though not superstitious, Tom couldn't help but feel a sense of foreboding over the incident. He suppressed a shudder, and though he didn't put it into words, he had a feeling that he would never return to Fort Lincoln.

The mirage only lasted for about fifteen minutes, for as the sun rose, it burned away with the mist.

Libbie, Custer's wife, and Maggie, his sister, had ridden along with the column for most of the morning. When the column stopped for lunch, the officers and their ladies picnicked on roast duck and wine. Many photographs were taken, and Mr. Kellogg, the special correspondent for the New York *Herald*, wrote up his impressions of the grand expedition's first day and presented them to Libbie to send in for him when she returned to the fort with Maggie after lunch. Young Autie Reed and Boston, though both too young for the Army, were to stay with the column. General Custer promised his sister to keep the two with him constantly for the duration of the expedition.

"Look at them, Maggie. Isn't that a magnificent sight?" Libbie asked as they watched the column.

"Yes," Maggie agreed. The two women were riding in the paymaster's car, which was to carry them back to the post. "I agree, there is no sight more beautiful or inspiring than this."

The column marched by as if on parade. Flags were snapping in the breeze, officers were holding shining sabers up in a salute, and row upon row of blue-clad soldiers stared straight ahead with pride. As they marched by, row on row, the band played stirring marches such as "Garry Owen", the ubiquitous regimental song.

Several times, the paymaster started to call to his horses, but each time Libbie put her hand out to stop him. Finally realizing that she intended to watch the entire procession, he sat quietly until the last of the column had passed. Then they watched the long blue line recede into the distance, listening to the music fade away until only the drum and the high notes of the flutes could be heard.

Finally, only a cloud of dust hanging over the horizon evidenced that the army had passed them by. It was deathly quiet save for the whistling of the wind.

A paper blew across the prairie and plastered itself to the wheel of the carriage. Libbie reached down for it, and looked at it.

"What is it?" Maggie asked.

"It's a poem," Libbie said.

"A poem?" Maggie asked with a little laugh. "What sort of poem? Oh, do let me see."

"It was written by one of the soldiers, I suppose," Libbie said, a strange, faraway look on her face.

"Well, what is it? Is it a love poem?" Maggie asked.

"No," Libbie said. "Here, read it for yourself." She handed the poem over to her sister-in-law, who began to read:

*There goes first call blowing,*
   *Sergeant Flynn,*
   *And it sounds like taps blowing,*
   *Sergeant Flynn,*
   *Oh my lad, that's only a fancy.*
   *Take a brace there, Private Clancy,*
   *You'll feel better when they strike up Garry Owen.*

*Ten thousand braves are riding,*
   *Sergeant Flynn,*
   *In the Black Hills they are hiding,*
   *Sergeant Flynn,*
   *Crazy Horse and Sitting Bull,*
   *They will get their bellies full,*
   *Of lead and steel from men of Garry Owen.*

*We'll dismount and fight the heathens,*
   *Sergeant Flynn,*
   *While there's still a trooper breathin',*
   *Sergeant Flynn,*
   *In the face of sure disaster,*
   *Keep those carbines firing faster,*

*Let the volleys ring for dear old Garry Owen.*

*We are Irish, Scotch, and thrifty,*
  *Sergeant Flynn,*
  *We'll sell troopers one for fifty,*
  *Sergeant Flynn,*
  *For each Seventh scalp that's lifted,*
  *Fifty heathen souls have drifted,*
  *To their Happy Hunting Ground for Garry Owen.*

*Here they come like screaming Banshees,*
  *Sergeant Flynn,*
  *Sioux and Blackfeet and Comanches,*
  *Sergeant Flynn,*
  *Let your blades run red and gory,*
  *In their blood we'll write our story,*
  *We will die today for dear old Garry Owen.*

Maggie lay the paper in her lap and looked at Libbie. "Oh, my," she said. "Oh, my, Libbie, you don't think..."

"What?" Libbie asked.

Maggie looked at the cloud of dust, which was now little more than a small puff on the horizon. "You don't think anything will happen to them, do you?"

"No, of course not," Libbie said. "Why, one company of the Seventh could handle the entire Sioux Nation. I've heard Autie say that I don't know how many times."

"I know," Maggie said. "Still..."

"Maggie, you saw the army as they left, didn't you? How magnificent they were. Do you really think they are in any danger from savages?"

"No," Maggie said. "No, I suppose not."

"Good. I thought you would see it that way. Now, driver, let us hurry quickly back to Fort Lincoln."

"Yes, ma'am, Mrs. Custer," the driver said, and clucked to the horses.

———

THE COLUMN COVERED thirty-two miles the first day, finally stopping to eat at about ten o'clock that night. Despite that, there was very little grumbling from the men, for most of them were more than willing at last to have left the long winter's garrison.

"There is nothing tastier than trail stew, gentlemen," Custer said, squatting beside the campfire, eating from his mess tin with great gusto. A tin cup of coffee sat on the ground beside him, and he periodically took a drink from it and smacked his lips appreciatively, mostly for the benefit of young Autie Reed, who was enjoying his uncle's antics.

"You'd better not let Aunt Libbie hear you say that, Uncle," Autie teased. "She would grab you by the hair."

Tom laughed. "She wouldn't have much hair to grab. The general shaved most of it off. Did you hope to cheat the Indians of their prize, General?" he asked.

Custer joined in the laughter, and removing his hat, ran his hand across his newly shorn hair. "I needed a change," he said. "And besides, there's no sense in making it easy for them."

"What does the newspaper think about the general's new look?" Tom asked Kellogg.

Kellogg, who was reading by the firelight, looked up and chuckled. "I don't think the readers will find him quite as dashing," he said. He ran his hand over his own hair. "But if I thought it would keep the Indians from being interested in me, I'd shave myself bald."

"Don't worry, Mr. Kellogg," little Autie Reed said. "If the going gets rough, I'll protect you."

"I'm certain Mr. Kellogg will sleep much easier for that, Autie," General Custer said. "Tell me, Mr. Kellogg. What do you find so interesting in the paper?"

"Oh," Kellogg said. "I just got these before we left the post, and I haven't had a chance to look at them before now. But they have all the latest news of the Republican National Convention."

"Oh?" Custer asked with interest. "And what is the news?"

"Mr. James G. Blaine has announced that he is withdrawing his intention to place a name into nomination in order that his own name may be entered."

"What?" Custer asked in a small voice. "What did you say?"

"Oh, it's all political strategy and hokum anyway," Kellogg said. "You see, Blaine's biggest opponent for the nomination is clearly Governor Rutherford Hayes of Ohio. So Blaine spread the rumor that he was going to place another prominent Ohioan into nomination for president, in order to dilute the support for Governor Hayes. Of course, nobody knows who the fellow from Ohio was who would be so base as to allow his name to be used for such a purpose. Certainly, it could be no one with political ambitions of his own, for such a thing would be the death knell to any future political aspirations."

"I see," Custer said in a small voice. "Did they find out who it was?"

"No," Kellogg said, looking through the paper. "No, I

don't think so. It may be, though, that the fellow whose name Blaine was going to propose had no idea of the real reason for the nomination, and when he realized it, he ordered Blaine to withdraw him."

Custer stood and looked down at Kellogg and the others for a moment, then turned and walked quickly away into the darkness.

"General," Kellogg called. "Are you all right?"

Tom set his plate down and went after his brother.

He found him standing by the front wheel of a wagon, his hands around the spoke, pulling on the wheel.

"Autie, are you all right?" Tom asked.

Custer pulled on the wheel so hard that the hub and axle squeaked.

"Listen to that," he said. "If the teamsters don't keep these wheels lubricated, we shall be having a great deal of trouble before this expedition is over."

"I shall take it upon myself to see that the wheels are all properly lubricated," Tom said.

"And not just the hubs," Custer said. "The tie joints as well."

"Yes," Tom said.

Custer walked around to the other side of the wagon and pulled at the wheel on that side, too.

"I was a fool," he finally said, speaking so quietly that Tom could barely hear him.

"No, you weren't, Autie."

Custer laughed, a quiet, self-deprecating laugh. "Oh, yes, I was. I sat there in Blaine's office in Washington, and I let him convince me that he would be submitting my name for nomination for the president because he really believed I would be the best man for the job. Who was I fooling? How could I have been so naive as to think I could be president?"

"You would make a fine president, Autie," Tom assured him. "And you weren't being naive, you were being confident. Your problem is you are too honest a man, Autie. You had no idea that Blaine intended to use you for his own purposes."

"I can tell you that never again will I be such a fool," Autie said.

"Autie, I hope you aren't considering withdrawing from all political considerations," Tom said.

Custer looked at his brother and smiled. "Oh no, Tom," he said. "Quite the contrary. I shall be even more forceful in my political pursuits. But I shall do it all myself, and never again will I depend on someone else."

"That's the boy, Autie," Tom said proudly. "And I'll be with you."

"Tom, we start here, now," Autie said. "Have you seen General Terry's orders to me?"

"No," Tom said. "They are secret."

"I authorize you to read them," Autie said. He reached into his pocket and removed the orders and a small reading candle. He lit the candle and handed Tom the dispatch from General Terry:

*Lieutenant Col. Custer, Seventh U. S. Cavalry Colonel:*

*The Brigadier General Commanding directs that, as soon as your regiment can be made ready for the march, you will proceed up the Rosebud in pursuit of the Indians whose trail was discovered by Major Reno a few days before. It is, of course, impossible to give you any definite instructions in regard to this movement, and even if it were, the Department*

*Commander places too much confidence in your zeal, energy, and ability to impose upon you precise orders which might hamper your action. He will, however, indicate to you his own views of what your action should be, and he desires that you should conform to them unless there is sufficient reason for deviating from them.*

*He instructs you to proceed up the Rosebud until you ascertain definitely the direction in which the trail spoken of above leads. Should it be found—as it appears almost certain that it will be—to turn toward the Little Big Horn, you should continue southward, perhaps as far as the head-waters of the Tongue, and then turn toward the Little Bighorn, feeling constantly, to your left, so as to preclude the possibility of the escape of the Indians to the south or south-east by passing around your left flank. The column of Colonel Gibbon is now heading for the mouth of the Big Horn. As soon as it reaches that point, it will cross the Yellowstone and move up at least as far as the forks of the Big and Little Bighorns. Of course, its movements will be controlled by circumstances as they arise, but it is hoped that the Indians, if upon the Little Bighorn, will be outflanked by two columns so that their escape will be impossible.*

*The Department Commander desires that on your way up the Rosebud, you should thoroughly examine the upper part of Tulloch's Creek, and that you should send a scout through to Colonel Gibbon's column with the results of your examination. The lower part of this creek will be examined by a detachment from Colonel Gibbon's command. The supply steamer will be pushed up the Bighorn as far as the forks of the river are navigable, and the Department Commander, who will accompany Colonel Gibbon's column, desires that you report to him there not later than the expira-*

*tion of the time for which your troops are rationed, unless in the meantime you receive further orders.*

*Very respectfully,*

*Your obedient servant,*

*E. W. Smith, Captain 18th Inf. Act'ng Asst. Adjutant General.*

TOM FINISHED READING the orders and returned them to his brother. Custer put them back in his pocket, then blew out the candle.

"As you can see," Custer said. "General Terry practically gives me the authority to do whatever I wish."

"Not really, Autie," Tom disagreed. "He gives you his own views, and states that he desires you to conform with them."

"Unless I see sufficient reason to depart from them," Custer said. "And I see sufficient reason." Custer smiled. "Tom...when we do locate the Indians, we aren't sharing them with anybody."

"What do you mean?" Tom asked.

"I'll tell you what I mean. I mean, the Seventh is going to report to General Terry at the Bighorn, with news not that we found the Indians, but that we defeated them. From this moment on, Tom, we aren't on a scouting expedition, we are on a hunting expedition."

"I see," Tom said.

Custer got a faraway look in his eyes. "It will be a clear message to the Republican National Convention and to the American people," Custer said. "I may have missed out on the nomination this time, but I will get it in '80. Not only the nomination, Tom, but the election as well. And it all hinges on this operation."

"Then we must make certain that we find the Indians," Tom said.

"Oh, we'll find them all right," Custer said. "And when we pick up their trail, we won't wait for anyone. We will close with and kill them ourselves. In this battle, Tom, I shall do something which will make my name go down in the history books forever."

# CHAPTER TWENTY-FIVE

HARLEY AND LUKE DIDN'T SPEAK MUCH TO EMILY AFTER they captured her. It wasn't that they were feeling charitable, they simply wanted to put as much distance as possible between themselves and the dead Indian, in case any of his companions were lurking nearby.

Though now Emily rode instead of walked, it was, if anything, more difficult. Crazy Wolf at least had ridden at a slow enough pace to allow her to keep up on foot. But Harley and Luke rode fast and hard, and Emily, whose hands were tied behind her and her feet were tied with a rope that passed under the pony's belly, was most uncomfortable. She had to hold on with her knees lest she fall and be dragged by the animal, and before long, the strain made her legs ache deep in the bone.

By the time the sun began to set, she was lightheaded from fatigue and the gnawing hunger. At last, Luke raised a hand.

"We may as well stop here 'n sleep a spell," Luke said. "Like as not 'ny injun as may have come up on the dead injun is far away."

"Fine by me," Harley said. "And besides that, I'm tired. But we ain't stoppin' cause of her."

They pulled up near a stand of scrub pines. Luke dismounted first and cut her loose, but only enough for her to slide from the saddle. Her legs almost buckled under her as her cramped muscles protested.

"Go do what you have to do and then sit over yonder," Luke ordered, pointing toward a patch of grass under one of the pines. "And don't try getting' away."

"Thank you," she said, as she lowered herself slowly. "Could I have a drink of water?"

Luke tossed her a small, battered canteen. "Don't drink too much. That's all we got for a while."

She raised it, finding the water had a metallic taste. She drank because she had no choice. Then she moved away to take care of her needs.

When she returned, Harley was rummaging through his saddlebag.

"Why'd you give her that?"

"Cause she was thirsty," Luke said, as he found a place to lie down. "I've got to get some sleep, 'fore I fall over dead. You keep an eye on her and if she so much as blinks wrong, you cuff her, you hear."

Harley nodded. "And if she tries runnin'—"

"You see them welts she's got," Luke said. "If she takes off runnin', she'll get a hell of a lot worse than that."

Harley stepped closer, his gaze cold. "You hear what my partner said, do you? You try and run, and I'll put a hobble on you where you can't take two steps in front of you, and your ankles will be raw as a piece of steak." He turned away, but stopped to add, "And to top that off, you can go back to walkin' like you done for the Indian."

"I won't run," she said. Her voice was steady, but her pulse rang in her ears.

"That's right," Luke said. "You won't, because you know we'll find you. And if we have to come lookin'..." He let the rest hang in the air, letting her imagination do the work.

Harley dropped a strip of dried meat in the dirt at her feet. "Here, eat. Don't say we ain't been good to you."

Emily's stomach churned. She took the meat without looking at either of them or at it. And she devoured it much like a ravenous dog would do, but she knew she had to. If there was any chance to escape, she had to have some sustenance.

Harley moved a short distance away and built a small fire, and Luke soon joined him beside it. She knew they were talking, but their voices were so low, she couldn't hear what they were saying. More than once, she caught them looking toward her. Whether they were planning something to do with her or just making sure she knew she was being watched, she couldn't tell, but the effect was the same. Her fear of Crazy Wolf had been immediate, but the fear she felt now was worse. The uncertainty of where they would take her, or what they would do to her, would be there as long as she was with these two cold-blooded monsters.

After a while, Luke stretched out beneath a pine, pulling his hat over his eyes. Harley propped himself against a saddle, still keeping her in his line of sight. Eventually, his head began to nod. Emily watched him, scarcely breathing.

Minutes passed. His breathing deepened. Luke was already snoring softly.

Emily's heart hammered. This might be her only

chance. She shifted slowly, every movement deliberate. Neither man stirred.

She rose to her feet and crept toward the horses, pausing once when Harley gave a low grunt and rolled to his side. When he didn't wake, she moved again, reaching the nearest horse. She untied it as quietly as she could, then led it away, putting distance between herself and the camp before daring to mount.

The moment she was on its back, she nudged the horse forward, keeping to a steady, quiet pace until the darkness swallowed her from sight.

She had escaped.

———

The steamer Far West was playing a very important part in Custer's expedition. It had pushed all the way up the Yellowstone, then up the Bighorn to the confluence of the Bighorn and the Little Bighorn, where it unloaded fresh supplies and mail for the troops in the field. Couriers from Custer's regiment brought mail to the Far West and hurried the incoming mail back to the soldiers.

The waiting wives in the fort were eager for word from their husbands, but their husbands in the field were no less desirous for word from home, talk of the daily routine, assurances of a stable domesticity.

Custer received his first letter from Libbie in the field and read it aloud to Tom, who had received no mail of his own.

"The servants are doing very well, and we are raising chickens," Custer read.

"Oh, what I wouldn't give to have a plate of Libbie's fried chicken right now," Tom said.

"Now, do you want me to read this or not?" Custer asked.

"Yes, yes, go on," Tom said.

Custer cleared his throat and continued.

"We have forty-three chickens. And we have so many cats about the garrison that our rat problem has disappeared. The weather is very hot, but the nights are cool. The lights about the hills and valleys are exquisite. The river now is too high for sandbars to be seen.

"About a hundred men with John Stevenson in command have gone to the Black Hills. Nearly twenty-five teams have passed by.

"Carter has returned and is chief trumpeter. He really sounds the calls beautifully. But his drawn-out notes make me heartsick. I do not wish to be reminded of the cavalry."

After Custer finished the letter, he handed it to Tom, who read it to himself. Then the two men sat quietly for a moment, staring into the campfire, which popped and snapped before them. Around them were over a hundred campfires. It was an absolute certainty that every Indian in the territory knew their whereabouts. But a hundred campfires could mean ten thousand men, and they knew that they were perfectly safe from any surprise Indian attack.

Off in the distance, someone began singing in a rich, clear voice, and soon he was joined by a few others until the valley rang with song.

Boston and little Autie were hopping around from campfire to campfire. Boston was only a couple of years older than Autie, but he was Autie's uncle and wore that position of authority as surely as if it were a military rank. In general, though, the boys got along well together and were much in demand by the soldiers who couldn't read or write, to read messages from their families back home and write letters for them.

Boston finally managed to settle down to write his own letter home to his mother back in Ohio.

My darling Mother,

The mail leaves tomorrow. I have no news to write. I am feeling first rate. Armstrong takes the whole command and starts up the Sweet Briar on an Indian trail with the full hope and belief of overhauling them, which I think he probably will with a little hard riding. They will be much entertained.

I hope to catch one or two Indian ponies with a buffalo robe for Nev, but he must not be disappointed if I don't. Judging by the number of lodges counted by scouts who saw the trail, there are something like eight hundred Indians and probably more. But be the number great or small, I hope I can truthfully say when I get back that one or more were sent to the Happy Hunting Grounds.

Now don't give yourself any trouble, as all will be well. I must write Maggie and Libbie, for if the mail should reach

LINCOLN WITHOUT A LETTER FROM ME, THERE
WILL CERTAINLY BE TROUBLE IN THE CAMP.

AUTIE REED IS GOING. HE WILL STAND THE
TRIP FIRST RATE. HE HAS DONE NICELY AND IS
ENJOYING IT. THE OFFICERS ALL LIKE HIM VERY
MUCH. HE WILL SLEEP WITH ME IN MY SMALL
TENT. TELL ANN HE IS STANDING THE TRIP
NICELY AND HAS NOT BEEN SICK FOR EVEN A DAY.

ARMSTRONG, TOM, AND I PULLED DOWN AN
INDIAN GRAVE THE OTHER DAY. AUTIE REED GOT
THE BOW WITH SIX ARROWS AND A NICE PAIR
OF MOCCASINS WHICH HE INTENDS ON TAKING
HOME.

GOODBYE, MY DARLING MOTHER. THIS WILL
PROBABLY BE THE LAST LETTER YOU WILL GET
TILL WE REACH LINCOLN. WE LEAVE IN THE
MORNING WITH SIXTEEN DAYS' RATIONS WITH
PACK MULES.

LOVE, BOSTON

Boston finished his letter and dropped it in an envelope, then carried it over to deposit it in the mail sack.
He saw Tom standing over by a rock, some distance
from everyone else, and he walked over to talk to him.

"Hello, Tom," he said. "Thinking about all the
Indians we are going to kill?"

"Bos, I think you and Autie should return with the
dispatches tomorrow," Tom said.

"What? Whatever makes you say such a thing?"

"I just don't think what's coming up will be good for
civilians, that's all."

"We aren't just civilians, Tom, we're family," Boston said. "Besides, Kellogg is going, and he's a civilian."

"Kellogg is a newspaper man," Tom said. "This is his job. But it isn't your job, and you don't have to go. Besides, being family has nothing to do with it, except maybe make me more anxious for your safety."

"Tom, are you afraid?" Boston asked, awed by the possibility. "I've never known you to be afraid."

"There are only two kinds of people who are never afraid," Tom said. "Fools and those who want to die."

"Then you are afraid," Boston said.

"No," Tom finally replied quietly. "I'm not afraid."

Boston gave a small laugh. "You said only fools and those who want to die aren't afraid. So which are you?" he teased.

"I'm not a fool," Tom said quietly.

# CHAPTER TWENTY-SIX

EMILY RODE AS FAST AND AS HARD AS SHE COULD. THOUGH she was so exhausted that she could scarcely stay on the horse, she pushed on, driven by the fear of what lay behind her. Finally, she topped a ridge, then stopped, gasping. For there, spread out in the valley below her, was the magnificent sight of a bivouacked army.

With a small cry of joy, Emily rode down the hill toward the encamped army, calling out to them. She was saved!

Emily was spotted by one of the outlying pickets, who notified his sergeant, who notified his lieutenant, so that by the time Emily reached them, nearly a dozen soldiers had turned out to meet her.

"Oh, thank God," she said, almost falling from the horse when she reached them. "You don't know how happy I am to see you."

"Who are you, ma'am, and what are you doing out here?" the lieutenant asked.

"My name is Emily Thomson."

"Emily Thomson? I'm sorry, ma'am, but that name doesn't mean anything to me, I'm afraid."

"You haven't heard of me?" Emily questioned. "Well, no matter. Take me to General Custer. He knows me."

"Ma'am, this is Colonel Gibbon's column. Custer is a long way from here. But General Terry is with us, if you'd like to see him."

"General Terry? Yes. Is there a Colonel Gray on his staff?" Emily asked, remembering the officer she and her father had met on the train nearly a year ago. Was it less than a year? It seemed decades ago.

"Yes," the Lieutenant said. "Come with me."

Emily followed the young officer, feeling the questioning stares of the soldiers.

"Bet she was an injun squaw," she heard one soldier say.

"She should'a had the decency to shoot herself," another said.

Emily closed her eyes and ears to the soldiers as she followed the lieutenant. Finally, they reached a tent, much larger than the others and with a flag flying out front. The two soldiers posted outside came to attention and brought their weapons up as the lieutenant and Emily approached.

"Lieutenant Kent to see Colonel Gray," the lieutenant said.

One of the soldiers went inside the tent, and a moment later Colonel Gray appeared in the door flap, a puzzled expression on his face.

"Colonel Gray, do you remember me?" Emily asked.

"No," Colonel Gray said. "No, I'm sorry, miss, but I don't."

"I'm Emily Thomson. You met my father and me on the train last summer."

"My God, yes, of course," Colonel Gray said. "Miss Thomson, what has happened?"

"I...my father...he was killed, and I was..." Suddenly, Emily felt so dizzy that she was afraid she would faint, and she put her hand to her forehead. "Forgive me," she said. "I am so tired and hungry that..."

"No, you must forgive me, Miss Thomson," Colonel Gray said. "I should have offered you food and rest before I began to question you. Lieutenant, see to it that Miss Thomson is fed at once. Also, see the quartermaster. I believe there are some dresses in his stock that are to be used as trading material with cooperative Indians. Select one for Miss Thomson."

"A new dress?" Emily said, looking at the tattered rags she was wearing. "As dirty as I am..."

"Sergeant, rig up a screen down by the river and post guards to see to the lady's privacy. Miss Thomson, if you wish, you may take a bath and change clothes while your meal is being prepared."

"Oh, thank you," Emily said. "You have no idea how grateful I am to you."

"As soon as you've cleaned up and eaten, we shall have our talk," Colonel Gray offered.

Soon Emily was bathing in the cool, bracing river. She used soap and even sand to scrub herself pink-clean. And when she emerged from behind the privacy screen a bit later, clean and fresh, dressed in a new if not stylish dress, she felt one hundred times better.

A small camp table and chair had been brought up for her, and she was invited to sit down to eat. The simple fare of beef stew and potatoes was as delicious as any meal she had ever eaten in the finest restaurant in New York.

After the meal, though, everything caught up with her, and she nearly passed out from exhaustion. Colonel Gray tried to question her, but after a few attempts, he realized how tired she was and invited her to lie down on his cot to sleep.

"Colonel, as tired as that girl is, she'll sleep right through until after we pull out," Emily heard one of the officers say.

"No matter," Colonel Gray said. "I can question her back on the post after this is all over. I say let her get all the sleep she can get."

"But what will we do with her if we have to leave before she wakes up?"

"Wright and Hill will be back from their scout by then. We'll leave her with them. They can take her back into the fort. I'll just talk to her when this expedition is over, that's all."

"Yes, sir," the officer said.

Their conversation diminished to a buzz, then grew silent altogether as Emily fell deeper and deeper into sleep.

———

JACOB HAD BEEN WATCHING the encampment for the last two days now. He thought he had it figured out, but he wanted to watch a bit longer, just to be sure. If he was right, this army would sweep up toward the Indians with Sitting Bull, while Custer's army swept down from the north. Sitting Bull and the others would be trapped in the middle.

Sitting Bull had prohibited Jacob from participating in the war that was to come, but he couldn't just stand by while the trap was being closed, either. If the Army was successful, a lot of people would die, people who were his friends and very nearly his family. He wouldn't let the trap be sprung.

Jacob watched for the rest of the day. If he was right, the army would leave by nightfall, starting in a generally northern direction. Then he would ride quickly to Sitting Bull and tell him what he had seen.

Jacob knew that he would be riding hard tonight, so he scratched himself a place out of the side of the gulley, crawled in, and went to sleep. It would be dark when he woke up, and if they had left while he was still asleep, it would be easy enough to follow them, for the number of horses the army had was astounding. That many horses would nearly leave a road paved in horse dung. It would be simple to follow, night or day.

———

IT WAS dark and quiet when Emily woke up. She lay in bed for a moment but could hear nothing, neither voices nor sounds of men at work. She swung her legs over the side of the cot and looked around the dark tent for a moment. Finally, she stood up and walked to the tent flap to look outside. She saw a campfire with a coffee pot suspended over the flames. Two men were squatting by the fire, staring into the flames. Then Emily remembered hearing Colonel Gray say that Wright and Hill, the two scouts who were out at the time, would be back to take her home.

"Well, you must be Wright and Hill," Emily said.

"Some folks calls us that," one man answered. The grin he gave her stopped her cold. "Others just call us Luke and Harley."

Emily gasped. It was the same two White men who had *saved* her from Crazy Wolf only to put her in more peril.

"No!" she screamed.

Luke stood up and started toward her.

Emily was rested and fed, and finding a strength in her legs she had not had before, she ran from Luke.

"Come back here, damn you!" Luke sputtered, starting after her.

Harley laughed at them. "Go get 'er, Luke," he called.

"Well, help me, damn it. Don't just stand there," Luke called back.

Harley took a swallow of whiskey, not moving from his spot. "I'll wait here for you to bring 'er back."

Emily looked back over her shoulder and saw that Luke was gaining on her. From somewhere, she summoned an extra burst of energy and started up the hill just behind the campsite.

"Hey, girl," Luke called to her. "You'll get lost in the dark, and the Injuns'll get you. Come on back. Ol' Luke'll be nice to you."

Emily ran pell-mell through the dark, her breath coming as rasping gasps in her throat. Bushes and low-lying scrub trees formed barriers, and the limbs seemed to grab for her. Finally, one of them tripped her, and she pitched headfirst into the briars.

"Where'd you go, girl?" Luke called. He had seen her fall, but it was so dark that he couldn't see her in the bushes on the ground. He was walking slowly, moving the bushes aside with his hand, squinting in the moonlight. "Come on, girl," he called again.

Emily began crawling through the bushes and stepped on a dry twig, which snapped loudly.

"Ahh, trying to sneak away, are you?" Luke said. "Well, not to worry, little girl. I'll find you."

Emily crawled away until she felt she had put enough distance between them. She darted into a patch of shadow, meaning to circle around and lose him, but instead she collided with a solid shape.

"No!" she screamed.

"Emily...it's me, Jacob!"

Emily, who had closed her eyes tightly the moment she felt the arms grab her, now opened them. She saw Jacob standing there in the moonlight, and she collapsed against his chest, giving herself over to his strong, protecting arms.

"Oh, Jacob," she said. "Jacob, thank God it's you."

"Well, well, well. Now, ain't this just fine?" Luke's voice was right behind Emily. She gasped and looked around. He was standing no more than ten feet from them, smiling the same evil smile.

"Yes, sir, this is really fine," Luke went on. "First off, I'm gonna kill me a traitor, 'n collect the reward. Then I'm gonna get me a woman."

It was only then that Emily saw Luke's knife. He was holding it out in front of him and tested the point with his finger.

"If you got any heathen gods to pray to, injun lover, you'd best get 'em said. 'Cause I aim to gut cut you."

Jacob pushed Emily around behind him, then quickly removed his buckskin shirt and wrapped it around his left forearm. He held his arm, padded with his shirt, crooked in front of him, and reached for the knife he carried in his waistband. Then he assumed a crouching stance similar to Luke's, right arm out, knife blade moving back and forth slowly and hypnotically.

It was obvious that the fight would not last long. Both men were going for a quick kill.

Luke danced in, light on his feet for a heavy man, and raised his left hand toward Jacob's face. He feinted with his right, the knife hand, and when Jacob raised his left arm to block, Luke brought his knife hand back down so fast it was a blur and went in under Jacob's arm.

The knife seared Jacob's flesh like a branding iron along his ribs and opened a long gash in the tight ridges of muscle. Blood began to spill down his side and over the top of his breeches. Jacob brought his left hand down sharply, almost by reflex, and knocked away the knife, which Luke was now holding with an air of careless confidence. He jabbed quickly with his right hand, sending his knife into Luke's diaphragm, just under the ribs.

They stood that way for a few moments, Jacob twisting the blade in the wound and struggling to stay on his feet in spite of the pain burning across his ribs. Finally, Luke began to collapse, expelling a long, life-surrendering sigh. Jacob turned the knife, blade edge up, letting Luke's body tear itself off by its own weight. When Luke hit the ground, he flopped once or twice, like a mortally wounded buffalo, then lay still.

Jacob staggered back, breathing heavily. The fight had not been physically exhausting, and it was over too fast. But it had totally drained him emotionally. He looked into Luke's face. The eyes of the fallen scout were open and unseeing, still registering surprise. He had not had time to know fear or to feel much pain.

Jacob felt along the cut in his side and tried to estimate its severity. He held his fingers up and examined the blood in the moonlight.

"Oh, Jacob, you're hurt!" Emily said.

"Come on," Jacob answered. "We have to get out of here. I don't want to fight the other one too."

Jacob pulled himself onto his pony, then reached a hand to her. Once she was settled behind him, he said only, "We ride to the village," and turned the horse into the darkness.

# CHAPTER TWENTY-SEVEN

THE NIGHT PASSED SLOWLY, ALMOST RELUCTANTLY, FROM the earth. When the darkness lifted, the slanting bars of morning sunlight revealed an army stretched out in a line nearly two miles long. The Army was divided into three mobile units and one supply train, and as they moved, each mobile unit was smaller and less impressive than had been the sum of all its parts.

All that day, Custer continued on the trail of the Indians. Throughout the day, many Indian camping places were passed. Every bend of the stream bore traces of a camp, and the Indian ponies had nipped almost every blade of grass. The ground was strewn with broken bones and cuttings from buffalo hides, and the carcasses of recently killed buffalo. One camp-site was much larger than the others, while still standing was the framework of a large sun dance lodge.

"Let's hold up the column," Custer said, raising his hand. The command was passed along the line of march, and the column halted. Soldiers turned in their saddles and looked over the site. None of them had ever seen a campsite so large.

"General, I don't like the looks of this," Captain Keough said. He took off his hat and wiped the sweat from his forehead.

Custer took a drink of water from his canteen and handed it over to Tom.

"What don't you like about it?" Custer asked, smiling broadly.

"Look at this place," Keough said. He took in the campsite with a wave of his arm. "My God, General, I'll bet there were ten thousand Indians here."

"You worry too much, Keough," Custer said. "This is nothing but a campsite that has been used over and over again, that's all. I don't think there are any more than eight hundred warriors ahead of us."

"There are ten times that many," Keough said. "General, we'd better wait until we link up with Terry's column."

Custer fixed a hard look at Captain Keough. "Keough, if we join Terry's column, then under whose command would the operation take place?"

"Why, as Terry is senior, it would be under his command," Keough said.

"That's right," Custer said. "He would depend on the Seventh Cavalry to haul his ashes out of the fire, but he and his men would get credit for the victory. No, sir, I don't intend to hand him such a prize. We will press on, Captain."

"Then would you at least abandon your plan to separate Reno and Benteen?" Keough asked. "I feel it would be unwise to divide our forces in the face of such numbers."

Custer laughed. "Don't worry about it, Keough. When the Indians see three disciplined units attacking from three different directions, they will become so demoralized that we can pick them off like shooting ducks in a barrel. I've enjoyed over a decade of successful campaigns, and I know what I'm talking about."

"Yes, sir," Keough said.

"General," one of the sergeants called from the door of the large sun lodge. "General, maybe you ought to come see this, sir."

Custer swung down from his horse. "Come along, Tom," he said.

Tom followed his brother to the lodge door. Inside, hanging from one of the lodgepoles, were two fresh scalps, obviously taken from White men.

"Who are they, General?" the sergeant asked.

"I'm afraid I don't recognize the gentlemen," Custer said.

"Here's a button on the floor," Tom said. He picked it up. "It's from the Second Cavalry."

"Brisbin's command," Custer said. He made a fist of his hand. "Good Lord, Tom, you don't suppose Brisbin is ahead of us, do you?"

"I don't see how he could be, Autie," Tom answered. "We've certainly seen no sign. These men may have been scouts."

"Or deserters," Custer said.

Several others came into the lodge to look around, including Bloody Knife, one of the Indian scouts who was riding with Custer's column.

"The Sioux had a big ceremony here," Bloody Knife said. "Look."

The scout pointed to a drawing in the sand. A line had been drawn with soldiers on one side and Indians on the other. Dead men were drawn with their heads pointed toward the Indians, which Bloody Knife said meant that all the soldiers would be killed.

Custer laughed. "That is what their medicine says, is it?"

"Look at this," Tom called. "What does this mean?" He pointed to a pile of stones, with the skull of a buffalo bull on one side and the skull of a buffalo cow on the other. A pole was leaning toward the cow skull.

"This says that when the Sioux are overtaken, they will fight like a buffalo bull, and the soldiers will run from them like women."

"Well, we shall see about that," Custer said.

Boston and young Autie Reed were among the others standing in the lodge.

"Armstrong, may Autie and I have these skulls as souvenirs?" Boston asked.

"Certainly," Custer said.

"Thank you," Boston replied. "Come Autie, these will make wonderful souvenirs," he said as he gathered them in.

Custer walked back outside.

"Tom, pass the word that we will rest for a couple of hours," Custer said. "Tell the men to make coffee if they want to. Then we'll press on."

"Very well," Tom said.

While Tom was relaying the message to the others, Custer walked to the edge of the campsite and looked out toward the valley that stretched before him. The trail was fresh, and the whole valley was so scratched up by thousands of trailing lodgepoles that it looked like a poorly plowed field. It was apparent that the quarry was not far ahead.

# CHAPTER TWENTY-EIGHT

Emily heard a sound and sat up quickly. Jacob was smiling at her.

"I'm sorry if I woke you," he said. A trout, tied to a green sapling and suspended across forked poles, was sizzling over a fire. "I'm just cooking breakfast."

"Jacob, the cut on your side," Emily said. "How is it?"

Jacob looked down at the wound, which he had packed with moss.

"The pain is gone," Jacob said. "The moss will keep it from bleeding more."

Emily stood up and looked around. It had been dark when they arrived here during the night. Jacob had constructed a rude shelter for them, and Emily had gone to sleep almost as soon as her head hit the ground. But now, in the light of day, she saw that there was much to admire about their campsite.

It was located in a glen of trees near a meandering stream. The valley before them was green with grass and dotted with wild flowers. Thousands of yellow and pink and red flowers dotted the plains. The wind softly whispering through the trees, the bubbling of the brook, and the delicate song of the birds surrounded them with music.

"This is like the Garden of Eden," Emily said.

"Garden of Eden?" Jacob asked. "I've heard of that somewhere."

Emily laughed. "Jacob, you are teasing. Don't you know what the Garden of Eden is?"

"No," Jacob admitted.

"It's from the Bible. It is the place where Adam and Eve lived."

"Oh, yes," Jacob said. "I think the White man's God is very angry with me because I took up the Indian's ways."

"He isn't just the White man's God," Emily said. "He is the God of all men. And He wouldn't be angry with you for taking up the ways of the Indian, for the Indians are His children just as is everyone else."

"Is the Garden of Eden a pretty place?" Jacob asked.

"It is beautiful," Emily said. "But in truth, I do not see how it could be more lovely than this place."

"Here," Jacob said, handing a goatskin to Emily and pointing to the stream. "Get us some water."

Emily walked down to the stream to fill the goatskin with water, and by the time she returned, Jacob had taken the trout off the fire and filleted it for them. After breakfast, Emily asked Jacob to stretch out on the ground and remove the moss.

"Why?"

"I'm going to clean the wound," she said. "Then I'll put fresh moss on."

Jacob did as she instructed, and Emily gingerly

pulled the old moss off. She used the water from the goatskin to loosen the dried blood around the wound.

"It isn't too bad," she said, examining the cleansed wound. "If you don't break it open again."

"Shall we put more moss on it?" Jacob asked.

"Not yet," Emily said. "I'm sure the air and the sun is good for it. Wait for a bit. We can stay here, can't we?"

"Yes," Jacob said. "We can wait here as long as we need to."

Emily lay down beside Jacob and put her hands behind her head, then looked up at the sky.

"It is so peaceful here," she said. "I wish we could stay here forever."

"It won't be peaceful for long," Jacob said. "There is going to be a great battle."

"I know," Emily said. She reached over and took Jacob's hand in hers. "I am glad you are not going to be in it."

"Sitting Bull will not let me fight in the battle," Jacob said. "He has told me that I am White."

Emily raised up on one elbow and looked down at Jacob. "You *are* White," she said.

Jacob sighed. "I know. I married Aiana, and I was a good husband to her while she lived. But when she died...something changed. It was not good to be an Indian anymore. And when Crazy Wolf killed Flynn and the other soldiers who were helping the Indians... my heart grew very hard against the Indians."

"Crazy Wolf bragged to me many times how he killed Sergeant Flynn and the others," Emily said. "And he bragged how he would kill you."

"Crazy Wolf was like his name," Jacob said. "He was crazy. I was sorry for him."

"I wasn't sorry for him," Emily said, shivering.

"I am sorry," Jacob said. He looked at her with eyes full of compassion. "I know he killed your father and held you captive. It was evil, and I came to find him, to kill him for it. But when I found him, he was already dead, and I saw a sign saying White men had saved you."

"Saved me?" Emily's tone was bitter. "Jacob, one of the men who *saved* me was the man you killed. They were beasts. They were worse than Crazy Wolf."

Jacob put his arms around her. "Then I am glad I killed him."

For a long while they sat in silence, drawing strength from each other. Emily felt the same deep closeness she had felt for Jacob from the beginning, not born of desire, but of trust and shared hardship.

Jacob spoke at last. "It is not the way of Indian men to speak of love to their women. And yet, I feel I must tell you that I have a great love for you."

"I'm glad you can say that," Emily said. "For I have a great love for you as well."

Jacob sighed and lay down beside her. "I don't know what we can do," he said.

"We can get married," Emily said easily.

"No. As long as Custer is alive, I will always be a wanted man. Hunted by the Whites...shunned by the Indians. I am a man without a place in life."

Emily laughed.

"Why do you think that is funny?" Jacob asked.

"Jacob, the world is bigger than this. Do you think Custer would chase you all the way to New York? Or Boston? Or Paris?"

"Perhaps not," Jacob said. "But can I hunt buffalo in

New York? Can I fish in Boston? Can I steal ponies in Paris? I know only the things an Indian knows. I do not know how to live as a White man."

"I'll teach you," Emily said.

This time it was Jacob's turn to laugh.

"You think I can't teach you?" Emily challenged. "You learned to be an Indian, didn't you?"

"Well, yes."

"Then you can learn to be a White man again. And it will be easier for you, because you are white, and things you may have forgotten, will come back to you."

"All right," Jacob said. "I will let you teach me the ways of a White man. And when I have learned, I want to go to Washington."

"Why?"

"I want to work for the president, to help the Indians."

Emily smiled. "You know, Jacob, you just might do it."

# CHAPTER TWENTY-NINE

IT WAS A DIFFICULT AND TIRING MARCH, AS CUSTER, after halting only long enough for supper, pushed his troops on through the night. They moved west, alongside Davis Creek, more than twenty miles north of where General Terry expected them to be.

No lights were permitted during the night march, and the only way the troops in the rear had of knowing which direction to take was by the dust cloud raised by those ahead. If they could not smell dust, they knew they were off the trail. Also, the men in the rear of the troop pounded their tin cups on their saddle horns to guide the troop following them.

When the first faint streaks of dawn broke in the east, the scouts told Custer that they could not possibly hope to cross the valley before daybreak, and they couldn't cross after daylight without being discovered by the Sioux.

"I don't want the Sioux to see us yet," Custer said. "I don't want them to get away."

"General, do not fear that the Indians will get away,"

Bloody Knife told him. "I think when you find the village, you will find all the Indians you want."

"How many?" Custer asked excitedly.

"Maybe three thousand."

"Three thousand?" Keough asked. He looked at Custer. "General, is he talking about three thousand warriors?"

"Oh, I scarcely think we will be that lucky," Custer said with a chuckle.

"Autie, perhaps we should stop here until dawn," Tom suggested.

"Yes, maybe you are right," Custer said. "Give the orders."

The troops concealed themselves in a wooded ravine situated between two high ridges. Some of the mules were unpacked and some troopers unsaddled, although most simply dropped down with the reins over their arms and went to sleep.

The campsite they chose was a poor one. There was very little grass for the horses, and the water was so alkaline that the horses refused to drink it. Even when the water was boiled and made into coffee, it was unpalatable.

Lieutenant Varnum, who had gone ahead with the scouts, returned at daybreak as Custer was eating his breakfast.

"Sit, Lieutenant, and tell me what you have seen," Custer said.

Varnum wore a shocked expression on his face—he walked over and took a long drink from a whiskey bottle protruding from a nearby knapsack.

"What is it, Varnum?"

"General," Varnum said, "the entire valley on the

other side of Crow's Nest is white with tipis. There are so damn many campfires that the smoke covers the entire valley. There are more hostiles ahead than there are bullets in all the belts of all the soldiers."

Custer smiled. "Well, then, I guess we are in for the fight of our life, gentlemen. But I guess we'll get through them in one day."

"Shall we break camp, Autie?" Tom asked.

"Let's go," Custer said, and without finishing his breakfast, he mounted his horse and rode bareback around the camp, shouting orders to his officers.

By eight-thirty, the command was ready, and they moved out. The men were in high spirits, and they laughed and bantered back and forth. The sun was clear and bright, and it was obvious that they were in for an extremely hot day.

Custer had not slept well, despite his exhaustion, because the mosquitoes had kept him awake. In his diary the evening before, he wrote that he would rather face ten thousand Sioux than ten mosquitoes. And now, as he rode in the saddle, he, like his men, hung on the edge of total exhaustion.

———

EMILY AND JACOB, after two days on the trail, rode down from the ridge and saw preparations being made by the Indians in the village below to leave their encampment. He hurried his pony on and arrived on the scene just as the equipment was being loaded onto a lodgepole travois.

"White Ghost," he said, spotting the old man. "It is good to see you."

"It is good to see you as well," White Ghost replied. "I see you have found woman who makes pictures. That is good."

"White Ghost, what is happening here?" Jacob asked. "Where is everyone going?"

"Long Hair has been seen," White Ghost said. "He is very near to here, and I think soon there will be a great battle. In the way of the sunset, there is a great village. Some say it is a village as large as the great cities of the White men. We are going there, for no soldiers would have the courage to attack such a large village."

"Custer might," Jacob said. "He is a very brave man."

"Yes, this I know," White Ghost said. "But if he attacks us there, it is he and the soldiers who will be killed. If he attacks us here, it is only Indians who will be killed. You must come with us."

"Sitting Bull has forbidden me to fight," Jacob said.

"All right, you will not fight. But if you stay here the soldiers will find you and they will kill you."

"You are right," Jacob said. "White Ghost, I need another pony for Emily."

"I will get one for you," White Ghost said, and started out on his task.

"Jacob, do you really think Custer will attack a village as large as the one White Ghost describes?" Emily asked.

"You know Custer better than I do," Jacob said. "What do you think?"

Emily sighed. "I think he will do it."

"He is a brave man," Jacob said. "But he is also a very, very foolish man."

"Here is a good pony for you," White Ghost said, returning a few moments later. "Also, a blanket and a buckskin dress. You will be safer dressed in the Indian way."

"He's right," Jacob said.

Emily looked around and noticed that all the tipis had been taken down. She gave a small laugh. "Where will I change?" she asked.

"Change here," White Ghost said. "I will watch."

Emily looked at White Ghost with a shocked expression. "What?" she asked.

"It will be good to watch," White Ghost said in perfect innocence, totally oblivious to Emily's reaction.

"Jacob, is he serious?" she asked.

Jacob laughed. "Yes," he said. "It is common for Indian women to bathe or change clothes in the open. And if she is a pretty woman, it is common for the men and boys to watch."

"I can't do that," Emily protested.

"You must do it," Jacob said. "Emily, don't worry. No one will harm you. No one will even touch you. And if you do, you will be accepted as one of them."

Emily sighed. "Then I suppose I must do it," she said. And gathering her courage, she began slipping out of her dress.

Soon, Emily, dressed as the others, was able to lose herself in the crowd of people milling about, so that from a distance, except for her hair coloring, no one would be able to tell that she was a White woman.

The camp moved out, and Jacob and Emily rode in the front with White Ghost, who was the chief of this camp. On the distant horizon, they could see a great dust cloud rising, and they knew that Custer was near.

———

CUSTER'S SCOUTS told him of the moving camp, and fearing that the Indians were going to get away, the general ordered Major Reno to report to him.

Reno's command was trailing at the rear of the column, so he had to ride hard to catch up. Finally, with his horse lathered from the exertion, he rode up to Custer.

"Marcus," Custer said. "The Indians are trying to get away. Take your three companies and cross the river to engage them."

"I'm to engage them with only three companies, General?" Reno replied.

"Yes," Custer said. "Engage them, then charge right through. I will support you with the rest of the command."

"Very good, sir," Reno said.

"Tom," Custer called, as the major rode off. "Send word to Benteen to attack in the center. We'll go down to the other end of the village and drive the hostiles back this way. Lt. Varnum, take Bloody Knife and join with Major Reno. We've got them cold now. There's no way they can escape."

Reno overheard the exchange between the general and his brother as he rode back to his battalion to execute his orders.

"What did the general want?" asked Captain French, the senior captain in Reno's battalion, when Reno returned.

"He wants us to cross the river here," Reno said. "We are to attack with vigor, and he will provide us with support."

"I don't like the idea of splitting our forces in the face of such superior numbers," Captain French said.

"I don't either," Reno said. "But Custer is the great Indian fighter. I can only hope that he knows what he is about."

"Well, you know the old cavalry axiom, Major: 'Ours is not to question why, ours is but to do or die.'"

"Somehow at this point, I don't find that a very comforting thought," Reno said. He pulled a whiskey flask from his saddle bag and drank deeply, offered a swallow to Captain French, who refused, then recorked it and put it back in his bag. "Prepare the troops for the advance," he said.

"Yes, sir," French replied, and passed the word to the others.

The men, excited by the prospect of imminent battle, shouted and cheered as the battalion broke off from the rest of the column and started toward the river.

"Knock off that noise!" Reno ordered. "We are soldiers, not savages!"

"Major, it's good to let the men yell," Captain French said. "It lets them get rid of some of their tension."

"The soldiers of my command will behave as soldiers," Reno said.

The column crossed the river, sending sheets of silver water from the hooves of their horses. On the other side, they formed into a line of skirmishers and started toward the Indian village.

"Forward at a gallop, men!" Reno called, and the battalion swept across the plain to the thunder of hooves.

Reno fully expected the Indians to retreat, but surprisingly, they stood their ground. Then, even more surprisingly, those on horseback started charging toward the soldiers.

"My God, they are attacking!" Reno said.

"No, Major, we are attacking. They are just coming to meet us," French replied.

"That gulley up there," Reno said, pointing to a nearby ditch about three feet deep and ten feet wide. "We'll dismount and take cover there!"

"Dismount?" French asked in disbelief. "Major, we can't dismount! If we do, Custer's forces will really be divided!"

"I am in command here, Captain French!" Reno said. "I can't worry about Custer's forces, I have my own men to worry about. Dismount!" he yelled. "Take cover in that ditch!"

As yet, few shots had been fired, but when the Indians saw that Reno had checked his charge, the few who had feinted toward him to fight a rear-guard action, suddenly took heart and began firing in earnest.

"Return fire!" Reno shouted, and a ripple of gunfire exploded along the ravine as the soldiers began firing.

"Major, we've got to get the men mounted," French insisted. "We can't fight here."

"This is a good defensive position," Reno insisted. "This is a very good place to fight."

"But we are supposed to be on the offense," French said.

"What do you want from me?" Reno yelled desperately. "Look out there! There are thousands of Indians in front of us! Where is Custer? He was supposed to support us!"

"Major, didn't you say he was going to hit them from the other side? We've got to keep moving or the Indians can crush us one at a time!"

An arrow stuck into the ground just beside Reno, and he looked at it with a shocked expression.

"We can't stay here," he said. "They can drop their arrows right down on top of us. We've got to get back into the trees."

By now, the soldiers were firing furiously and had nearly checked the Indians' advance.

"Major, look," French said. "The Indians are beginning to pull back. Come on, let's charge them. We can yet link with Custer."

"No. It's a trick. Move back to the woods," he called. "Move back to the woods!"

Reno started back to the woods, and the soldiers climbed out of the gulley and followed him.

"French, what the hell is going on?" Lieutenant Varnum called. Custer had sent him to Reno as a liaison officer. "Doesn't Reno know the general expects him to attack?"

"He is attacking," French said dryly. "He's attacking the woodline."

With the realization that the soldiers were leaving, the Indians pressed their advantage, and a whole flight of arrows whistled down toward the two officers, who now found themselves virtually alone in the gulley.

"We'd better get out of here!" French said. He and Lieutenant Varnum scrambled up the opposite side of the gulley and ran like deer toward the tree line. Arrows and bullets kicked up the dust around them, but miraculously, they weren't hit.

The soldiers, having taken a position in the treeline, opened fire at the Indians and once again had them nearly in check. French and Varnum tried again to convince Reno to rally the men and charge the village.

"You are asking me to lead my men into a slaughter pit," he said. "I simply won't do it!"

"Major, you don't know what you are doing," French insisted. "You are just giving this battle to the Indians! You don't understand the Indian mind."

"I don't, do I?" Reno said. "Bloody Knife! Bloody Knife, come here at once!"

Bloody Knife, who had come to Reno with Varnum, hurried toward the commander.

"We'll just see about the Indian mind," Reno said. "Bloody Knife is an Indian. I'll get his opinion."

Bloody Knife joined them and stood before Reno.

"Bloody Knife, these *gentlemen* are advising me to charge the enemy. They say I don't understand the Indian mind. What do you think?"

Bloody Knife opened his mouth to speak, but at that very moment, his head nearly exploded as a bullet crashed into it. Blood and warm, gelatinous brain matter gushed out of the wound and splashed onto Reno's face.

"Oh...oh...oh my God!" Reno said. He backed away, horror-struck, holding his hands out in front of him as if afraid that Bloody Knife's collapsing body would fall on him. "My God...oh...my God!" Reno said again.

"Major, get hold of yourself," French said.

Reno ran to his horse and leaped on the animal's back, then spurring it, started back toward the river. "Retreat!" he yelled. "Retreat!"

"Major Reno, come back here!" French shouted. Captain French raised his pistol and took a long, careful aim at the retreating major's back.

"French, no," Varnum said softly. "It isn't worth it."

French sighed and lowered his pistol. "I should have

shot the son-of-a-bitch when he dismounted at the gulley."

The soldiers, hearing a second order to retreat, feared the worst. In the space of a few moments, they had seen what they thought was going to be a victory turn into a setback, then a defeat, and now a rout. Panic-stricken, they made a mad dash for the river, a mad, scrambling run, with the frightened horses running out of control.

"M Company, form as skirmishers to protect the crossing," French called. But M Company, taking a page from the book of their senior commander, leaped into the river. The pursuing Indians were having a field day, picking off the soldiers as they struggled across the water.

Until the moment Reno's battalion retreated across the river, only four or five had been killed and four wounded. But at the river, more than thirty were killed as the Indians came up to the riverbank and fired down at the hapless victims.

The soldiers who made the opposite bank started returning fire, and the Indians were driven back slightly. His command decimated by the river crossing, Reno moved into position on the bluffs overlooking the river, where he directed that breastworks be prepared.

The shooting stopped, and an unearthly quiet came over the scene. All that could be heard was the heavy breathing and low moans of the wounded who had made it back to the bluffs.

They stayed in position for about fifteen minutes, waiting for what they were sure would be an Indian assault, when Lieutenant Varnum sat up and held up his hand.

"Listen," he said. "Do you hear that?"

From the distance came the low, muffled sound of gunfire.

"It's Custer," he said. "He is engaged."

"Why doesn't he come help us?" Reno asked petulantly.

"Major, I imagine he's got about all he can handle and then some," Varnum said.

"Major...Major...we are saved!" a trooper yelled. "It's Captain Benteen!"

Reno smiled for the first time since the engagement had begun. He ran down the bluff to meet Benteen, who was approaching from the opposite side.

"Benteen, am I glad to see you!" Reno said. "For God's sake, stop and help us. We've been badly beaten here, and I've lost half of my command."

"I've just got a message from Custer to come quick," Benteen said.

"Custer? You know Custer, he's in his glory. I'm the one that needs help."

"I don't know," Benteen said. He ran his hand through his thick, white hair and twisted in his saddle to look at the men he had brought with him. "Maybe he meant join up with you. He said bring packs. I'm sure he didn't mean bring them while he was on the attack."

"Yes, yes," Reno said. "I am certain that is what he meant. Now, get your men dismounted and stay here with me. Our situation here is critical."

# CHAPTER THIRTY

JACOB AND EMILY HAD REACHED THE NORTH END OF THE big village when they heard the sounds of fighting from the south. They were actually hearing the sounds of the rear-guard's engagement with Major Reno, though they supposed it was Custer himself.

The village was the largest Jacob had ever seen. In fact, though he had no way of knowing it at the time, it was the largest concentration of Indians ever to gather on the North American continent.

Sitting Bull was standing by his tent in an open area in the center of his village when he saw Jacob.

"Why are you here?" he demanded angrily. "I do not want you to fight against the White man anymore."

"I had to come to the village," Jacob said. "It was not safe for us."

"I will not turn you away," Sitting Bull said.

"I am glad. Now, tell me where I must go to fight."

"No," Sitting Bull said. "I will not let you fight. You will stay with the women and the children and the old men."

"And the cowards?" Jacob asked sharply.

The expression on Sitting Bull's face softened. "Any who would call you a coward must call me a coward as well," he said. "For it is my wish that you not fight."

"Sitting Bull is right," Crazy Horse said. "It is not right that you should fight in this battle." Crazy Horse, dressed in war paint, reached down and patted his horse on the neck and spoke soothingly to the nervous animal.

"Long Hair comes now," Crazy Horse said.

"So," Sitting Bull said, with a faraway expression on his face, "now the vision will be proven true." Sitting Bull held up his hands for attention. "Warriors, Long Hair comes," he said. "We have everything to fight for. If we do not fight, we have nothing to live for. Go, fight well, and be brave."

Crazy Horse let out another whoop and dashed toward the river.

"Brave hearts to the front," Crazy Horse yelled. "Cowards to the rear! This is a good day to fight! This is a good day to die!"

From all over the village, warriors swarmed to join Crazy Horse. Many were mounted, but most were on foot, and they crossed the river and quickly disappeared into the ravines and behind rocks and hills. To the person who had not seen the warriors hide, the approach to the river looked deceptively peaceful.

"Oh, Jacob, what is going to happen?" Emily asked.

"If Custer tries to cross the river, he will be defeated," Jacob said. "In fact, he will be killed, as will all of his men."

"Can't we...can't we stop it?" Emily asked in a small voice.

"No," Jacob said quietly. "If we tried now, we would be killed as well...and it would do Custer no good."

"But we've got to do something," Emily said. "Jacob, we can't just sit here and watch Custer's entire army be massacred."

"Emily, believe me," Jacob said. "We can do nothing."

"What a cruel twist of fate that I should be a witness to this," Emily said.

———

As CUSTER CRESTED the bluffs on the opposite side of the river from the village, he saw that the Indians would not run from him as he expected, but would stand and fight. He also realized for the first time that there were more Indians than he, or anyone else, had expected. At that, he couldn't see all of the village because his view of the section furthest downstream was obscured by the bends in the river and the timber growing along the banks.

"Damn, Autie, look at that," Tom said.

"It looks like New York City, only with tipis, doesn't it?" Custer said. He held his hand up and stopped the column.

"Where is Lieutenant Varnum?"

"You sent him with Reno," Tom informed him.

"Oh, yes, I did, at that. Well, Captain Cooke, select a messenger for me, would you?"

"Yes, sir," his adjutant said, and signaled a nearby trooper, a trumpeter named Martin.

"Trooper," Custer told him. "Get back to Benteen as

fast as you can. Tell him we have spotted a big village here. Tell him to come quick and bring packs."

"Yes, sir," Martin said.

Captain Cooke was scribbling a message on a page in his notebook, and he tore the page out and handed it to Martin.

The trooper put the message in his shirt pocket and started off at a gallop. As he reached the bottom of the hill, he saw young Boston Custer coming toward him. Boston had been back with the pack train, but anxious to be in on the excitement, was hurrying to join his brothers.

"Where is the general?" Boston yelled.

"Go over this hill and you'll find him," Martin replied, the two riders passing each other at a gallop.

Boston spurred his horse on faster, and as he crested the hill, he was rewarded by seeing his two brothers in front of a line of skirmishers.

"Wait!" Boston called. "Wait for me!"

"Dammit, Boston, what are you doing here?" Tom asked angrily. "I thought you were going to stay with the pack train."

"What? And miss all the fun?"

"You call it fun, do you? We'll see how much fun it is about ten minutes from now."

Tom turned back in his saddle and looked down toward the village. If they turned back now and rejoined forces with Reno and Benteen, they might be able to hold off the Indians until General Terry's column arrived. If they attacked, they would probably all be killed.

"Are you ready, Tom?" Custer asked quietly. Tom looked over at him and nodded. He knew that his brother was aware of their situation. He also knew that they would be attacking.

So it had come down to this, he thought. This would be the end of the Custers. The great dynasty that Libby spoke about would be no more. He had been prevented from marrying Emily, and now, it was going to end in a lonely valley in Montana. No cheering crowds, no fawning politicians, nothing but Indians.

Tom laughed.

"Well, brother Tom, I am pleased to see that you have maintained a sense of humor through it all," Custer said. "Perhaps you'll share the laugh with me."

"It's a joke," Tom said.

"What is the joke?"

"I don't have time to tell you now," Tom said. "I'll tell you tonight, over drinks."

"Over drinks?"

"In Fiddler's Green."

Custer laughed out loud. "Tom, my boy, you are on," he said.

He stood in his stirrups and looked back over his command. "Shall we, then?" he said.

"Why the hell not?" Tom replied, and nodded at the bugler, who sounded the charge.

———

THE NOTES of the bugle call drifted down across the stream and into the village. Emily stood beside Jacob, a cold chill traversing her body at the sound. Then she saw the soldiers charging down the hill toward the village. At first, she could hear only the beat of the hooves, then the jangle of gear and the rattle of sabers.

Finally she heard the soldiers themselves, shouting and screaming at the top of their lungs as they approached.

Closer and closer they came, until the great blue mass became distinguishable as horses and riders, then closer yet until even the individual faces were visible. Emily saw General Custer riding in front, but she didn't see Tom.

The Indians who were waiting in ambush held their fire until the soldiers hit the stream, then opened up. Several soldiers were hit, and the column was divided. Custer and several more crossed the stream and made it to the edge of the village, but the soldiers on the opposite side of the bank were caught in a murderous crossfire and were driven back.

"General, our line has been cut!" Captain Keough called.

"Damn, they must come across!" Custer called. He turned his horse and with his hat began to wave his troops over. But the soldiers wouldn't abandon their positions.

"Tom, start killing the women and children!" Custer called.

"What?" Tom replied. "What are you saying?"

"Do it, Tom, do it!" Custer shouted. "It's the only way to get the warriors over here!"

"Autie, I can't," Tom said.

"Do it, Captain! That's an order damn you!" Custer shouted.

Tom rode up from the bank of the stream, and pointed his pistol toward a group of children. A pained expression on his face, he cocked the hammer.

"Tom, no!" Emily screamed, darting out from behind one of the tipis. Jacob ran out with her.

Tom couldn't have been more shocked if his own mother had suddenly appeared before him. He lowered the gun and stared at Emily, then at Jacob, and his face grew deathly white.

"Emily...you...what are you doing here?" he asked.

"Please, Tom, don't kill any of the children," Emily begged.

"If you do, I'll kill you," Jacob promised.

Tom laughed. "Jacob, don't you know I'm going to be killed anyway? What difference does a few minutes make?"

Jacob put his arms around Emily and pulled her to him, and they gazed at Tom. Finally the bitter smile left Tom's face, and Emily saw in it the most incredible sadness she had ever beheld. Not fear...sadness. Finally he saluted with his pistol, then slipped it back into his holster.

"Kill the kids by yourself, General," Tom called, turning his horse back toward the river. "I'm going back to help our men."

Tom and the troopers started back across the river and Custer had no recourse but to follow them. On the other side of the river, the Indians were swirling around the soldiers like a swiftly flowing stream around pebbles. The soldiers rallied when Custer reached their side of the stream, and he led them in an organized withdrawal. Gradually they worked their way to the north end of the ridge, where they dug in to make a defensive stand.

Custer may have been able to mount a spirited enough defense here had it not been for the influx of hundreds of Indians from the south end of the valley.

With Major Reno retreating, Gall and his warriors were able to join with the ones who were fighting Custer.

Gradually the volume of shooting diminished, and then the women and children of the village rushed across the stream and up onto the battlefield to witness the final stages of the battle.

Emily was swept along with the others, and she had no choice but to go along with the swirling mob or be trampled. She found herself in the front rank of the spectators crowding around the battlefield to watch the final scenes as if they were the audience of a macabre play.

The horror and shock of what she had been subjected to so benumbed Emily that she was able to watch almost with a sense of detachment. Her mind suspended reality, sparing her from further anguish as the grisly scene unfolded.

All around her, Emily saw dead soldiers. Among the dead, she noticed with the same surrealistic sense, was Tom. One by one the remaining soldiers, were gunned or clubbed down, until finally only General Custer himself remained alive. He had been shot through the side, and he was on his knees, holding his pistol in front of him. He pulled the trigger and the hammer fell on an empty chamber.

Custer looked at the pistol with bewilderment, as if unable to understand why it didn't fire. Then he looked at the Indians who surrounded him and laughed.

Even in Emily's numbed state, she was shocked by his laughter, a strange, high-pitched eerie sound, as if it were echoing from the halls of hell.

One of the Indians nearest Custer raised his rifle

and pointed it at Custer's head. Custer began to laugh even harder, and he shook his head.

"Yes," he gasped. "Yes, yes, yes!"

One dull, cracking sound, and Custer pitched onto his back, his laughter silenced forever. The sound of the rifle shot rolled back from the hills, and for several seconds after the echo of the shot died away, there was absolute and total silence.

The Indians stood around for several moments, too shocked by what had happened to do anything. There was no celebration of victory, nor wailing for the dead. No one spoke a word.

Quietly Jacob took the reins of two unwounded horses that were standing by their dead cavalrymen, and he walked over to Emily, leading the animals. He helped Emily mount her horse, then climbed onto his, and slowly, without looking back, they rode away.

# CHAPTER THIRTY-ONE

It was late afternoon. Major Reno, Captain Benteen, and the other soldiers in the hills at the south end of the valley saw the Sioux pulling out of the village. In an orderly fashion, the Indians headed south down the valley of Greasy Grass toward the Big Horn Mountains. The column of Indians was from two to three miles long, and consisted of from eight to ten thousand people, including about 4,000 warriors and countless ponies.

"Major," Benteen said, watching the exodus. "It's been several hours since we've heard the last gunshot. I think we had better go north now and link up with Custer."

"No," Reno said. "We will stay here. Suppose they have Custer surrounded, just as they do us. If we tried to link with him, we would walk right into a trap."

"A trap? Major, who is left to close the trap? My God, half the Indians in North America were in that column we just saw."

"That may be, Captain," Reno said. "But the other

half may be up there, just waiting for us." He pointed north, and from the agitation in his voice, it was obvious that he wasn't going to be persuaded to leave his position of safety on the hill.

"Then if you have no intention of attempting to link with Custer, you should at least consider moving to a better position," Benteen said. "The hills just to the north of us would be easier to defend. Also, the stench from the dead men and horses is unhealthy."

"Yes," Reno said. "Yes, perhaps you are right about that. All right, we'll move upstream and take up a new defensive position."

"And, don't you think we should send out messengers to try and make contact with Custer?"

"No," Reno said. "Custer is the senior commander in the field. It is his responsibility to make contact with me. My only responsibility is to the safety of my men."

Benteen made a few more suggestions to Reno, but Reno was unresponsive. Finally, Benteen took upon himself the responsibility for the soldiers, becoming commanding officer in fact if not in name. He saw to it that the cooks prepared as good a supper as was possible under the circumstances, and the troopers relaxed for the first time in almost two days.

At dusk, Benteen had the horses and mules led down to the river, where they were watered and put out to graze. The animals had suffered severely. Many had been killed, and many more were so badly wounded that the soldiers had to kill them as well.

During the night, a few stragglers returned, men who had been separated from the troops during the fighting. The men slept half on and half off during the night, and they kept their weapons at the ready for any contingency.

———

JACOB AND EMILY slept the sleep of the exhausted that night. Emily's fatigue spared her any nightmares she may have had as a result of having witnessed the horrible battle the day before. Jacob, who normally slept so lightly that the landing of a butterfly could awaken him, was also totally exhausted, which may have accounted for the fact that the four men dressed in soldier blue were able to sneak up on the two sleeping figures.

"Wake up injun lover, or I'll kill you where you lay," said the man wearing sergeant's stripes on his arm. He was in a semi-crouch position with his pistol in front of him, steadied by both hands and aimed right at Jacob's head.

Jacob sat up quickly and just as quickly appraised the situation. He froze, not wanting to startle the four men who were pointing pistols at him.

Emily woke up and let out a little gasp and sat up. Jacob put his arms around her to comfort her.

"What is it?" she asked. "What is going on?"

"Hey, she speaks English, Sarge," one of the soldiers said in surprise.

"Of course she speaks English," the sergeant said. "She's a White woman. You ever see an injun with hair that color?"

"You mean she's a squaw?"

"You might say that," the sergeant said. "Then again,

you might not. You see, we got us a good bit o' fortune here."

"Who are you?" Emily asked. "What do you want?"

"Who am I?" the sergeant asked. "Well, I'll just tell you, missy. I'm Sergeant Tucker of the Second Cavalry, and these here men is my patrol. We was supposed to be lookin' for Injuns, but we ain't found any." He smiled broadly. "What I found though, was a lot better. 'Cause what I found has just earned me a furlough, and enough reward money to have a fine time while I'm furloughin'."

"What are you talkin' about, Sarge?" one of his men asked.

"You mean you don't know?" Sergeant Tucker answered. "Why, unless I miss my guess, this White man here, who is all dressed up like an injun, is Jacob Two Hearts. He's a traitor. The question is, who are you, missy?"

"I am Emily Thomson," Emily said. "And this gentleman has saved my life."

Sergeant Tucker squirted a stream of tobacco from between his teeth, then wiped his mouth with the back of his hand and smiled.

"Well, now, you don't say. Saved your life, did he? That's a mighty fine thing, ain't it?"

"I think so," Emily said.

Sergeant Tucker laughed. "From the looks of things, I mean, the way you two was all cozied up when me 'n my men come sneakin' up here, why, I'd'a thought there was a little more to it than that. 'Course it could be that you was just bein' grateful to 'im. Was that it, missy? Was you bein' grateful?"

"Sarge, let's get 'em back to the column," one of the

other soldiers said. "I'm gettin' spooked bein' this far away from the others."

"Yeah, me, too," one of the other soldiers said.

"All right," Sergeant Tucker replied. "But I think we ought to tie this feller up good 'n proper. I don't want to take no chances on loosin' him."

"Yeah, Sarge, I'm with you. From the looks of this guy he might be pretty sneaky. I don't want him around me iffen he gets loose."

Jacob's hands were tied roughly, and he was shoved toward his horse.

"Hey, Sarge...look at these two horses. Did you see the saddle blankets and the brands?"

Sergeant Tucker walked over to the horses. The blankets were blue with a gold stripe and crossed sabers in the corner. On the flank of the horse was the brand 3/7 and another crossed saber.

"These here animals belong to the third of the Seventh Cavalry," Sergeant Tucker said. "Where'd you come by them?"

Jacob, who hadn't spoken a word yet, was silent. "Maybe he don't savvy White man's lingo, for all him bein' White," one of the soldiers said.

"He savvy's all right," Sergeant Tucker replied. "Maybe he just don't want to talk for no mere sergeant. Maybe he wants to talk to General Terry."

"General Terry?" Emily asked. "Are you with General Terry's command?"

"Yeah," Sergeant Tucker said. "What of it?"

"Is Colonel Gray with your column?"

"Yeah, I think he is," Sergeant Tucker said, his face reflecting surprise over her comment. "How come you know him?"

"Never mind, Sergeant," Emily said. "I just know him, that's all. Jacob, don't worry. Everything will be all right now."

"Yeah?" Tucker said. "Well, we'll just see about that. Now mount up, girl. We're gonna just go see General Terry and your friend Colonel Gray."

With Jacob and Emily mounted, the soldiers surrounded them, and they rode down the side of the hill and out into the broad valley below. This valley looked exceptionally peaceful when contrasted with the valley of death by the Little Bighorn. Under the morning sun, the valley was especially green, and the river, which snaked through the valley like a large letter $\underline{S}$, was shining gold.

They rode at a jog for about an hour before they reached the approaching column. The officer at the head of the column called for a halt.

"What do you have here, Sergeant?"

"General Terry, this is that White traitor that General Custer put out a paper on. His name is Jacob Two Hearts."

"Is that right?" General Terry asked Jacob. Jacob didn't answer.

"Sir, lookit the horses they's ridin'," the sergeant said. He squirted another stream of tobacco between his teeth.

"Third of the Seventh," General Terry said, looking at the brand. "Those animals belong to Custer's regiment."

"That's right, General," the sergeant said.

"Who are you?" General Terry asked Emily.

"I can answer that," another officer said, riding abreast of the two prisoners.

"Hello, Colonel Gray," Emily said.

"You know this woman?" General Terry asked.

"This is the lady I told you about," Colonel Gray said. "This is Emily Thomson."

"The daughter of the artist?"

"Yes, sir."

"I see," General Terry said. He looked back at Emily. "Well, madam, I imagine there are those who will be glad to discover that you are safe. Just as there are those of us who will be interested in your explanations."

"It's as I told these men," Emily said. "This gentleman saved my life."

"What are you doing here in the first place?" Colonel Gray asked. "I left you under the protection of two of my scouts."

"Some protection," Emily said. "If it hadn't been for Jacob, I'd be dead by now. Your scouts were...despicable men, and they attempted to assault me. Jacob saved me from them."

"Jacob. So you are Jacob Two Hearts?" General Terry said. "You admit it?"

"That is what the Indians call me," Jacob said, speaking for the first time since his capture.

"Well, I'll be damned, he does know our lingo," one of the soldiers who had been with Sergeant Tucker said.

"General, you'll keep it in mind who it was that brung him in, won't you?" Sergeant Tucker reminded him. "When it comes time for the reward, I don't want to miss out none."

"I don't have anything to do with a reward," General Terry said.

"They's paper out on this fella, I know they is," Sergeant Tucker said. "General Custer put it out."

"Then we shall let Custer handle the matter. I imagine he will be pleased enough to see him. I guess he'll be glad to see you, too, Miss Thomson. After all, I understand you were his guest at Fort Lincoln for the winter."

"General Custer?" Emily said weakly.

"Yes. We are going to link up with him shortly."

"General Terry...Colonel Gray...you mean you don't know?"

"Know what?"

"Custer," Emily said. "He...he..."

"He what? Come on, girl. Speak up."

"Custer is *dead*," Jacob said.

"Dead? How, when?"

"He was killed in battle yesterday afternoon," Jacob said.

"No," General Terry said. "No, I am certain you are mistaken. If he had been, a messenger would have reached me with the news by now. It is standard procedure. His next in command would have kept me informed."

"There is no next in command," Jacob said. "And there is no one to send as a messenger. They are all dead. Custer's entire command was killed."

General Terry laughed. "What are you trying to say? Are you trying to convince me that a handful of half-naked savages not only defeated Custer, but killed every man jack in his command as well?"

"Yes," Jacob said.

"General, you don't think that could be true, do you?" an officer asked.

"No, no, of course not," Terry said. "You two, ride up here in front with me so I can keep an eye on you.

Colonel Gibbon, order the column forward. We'll have a look-see."

"Very well, General," Colonel Gibbon said, and the order was passed down through the troops.

"Miss Thomson," Colonel Gray said, riding beside her. "What is this preposterous tale you and Jacob Two Hearts are trying to tell us?"

"It's true, Colonel Gray. Every word of it, I swear. Though, God in heaven, I wish it weren't."

Colonel Gray, a strained expression on his face, hurried his horse up to catch up with General Terry, who was now riding about twenty yards in front of the column. Colonel Gray said a few words to General Terry, speaking too quietly for Emily to hear, then hurried back and gave some instructions to Colonel Gibbons.

"Lieutenant Bradley," Colonel Gibbons called.

A young officer pulled his horse out of the formation and rode quickly up to Colonel Gibbons.

"Take a scouting detail out and survey the area. Be especially watchful."

"Yes, sir," the lieutenant said. He stood in his stirrups and yelled for the first platoon of D company to follow him. They broke away from the main column at a gallop and shortly disappeared over the hills ahead.

Several more minutes after the scouts left, the column ascended a line of low sandstone bluffs. From the top of the bluffs, they looked down into the Little Bighorn valley for the first time since the battle. General Terry halted his men, and they stared down at the valley that the day before had rung with the sounds of battle.

Today, the valley was very quiet. From this vantage point, they could see some abandoned tipis and a few horses grazing in the timber near the stream. Nearly all the river was black and smoking, and Emily dimly remembered the smoke rising behind them as they left yesterday.

Where the great Indian camp had stood yesterday, there was now only the funeral tipis and a great pile of garbage abandoned by the Indians.

"It looks quiet enough, General," Colonel Gray said.

"There is no danger," Jacob said. "The Indians have gone. They left last night."

"Mr. Two Hearts, I wouldn't trust you any further than I can throw you," General Terry said.

"He's telling you the truth, General," Emily said. "Why don't you believe him?"

"Miss Thomson, you are scarcely in the position to vouch for him. I'm not convinced of your credibility either."

"Shall we send scouts down first, General?" Colonel Gibbon asked.

"No," General Terry said. "Inform the men to be on extra alert, and we'll go on down together."

"Yes, sir," Colonel Gibbon replied, and the command started down into what was left of the village.

As the soldiers rode into camp, they were greeted with a smell which let them know in no uncertain terms that here was a place of death. Dogs running in packs darted around, barking and snarling at the invading army and nipping at the heels of the horses. But the dogs were the only resistance they encountered.

Terry halted his men just inside the perimeter of where the village had been and pointed at one of the lodges which was still standing. "Check that out," he ordered.

A lieutenant and a sergeant dismounted and stepped inside, then came back out after a few seconds.

"There are eight warriors in here," the Lieutenant said. "All dead. "They're dressed up in their finest costumes and laid out on scaffolds."

"General, look at that," one of the soldiers said. He slid off his horse and ran over to pick up an object lying on the ground. He examined it, then brought it back to the general.

"What is it?"

"It's a pair of underdrawers, sir," the soldier said. "There's blood on them, and the words, *Sturgis—Seventh Cavalry*."

"General, look at this...there's an officer's tunic with a bullet hole in it," Dr. Paulding said.

"Oh, my God!" someone called, his voice tinged with horror. He came running from one of the other lodges. "Oh, my God, do you know what is in there?"

"What? What is it?" one of the men called.

"Heads," the trooper screamed. "Dozens of heads. Heads of White men."

Emily felt dizzy and nauseous, and she leaned forward in the saddle, grabbing onto the saddlehorn.

"Are you all right, Miss Thomson?" Colonel Gray asked.

"Yes," Emily said quietly.

Lieutenant Bradley, who had ridden out on the scouting party, returned then, and in a voice trembling with emotion, reported to General Terry and Colonel Gibbon.

"I have a very sad report to make. I have counted one hundred and ninety-seven bodies lying in the hills."

"White men?"

"Yes, sir. I've never seen General Custer in person, but from pictures I've seen, I believe one of the bodies to be his."

A ripple of shock passed through the men. "Where did these two get Seventh horses?" one of the soldiers shouted.

"Yeah, that's what I'd like to know."

"How'd they know Custer was dead?"

"He's a traitor, you heard him say he was Two Hearts."

"Let's kill this son-of-a-bitch!"

"Hold it!" General Terry ordered, riding back quickly to position his horse between Jacob and the angry soldiers of his command.

"General, what are you protecting him for? Custer and all his men are dead because of him."

"You're a general," one of the others shouted. "You got the right to execute the bastard right here. Give us the word 'n we'll do it for you!"

"No," General Terry said, holding up his hand. "Men, listen to me. If we killed him here, it would be no more than a lynching, no matter what power I have. We've got to take him back to Fort Lincoln where the full story can come out. If he is guilty, he'll hang there, I promise you. And the woman..." General Terry looked at Emily, and his lips curled into a snarl. "By God, she'll hang, too."

# CHAPTER THIRTY-TWO

THE SLANTING BARS OF A LATE AFTERNOON SUN SHONE through the barred windows and made squares of light on the floor. Emily lay on the bed and watched the floating dust motes, wondering about her fate. It had been almost two weeks since she and Jacob were returned to Fort Lincoln. Two weeks, and in all that time she had talked to no one, except the private who brought her meals.

Her *jail* wasn't all that uncomfortable. In fact, it had been the quarters of one of the officers who had been killed with Custer. She was thankful she hadn't been given Tom's quarters. They had not been offered to her, but she wouldn't have wanted them if they had.

Emily had been certain that Libbie would come to speak to her, and hoped that she would. But in the two weeks since she returned, Libbie hadn't come, nor had she even sent word.

Emily was desperate to know about Jacob, but no matter how often she begged for information, the private who brought her meal told her nothing.

The one encouraging sign she did have was the fact that a scaffold hadn't been built. There could be no hanging without a scaffold. And from that, at least, she was able to take scant comfort.

But why hadn't anyone come to see her, or to tell her anything? That was what bothered her the most—the waiting and the uncertainty.

And then one afternoon, there was a change in the routine. She heard the door being opened, and by the position of the sun, she knew that it was much too early for her supper to be brought to her. She had a visitor!

Emily sat up and self-consciously put her hand to her hair as if to adjust it. Despite herself, she nearly laughed at this bit of vanity.

"She's right in there, sir," the private said, pointing to the bed where Emily sat. "If you need me, I'll be right outside."

"Why should I need you, for heaven's sake? Do you suppose she is going to try and attack me?"

"Paul!" Emily shouted happily. "Paul Gideon! My God, you have no idea how happy I am to see you! What are you doing out here?"

Her father's art agent smiled broadly and held his arms out to her. She ran to them with a short cry of joy, and feeling the comforting embrace of another human being for the first time in over two weeks, began crying.

"There, darlin', you just go ahead and cry all you want," Paul said comfortingly. He patted her on the back and rocked her back and forth soothingly. "Paul's here now. Everything is going to be all right."

Finally, after a few moments, Emily regained some of her composure. She walked back over to her bed and offered him a seat.

"I'm sorry, they don't allow me to have a chair," she said. "I hope the bed is all right."

"It's fine," Paul said. "Really, it is."

"Paul, have you heard about Jacob? How is he?"

"He's fine," Paul said. "In fact, that is one of the reasons I am here."

"Why? What do you mean?"

"Well, it seems that Fort Lincoln has a most interesting visitor right now...and Jacob's services are needed."

"Paul, don't be so mysterious," Emily said. "What are you talking about?"

"I'm talking about Sitting Bull," Paul said. "He's here, in the fort."

"Sitting Bull? You mean the Army captured Sitting Bull?"

"No, not exactly," Paul said. "He came under a flag of truce to hold a peace conference with a personal representative of President Grant. But he insisted that Jacob be used as his interpreter. And Jacob refused to interpret unless you are allowed to attend the sessions. He said he wanted to see you."

"Oh, I want to see him, too," Emily said. "Yes, yes, I'll go. Besides, I'll be glad to get out of here for a while." She looked around the room. "I know Jacob is being kept in the guardhouse, and I know it is much worse than this. But believe me, Paul, when you are a prisoner, anywhere is bad."

Paul smiled. "Well, then, perhaps I can tell you the second reason why I am here."

"Oh? What is the second reason you are here?"

"To tell you that you are free," Paul said. "The Army is dropping all charges against you. It seems that people are already beginning to ask a few questions about the battle. Questions like, was Custer a gallant leader who died a brave death with his men, or was he a glory-hunting fool who, in self-serving violation of orders, led his men into a senseless slaughter? That's why they are so anxious to talk to Sitting Bull. He is the first spokesman from the other side."

"Jacob or I could have given an account of the battle," Emily shivered. "Though I don't believe I would want to."

"No, nor would the Army want you to. Especially now that they are dropping their charges."

"What about the charges against Jacob?"

"No, they still stand," Paul said. "In truth, the Army never really had much of a case against you, anyway. You and your father clearly had permission to paint the Indians, and they were clearly unable to protect you. But the case against your Mr. Two Hearts is quite another matter."

"Oh, Paul, please, you must do everything you can to save him. Promise me that you will," Emily said.

Paul looked at Emily, then sighed. "You must really love that savage."

"He's *not* a savage!" Emily said hotly. And then, when she realized how loudly she had made that declaration, she gave a little laugh.

"I'm sorry," she said. "But he isn't a savage. He is a gentle, honest, and honorable man. And yes, I do love him. I love him more than I ever thought I could love anyone. Now, Paul, you must promise me you will help him."

"I'll do what I can," Paul said. "Now, come on. You do want to see him, don't you?"

"Yes," Emily said. "Yes, very much."

"Then you shall." He walked over to the door and rapped on it. The private opened it and looked inside.

"We are both ready to come out," Paul said. He pulled a paper from his pocket. "Here is an order signed by the general, authorizing her release."

"What?" Emily said. "You mean you had that all along, and you made me stay here while we talked?"

"Believe me, Emily, this was the best place to talk," Paul said. "Wait until you see the Sutler's store where the hearing is."

Paul was right. Emily had never seen so many people at the store, even during the dances. Soldiers were crowded around outside as Paul and Emily approached.

Emily heard a buzz of excitement from the soldiers, but she could not make out what they were saying. But for the moment, she was so happy to be free from confinement that it wouldn't have made any difference, anyway. Let them say whatever they wanted. She was free, and in just a moment, she would be seeing Jacob.

"Make way, men, make way and let her through!" Colonel Gray called from the porch of the store. "Miss Thomson, come right on up this way."

The crowd of soldiers parted further, and Emily walked up onto the porch, where Colonel Gray saluted her.

"Thank you for coming," he said. "Your friend is being most difficult for us. He knows how desperately we wish to talk to Sitting Bull, and he won't interpret for us unless you are present."

"I'm not doing this for the Army, Colonel Gray,"

Emily said resolutely. "I'm doing this for one reason and one reason only—so I can see Jacob."

"Very well, madam," Colonel Gray said. "But whatever the reason, you have the Army's gratitude."

Colonel Gray opened the door to the store, and Emily stepped inside. A few lucky enlisted men had managed to find room along the walls to stand, and one or two of them even had a barrel to use for a seat. But the chairs were all taken by officers and civilians, both commissioners and journalists. A photographer set off a flashpan of magnesium powder the moment Emily stepped inside.

A swell of sound greeted her arrival, and a civilian seated behind a table in front of the room pounded a gavel until the sound quieted.

"Please, ladies and gentlemen," the man said. "This is not a court of law, but an official inquiry into facts surrounding the incidents that occurred in the field two weeks ago. I am representing the President of the United States, and as such, have the authority to conduct this hearing behind closed doors if necessary. If you are to witness it, you must be quiet."

The man's words had their effect, and the crowd quieted.

Emily looked toward the front of the room, where she saw Libbie. She smiled at her, and her heart went out to her for her sorrow, but Libbie looked away. Emily looked at the floor in sadness.

"Now, would you bring in our witness and the interpreter, please?"

Emily looked toward the back door, and then her heart leaped for joy, for there was her Jacob. How wonderful it was to see him! And yet, sad too, for Jacob was in handcuffs. Instead of the buckskin breeches she had become used to seeing him wear, he was dressed in denim trousers and a red flannel shirt. It was the first time she had ever seen him in White man's clothing.

He looked over at her and smiled broadly. Emily returned his smile, and started toward him, but Colonel Gray restrained her.

"I'm sorry, Miss Thomson," he said. "But they won't let you get near him."

"But I must," Emily said. "Don't you understand? I must!"

"I'm sorry."

Emily looked back at Jacob and smiled again, only now there were tears in her eyes, her joy at seeing him again made bittersweet by the distance between them still.

Sitting Bull came in then, and Emily looked over at him. It was the first time she had seen him since that terrible afternoon in the village during the battle. Sitting Bull was wearing a black-and-white calico shirt, black cloth leggings, and moccasins magnificently embroidered with beads and porcupine quills.

Sitting Bull began to speak in his own language. It was sometimes guttural and barking, sometimes musical and lilting, but always spoken with the force of a man who knew his words would be listened to. He spoke quietly so that Jacob's simultaneous translation could be clearly heard.

"This land belongs to us. It is a gift to us from the Great Spirit. The Great Spirit gave us the game in the country. It is our privilege to hunt the game in our country. The White man came here to take the country from us by force. He has brought misery and wretchedness into our country.

We were here killing game and eating, and all of a sudden we were attacked by White men. Now we are tired of fighting and we want the soldiers to stop fighting us. The Great Spirit sees the bloody deeds going on in this country. Though he gave us the country, he did not give us the right to dispose of it. It is our duty to defend our country. We did not want to fight the White man, but now, if they wish to withdraw, they may. We do not wish to fight them, but if the Whites wish to keep up the war, we can fight for three years. We have plenty of game and everything else."

"Yes," said the commissioner, a man named Morris. Morris was a small man with wire-rimmed glasses and a tiny mustache, which he rubbed with his finger as he talked. "Yes, well, that may be so. But you will never be able to withstand the forces of the entire United States. So, we won't speak of wars yet to come. Though I do wish to speak to you of the war which was. Now, I know you are a great chief, but—"

"I am no chief."

"You aren't a chief?" Norris asked in surprise. "No."

"Then, what are you?"

"I am," Sitting Bull said, crossing both hands upon his chest and smiling slightly, "a *man*."

"What does he mean by that, Mr. Two Hearts?" Morris asked.

"It is difficult to explain," Jacob said. "But White men tend to use the word *chief* far too much. Sitting Bull has influence over his people. He speaks and they listen. But he does not demand."

"You mean he is only a medicine man?"

Jacob smiled. "Don't use the term *only* in that way when you are talking about Sitting Bull: as a *medicine* man. In fact, he is a medicine man, but a far more influential one than any I have ever known."

"I see," Morris said. "And it is my understanding Mr. Two Hearts, that you have known a few."

"I have," Jacob said. "I am a member of the Soldier Lodge. It is impossible to be a member without knowing a few medicine men."

"What is the Soldier Lodge?" Morris asked.

"Mr. Morris, may I answer that?" General Crook suddenly said, standing quickly.

"You, General? Yes, of course you may."

"Mr. Morris, I, too, am a member of the Soldier Lodge," General Crook said.

There was a gasp from many of the onlookers, and General Crook went on.

"It is a privilege reserved for very few people of any race. Besides Mr. Two Hearts, whose real name is Andrews, I know of only one more White person besides myself who is a member. It is a unique honor in Sioux society, akin to the highest order in Masonry. I have nothing but respect for anyone who would hold such a position."

"But General, I don't understand," Morris said. "How did you come by such an honor? You have been the enemy to the Sioux."

Sitting Bull spoke then, with Jacob interpreting. "For the Indian, there is as much honor in being a good enemy as in being a good ally. General Crook is a man who is much feared and hated by the Indians. And for that, he is much honored and respected. Hate is a prized emotion among Indians and is given away no less easily than love."

"I see," Morris said, then looked up in surprise. "How did Sitting Bull know what we were saying?"

"He speaks English," Jacob said. "But he understands easier than he speaks, so he wishes to speak with my tongue."

"Very well," Morris said. "So, Sitting Bull is not a chief, he is a medicine man. How did he become a medicine man?"

"I see. I know," Sitting Bull said. "I began to see when I was not yet born, when I was not yet in my mother's arms, but inside of my mother's belly. It was there that I began to study about my people."

"I don't understand—" Morris began, but Jacob interrupted him.

"Let him speak," Jacob said. "He is explaining his medicine. This is a rare thing."

"I was," Sitting Bull went on, "still in my mother's insides when I began to study all about my people. The Great Spirit gave me the power to see out of the womb. I studied there, in the womb, about many things. I studied about the smallpox that was killing my people. I was so interested that I turned over on my side. The Great Spirit must have told me at that time that I would be the man to be the judge of all the other Indians. A big man to decide for them in all their ways."

"And you have since decided for them?"

"I speak. It is enough."

"Well, we must move on, Sitting Bull. I want to speak to you about the battle in which General Custer was killed. Here is a map of the valley where the battle took place. Can you understand the map?"

Sitting Bull looked at a large map, showing a long village stretching up and down on the east side of the map, a river running down the middle, and a ridge of hills running down the west side.

"Now, where was the Indian camp first attacked?"

"Here," Sitting Bull said, pointing to the south end of the village where Reno made his first assault. "About what time was that?"

"It was two hours past the time when the sun is in the center of the sky."

"What White chief attacked you here?"

"I believe it was Long Hair," Sitting Bull said. There was a buzz in the store, and Mr. Morris looked up warningly.

"It was actually Major Reno," Morris said. "But of course, you had no way of knowing that. Was there a good fight there?"

"No," Sitting Bull said. "That was a trick. The soldiers did not fight hard there, because they thought to fool us. The real fight was here." He pointed to the north of the village at the place where Custer made his attack.

"But what of the fight here?" Morris asked, pointing again to Reno's position.

"Not much fighting there," Sitting Bull said. "The soldiers come, and the soldiers run away. Some stay on the hill, I think, and the others come to attack the village up here. So all the warriors came up here."

"But what about the warriors down here? Major Reno was pinned down on that hill for twenty-four hours. How many warriors were there?"

"No warriors," Sitting Bull said. "Only some old women and young papooses."

One or two enlisted men laughed derisively. But the

officers who had been at the hill saw no humor in the situation.

"I see," Morris said. "Now, tell me about the fight here." He pointed to the point on the map where Custer made his attack.

"Our young men rained lead across the river and drove the White braves back," he said.

"And then?"

"And then they rushed across themselves, from the sides. The soldiers were exhausted, and their horses got in the way, and they could not take good aim. Some of the horses broke away and left the soldiers to die. Long Hair had the bugle blow, and the soldiers fell back, still fighting, but they could not fire fast enough because there were too many Indians."

"Did the command fight until the last?" Morris asked.

"There were no cowards," Sitting Bull said.

"What about Long Hair," General Crook asked from the floor. "How did Long Hair equip himself?"

Long Hair stood like a sheaf of corn with all the ears fallen around him.

"Not wounded?"

"No."

"How many stood by him?"

"A few."

"When did he fall?"

"He was the last to fall," Sitting Bull said. "He tried to shoot his pistol, but it would not fire. And then he laughed, and then he was killed."

"You mean he cried out?"

"No, he laughed," Sitting Bull said. "He laughed at death. He was a very brave man."

A chair scraped across the floor, and everyone looked over to see Libbie standing. At first, they thought it was because the testimony was too painful for her, and General Crook opened his mouth as if to apologize. But then they saw that Libbie was smiling proudly.

"Thank you, Sitting Bull. Thank you very much," she said. "You have made me very happy to confirm my belief in my husband's bravery."

The audience gasped as she left the Sutler's store in haughty pride.

# CHAPTER THIRTY-THREE

EMILY WAS IN HER QUARTERS, THE SAME ONES SHE HAD occupied during her confinement. But now the door wasn't locked, and the cabin wasn't guarded. But with no word as to the fate of Jacob, she felt just as miserable as she had when she was a prisoner.

Then, one week after the hearing, Paul came into her quarters, a large smile on his face.

"Paul, you have something?" Emily asked excitedly. "You have some news for me?"

"Sort of," Paul said.

"Well, tell me. Don't keep me in suspense."

"You shall be happy to hear that I have negotiated a painting for you."

"You have what?" Emily asked, crestfallen. She had hoped for news about Jacob, and he brought her word of the sale of a painting.

"After all," Paul said. "You are a painter, and you must continue your work. And now that your father is gone, you must carry on."

"I don't know," Emily said.

"Emily, what do you mean you don't know? This is Paul Gideon speaking. Remember me? I'm your agent. You have me to look out for, too, you know."

"But Paul, I can't work now. Not until I know what is going to happen to Jacob."

"Wait until you find out what the painting is before you say you can't do it," Paul said.

"All right, what is the painting?"

"It's Custer's battle."

"Custer's...oh, Paul, no," Emily said. "No, I couldn't... I wouldn't do that. It's too...it's just too horrible. I don't even want to think about it. And I especially don't want to paint it."

"Emily, it might be good for you," Paul said gently. "If you paint it, you might be able to get it out of your mind, once and for all."

"No," Emily said. "Even if you were right, even if it would help me forget...I couldn't do it to Libbie. I couldn't put her through it."

Paul laughed.

"What's funny, Paul? I mean it, I don't want to hurt Libbie any more than she has already been hurt."

"I'm sorry, Emily," Paul said. "I shouldn't have laughed. It's just that...this painting is for Libbie, didn't you know that? She is the one who wants it done."

"Paul, surely you are mistaken," Emily said with a horrified gasp. "Why would she want anything so...so terrible?"

"Oh, no, my dear. You misunderstand. She doesn't want it terrible...she wants it heroic."

"Heroic?"

"Oh, absolutely," Paul said. "She is a fascinating lady, that woman. Do you know what she intends to do?"

"What?"

"She intends to make Custer into the greatest hero in American history. In fact, she told me she intends to spend the rest of her life doing just that."

"Yes," Emily said with a sigh. "Yes, I can understand that. She couldn't make him a president while he lived, so now that he is dead, she'll promote him to an even higher honor. Well, she's going to have to do it with someone else, because I won't help her. It's just too bizarre."

"Emily, wait until you hear the price she is willing to pay," Paul said.

"The price? Paul, I won't do it at any price," Emily said.

"At least listen to it, will you?" Paul pleaded. "I'm telling you, this is a good price. I'm a good agent, aren't I? Do you think I would even let you consider such a thing if I didn't think you were getting a fair price for it?"

"I don't care what it is," Emily said. "She could offer me five thousand, ten thousand, even twenty thousand dollars, and I wouldn't do it."

"She's offered two hundred and fifty dollars," Paul said. "That's all she can afford."

"Paul, it isn't the money, and you know that," Emily said.

Paul smiled. "Yes, I know it," he said. "That's why I got another concession. The Army is dropping the charges against one Jacob Andrews."

There was a moment of stunned silence, as Emily looked at Paul with an incredulous look on her face. "Paul, you aren't just telling me this, are you?" she asked in a small voice. "Because if you are..." She let the word hang.

"No, darling, I'm not just telling you this," Paul said. "I've made a bargain with her. If you will paint the heroic picture she wants, she will use her influence with General Terry to have the charges against Jacob Andrews dropped."

Suddenly, Emily screamed and flew through the door of the small cabin.

"Jacob!" she yelled. "Jacob, you are free, you are free!"

Emily ran across the quadrangle so fast that she scarcely felt her feet touch the ground, she didn't even see the formation of soldiers under the flagpole.

When she reached the guardhouse, one of the guards stepped in front of her.

"Get out of my way, you fool!" Emily shouted. "Don't you know he's free?"

The confused guard looked toward the officer who was drilling the soldiers in the quadrangle, and the officer looked toward the commandant's house. There, on the front porch, Libbie nodded her head ever so slightly, and the officer signaled for the guard to step aside. Emily threw the latch, and a second later, Jacob was outside, holding her in his arms, smothering her lips with kisses.

On the porch, Libbie watched the scene, and for just a moment it wasn't Emily and Jacob, but Libbie and Autie...Sunshine and Bo...and the guidon snapping sharply red and white in the afternoon breeze wasn't held by an orderly but her own sweet Armstrong. Her eyes dimmed with tears, but her heart surged with joy. Custer would live in the pages of history forever.

On the parade ground, the band suddenly struck up a song. It was "Garry Owen."

## IF YOU LIKED THIS, YOU MIGHT ALSO ENJOY: RIDERS OF GLORY

### A WESTERN HISTORICAL FICTION NOVEL BY ROBERT VAUGHAN

**In the crucible of war, courage and conviction are forged like steel.**

Colonel Nelson Pickett has spent his career carrying the scars of choices made and battles lost. Marked by the massacre at Wounded Knee and burdened by the weight of command, he believes a soldier's duty leaves no room for attachments. But as the Spanish-American War looms, his unwavering focus is tested by a spirited young journalist whose courage matches his own.

Marty McGuire is determined to prove herself in a world ruled by men. When she embeds with Pickett's Lightning Cavalry, she becomes an eyewitness to history—and a challenge to the hardened officer's rigid beliefs. As the horrors of war unfold, Nelson must face battles both on and off the field: the ruthless enemy ahead and the feelings he's tried to bury deep within.

When Marty is captured behind enemy lines, Nelson is forced to confront the cost of his decisions and the meaning of honor. In a world where survival demands sacrifice, can he reconcile duty with the stirrings of his heart?

*AVAILABLE NOW*

# ABOUT THE AUTHOR

Robert Vaughan sold his first book when he was 19. That was 57 years and nearly 500 books ago. He wrote the novelization for the mini series Andersonville. Vaughan wrote, produced, and appeared in the History Channel documentary Vietnam Homecoming.

His books have hit the NYT bestseller list seven times. He has won the Spur Award, the PORGIE Award (Best Paperback Original), the Western Fictioneers Lifetime Achievement Award, received the Readwest President's Award for Excellence in Western Fiction, is a member of the American Writers Hall of Fame and is a Pulitzer Prize nominee.

Vaughn is also a retired army officer, helicopter pilot with three tours in Vietnam. And received the Distinguished Flying Cross, the Purple Heart, The Bronze Star with three oak leaf clusters, the Air Medal for valor with 35 oak leaf clusters, the Army Commendation Medal, the Meritorious Service Medal, and the Vietnamese Cross of Gallantry.